The
Jicker Man

The Jicker Man
Ben Mears

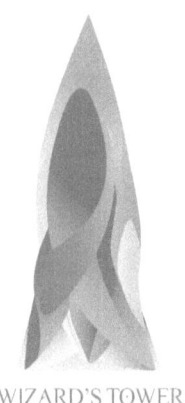

WIZARD'S TOWER

Wizard's Tower Press
Rhydaman, Cymru

The Jicker Man

Contents

THANKS & CREDITS

With thanks to my beta readers Keith Munro, David Warby, Revd Dr Simon Woodman, Jeff Parke, Joy and Henna Mears, Anne Corlett, Joel Cornah, Tej Turner and all at WiFi SciFi.

Special thanks to my good friend, saver of lives, Matt Cooper, who has by now probably read just as many versions of this story as me, and without whom I would likely have given up. I have a deep love of unexpected heroes, and you are one of the best. Matt, this one's for you.

And lastly, but by no means least, special thanks to author and editor Jo Hall, and to Cheryl Morgan at Wizard's Tower Press.

MAP

BEN MEARS

*K*ing Doon the Great ruled Londaland in peace for a grand total of 43 years. Those years were good. They saw the developing world into a new era, with the rebuilding of cities long fallen, and established a society edging ever closer to civility. It wasn't fair, of course, but it was better than what had come before. There were established two sects: the silkers, who were the nobles, rich and powerful, and the threaders, who lived like slaves, and whose lives were made hard by toil.

Doon's reign marked a point in time when things began to change. Old London was under water, had been submerged for an age, and was little more than legend. Though among the new centres grew one that quickly became the King's seat and the country's new capital. And so it was that Camdon City grew in stature.

But other things had altered since the cataclysm that had brought ruin to the world and put Old London under the Eastern Sea. A change had manifested in the caverns beneath the toxic deserts of Mors Zonam, that land poisoned by ancient war. A new race evolved to lie hidden for a great many years. Among the people of Londaland, this different kind were perceived as myth. Like ghosts, they appeared fleetingly to a hapless few—most of whom did not survive to make report—and like ghosts, their existence was denied. Yet one day the king of that race would reveal his kind to the world. It would be a day forever remembered as the Gawper Dawn.

An excerpt from *The Histories of Londaland*
by *Nathanual Dvorovich*

9

1. SURVIVING

1801 AD (After Doon)

Tower Bridge, a district of

Camdon City, Londaland

Musket blasts echo down the debris-strewn alley. More soldiers up ahead. Tucking my head low, I watch their long shadows drift by my hiding place in a haze of dust and smoke. Are they Londalanders or Urthian? I listen to them pass before risking a peek over the rubble that shelters me, though a glance upwards with my good eye tells me it ain't safe here. The ruined building towering overhead may topple at any moment and bury me alive or crush me to death.

Time to move.

I climb a mound of stones, limp to the alley's end and glimpse the rust-brown of the Urthian battle garb as bronze-skinned soldiers trudge out of view. Not ours, then, though it wouldn't make much difference at this point. The few survivors on either side are desperate. Usually scared and hungry. They shoot first and don't bother with questions.

Snippets of the Urthian language sound harsh on the smoggy air.

'Hakkard-toth, lakkan darh morhcantai.'

'Vlastrakken zah hagblaten haw. Darh doth atta-dran!'
The foreign voices drift away.

I'm kinda numb inside after all that's happened. I'll tell you about it, if you like. I'll tell you everything, though my words ain't always right. I was a street boy, see? 'Til I met Michael. Michael taught me to write.

Resting a moment, I rub at my twisted foot through the cracked leather of my old riding boots. It never healed right—my foot. It's turned in at the toe, the ankle forever buckled, but kneading it sometimes eases the ache.

To my left a terraced house remains standing, almost whole. That is, it *used* to be a terraced house. Now it's just a house. I'm wary because it's unusual—a building intact like that. It looks useable, which means it could be occupied, right? But by what? Terrified, I force myself to approach. It could be a lair. I need to know because my mission demands it.

Cautiously, I slip along the roadside wall to the door. I couldn't see it properly, back there, but it's ajar, an inch of thick darkness showing through the crack. The toe of my boot eases it open further. A shaft of light shows the trappings of a former life: chairs set around a kitchen table, the remains of a half-eaten meal mouldy on plates, a dusty sink, towels hanging from a row of small hooks. The place awakens another kind of ache. This one deep down inside. I rap my knuckles against the wooden door, catch a muffled noise and wait. Was that a sound from within or is my imagination toying with me? I can't decide. Pushing the door wider, I wince at the squeal of rusting hinges before stepping inside. I stop, and peer around in the gloom. Insects have nested here, their papery nests bulge from the corners. Hanging from the ceiling, hag bats twitch, disturbed by my invasion.

I creep through the room, my ears straining. There's a nasty, damp smell. My senses warn me there's something in here with me. It's a feeling, a scent in the air, the knowledge of that *maybe* noise. A door leads into a hallway which is lit only by light squeezing through a fissure in the wall and there a staircase rises to the first floor. A framed imograph of a mother and child lies fallen. Its shattered shards of glass catch in the fissure glow and crunch beneath my boots.

The stairs lead to several upper rooms. A closet in a bedroom holds Draker uniforms hanging in a neat row. The Drakers were Camdon City's watchmen. Before the war, that is. I sluff off my old, patched jacket and slip into a Draker long coat. It's on the loose side but better than my old one and it don't smell too bad. I catch a hint of stale cologne that lingers from its last owner. It's thick, warm and black, with shiny brass buttons and two red strips on the epaulets and cuffs.

A Draker's reinforced top hat sits on a side table. I ain't interested in that but there's a drab coloured blanket on the bed. It's clean, apart from a little dust. I shake it out, filling the air with motes that swirl and blaze in the light from broken windows. I roll the fabric to stow it with the few other belongings in my pack.

There's a good pair of boots under the bed but they're too big for me. Shame. Mine leak and my feet have been damp and cold for ages. I leave the boots but bag a pair of good woollen socks from a drawer.

In the grimy bathroom, I catch broken reflections of a youth in a cracked mirror. The face is old beyond its years, the left eye unseeing, scarred and occluded white. I wipe the glass to see better, rub a hand over my stubbly face, in need of a wash and a shave. A cutthroat razor rests on the wooden edge of the sink. I fold and pocket the razor, prise a corner of the mirror free with my fingertips and take that too.

BEN MEARS

Returning to the ground floor, I check the back room and, pushing the door wider, step into the half-light. I freeze at a sound: the scurry of feet. Or was it paws? That feeling again. That smell, only stronger. Annoyance taps at my mind. A Draker's house, yet no gun, no ammunition, not even a watchman's club. Disappointing to say the least. And now I'm in a room with something living, and I wish I wasn't. My eye adjusts to the murk as I deliberate: stay and make a wary search for perks, or hang it and run for the door?

The *something* shuffles in the corner, a low shape, close to the floor amid a range of other similar forms.

When nothing attacks, I edge to the side wall to tear back the curtain from the window. In the sudden stream of light, a small pup cowers amid its dead mother and siblings. It seems lost yet unwilling to leave its mother's side. I count seven others—two black, the rest tan with black faces. All skin and bones. All dead. The survivor, jet black with darkly golden eyes, watches me and I wonder what it's thinking. Is it afraid, terrified, relieved, glad of the company? Who knows? It seems sad and curls up, nuzzling into the crook of its mother's throat to settle down on the filthy floor.

If it stays here, it will die like its brothers and sisters. I don't know what killed them. Perhaps the mother was shot or injured, her master blown to the wind in some street battle when the Urthians came. They probably starved. I'll never know. Whatever the truth, there seems only one thing to do. I cross to the pup and scoop him up for a closer look. He's a scrawny fellow. He licks my fingers, sniffs, peers at me, pees, chews my thumb with needle-sharp teeth.

'Ow!' I catch a whiff of him. 'Blinders! You stink!' Lifting him by the scruff of his neck, I hoist him away from my nose. I swing the pack from my shoulder and widen the entrance to lower him in.

*

Winter 1802, Londaland—somewhere
north of Camdon City

Stink wakes me at close to ten o'clock. At least, that's the time according to my favourite pocket watch. I've collected five along the way. Found them here and there. I don't like to think about where or how.

Watches ain't in short supply. Watches ain't the problem.

I give each one a winding and shiver as a savage wind bites in from the Eastern Sea to chill my bones. My stomach growls like a caged bear. There's never enough food and my stock of dog biscuits ran out long ago. Food. Food *is* the problem. I fend off Stink's slobbery tongue and wipe my cheek on a sleeve as his tail fans the air.

He looks at me with those golden eyes before pointing his snout in the opposite direction, as though he suspects a morgue rat is lurking in the burned out halker that's splintered on rocks further up the beach. It would be hard to know for sure. Dunes lie between, partially blocking our view, the ashen sand cracked and spiked with dead grasses.

I take the telescope from my pack and survey the open beach and billowing sea.

Stink's ears pivot as he homes-in on sounds beyond my range, sounds that lie beneath the moan of the easterly, the waves and the raucous cries of gulls. His ears are upright and pointed, not floppy like some dogs'. I don't know what breed he is, but he looks like the sort the Drakers used before they lost control of Camdon City—before everything fell apart—which makes sense as he came from a Draker's house.

He's black and kinda wolfish although from certain angles his face looks almost bear-like. So, I've taken to calling him Bear Dog when he's good. He's grown quickly in the year and a half since I found him and he's now so large I doubt he'll get much bigger. In that time we've practised a few basic commands, clicks and hand gestures mostly, 'cause anything else can get you noticed when it ain't safe. There are a few whistles I use, which sound like bird calls, but I still speak to him all the same. He'll *sit*, lie *down*, *come* to heel, jump *up*, *take*—he's good at that one—whenever I say. But his best trick is to steal.

'What is it, boy? What's there?' I whisper. Experience has taught me that caution is a good thing. And Stink only reacts when there's a reason. I've learnt that, too.

He ignores me, of course. He's a dog and dogs don't speak—not in the same way people do. But if you watch him closely, you can understand everything he's saying. It's just a different sort of language.

The pocket watch I use most is cased in gold. I run a grubby thumb fondly over its polished surface, tuck it back into my waistcoat pocket and peel myself away from a bedroll that's clammy with damp. Suppose that's what you get for sleeping in a wreck. I glance up at the half a deck that forms my roof, the jagged edge smashed where it was driven onto rocks. Now it's stark against the bleak Twinemoon sky. Suppose it's better than no deck at all, like a lot of the others. It was the best I could find by last night's thin moonlight when we crawled inside to shelter. Stink soon curled in tight to my body beneath the skirts of my coat, and that is how we slept. That's how we always sleep.

I glance south at the coastline I've walked for days, keen to turn inland away from this cursed wind.

The wrecks huddle along the shore like the fallen skeletons of giants, their naked ribs battered to dark lines. Washed in by a sinister tide, there are both merchant galleons and gunships with a scatter of smaller vessels. An ironclad rusts in the shallows, jutting from the waves at a hapless angle. To my right, the sea reaches to the horizon, grim and grey, broken only by the storm brakers that tower heavenward. To my left the land rises and falls, patched with charred woodlands and settlements, scarred by the craters of bombs that fell during the war. *The Gawper War*, they call it, but I've a feeling the Gawper War has barely begun.

The air is damp and heavy with salt and decay. Below me, bodies litter the beach, lapped by the low tide. I'm sure they weren't there when I crawled into the steam-tug.

I make the sacred sign and squint into the nearby wreck, trying to discern movement in the shadows of its belly. Then Stink emits a low growl, a sound that tells me he's planning something. Normally what follows is loud and aggressive, though sometimes the growl rumbles away to become a moan or whimper, which might signify any number of things. Mostly I take it to mean *I'm hungry*, 'cause I feel the same.

Peering out at the halker, I wonder what's onboard.

'There could be food,' I mutter to Stink under my breath, still afraid that something deadly might explode from the murk of the ship, that a creature from Mors Zonam has nested in there or another desperate soul—like me, only better armed—is lurking there. I finger the slingshot in a pocket of my long coat while selecting a good round pebble from another pocket with my other hand. It's a better weapon than a gun, these days. Bullets and black powder run out and are hard to replace. You can find stones almost anywhere.

Taking out the slingshot, I slot the pebble into its leather pouch. Stink whines, glancing at me briefly before fixing back on the halker.

'Come on,' I tell him. 'We can't sit *here* all day.'

I scramble up the tug's storm-battered boards and drop myself over the edge of the bow to land on the beach. Stink shadows me, leaping down and stalking nearer, his chest low to the sand. Closer we creep, until we reach a dune from where we spy.

'What d'you think?'

Stink's gaze remains locked onto the halker's dingy innards.

BEN MEARS

I wonder if anything of use might have survived the fire. The damage to the hull looks bad—a gaping wound in the side—and I think it's seen battle. A smaller hole further up the clinkers is suspiciously cannonball-sized. Scrambling up to the peak of the dune, I see the stern is peppered with red-feathered arrows, each lodged in the timber, some fire-blackened.

It's true, there could be food in there. I weigh the risk, my stomach refusing to still. Jarred, canned or bottled goods would work: beans, meats, hallard eggs, pickles, sweet preserves, cherries in brandy, whisky or wine—not that alcohol would be much help. Barrels might be unspoiled and could contain salted fish or meats, olives or oil. I bite my lip and remind myself to stop thinking about food. It don't help when you're starving.

Despite Stink's continued growl and my jittering nerves, I decide to investigate.

He pauses around eight yards from the hull, shoulders hunched, his growl building.

I whisper. 'You really think there's a big old rat in there, huh?'

He has a thing for morgue rats. Hates 'em. I limp past him. Reaching the hull, I jump up to grab a hold of its edge—nice and quiet—heave my body slowly up to peer into the halker. I sense my eyes grow wide as something shifts in the darkness before me. My heart thumps in my throat.

A sudden flash of white startles me as a gull launches, squawking from the shadows. I fall to the beach while Stink barks like crazy, leaping at the bird but coming nowhere near it. Pulling myself up again, I climb aboard, ease down into the ship. We're in luck. Barrels. Twelve in a row, all roped up and secured for a voyage, though I've no way of knowing what's inside each one without breaking the seals. I don't see anything else that might prove to be food. There's no rats, morgue or otherwise.

With a sigh of relief, I unbind a cask, roll it across the sloping floor and up the broken hull. The beach below is empty, except for Stink who peers up at me imploringly: *What's taking so long?*

I click my tongue twice—a signal I use to tell him, *Watch it!* He tilts his head at me before darting aside as the barrel falls to the sand. I hunt below deck for something with which to prise open the lids. There's nothing much: the remains of a smashed windlass lamp, a clutch of cannons and some shot that's been thrown around. I find a mariner's satchel but ditch it when its contents prove to be only an empty tobacco pouch, some ruined maps and damp matches. Useless.

There's a burnt body at the far end, adhering to the lower clinkers and the deck. Moving closer, I see there's been a spill of tar and the body's held by the tacky burnt remnants of the puddle. When I blink, I see the body of a spy, the one who had seemed to set everything in motion.

Six months earlier, I'd found myself in Camdon City's Museum of Unnatural History, which towered over the dark waters of the Tynne, though from where I had stood the river couldn't be seen at all. I was deep in the building on the first floor, surrounded by glass cabinets full of ancient things. In the case before me were some machines that sat open, like the splayed covers of books. Only they weren't books at all. They were devices, each with a blank panel on the inside of the front cover and rows of little square buttons on the inside of the back. On each of the buttons was a letter or number. Some of the machines were mangled and burnt. Others half missing their parts. There wasn't a single one whole. A card behind the glass explained that no one knew what made them work, although they were probably for writing or for sending messages somehow. It said they were built by the Old People, those who lived long ago. At nineteen years of age, I didn't much care. I wasn't there for the artefacts.

I was there to find a spy.

My employer, who at that moment stood at my side, was
a wiry fellow named Michael Banyard. He was a young man
in his prime—though older than myself—a silker with a
head of black hair, a slender face and a large nose, which had
something of the nobleman about it. I thought of him fondly
because he was much more than my master. He'd become
my mentor, having taken me in from the rat-infested city
streets, for which I was grateful.

He leaned closer to whisper in my ear.

'Remember—green jacket, missing button. If you make
contact, bring him directly to me, Ebadiah.'

I gave a nod. 'Right you are, boss.'

Michael strode away to lurk beyond the doors in the next
room, leaving me to nervously watch for a man wearing the
green jacket of a Londaland gunner. There were others like
him in the city, but *this* gunner's jacket would have a gap
somewhere on the double-breasted rows of buttons, where
one was missing. That's how I'd know him.

For half an hour I waited there, wondering if he'd show,
hoping he would. For then we could take his message and
at least go home. I was well acquainted with those museum
artefacts by the end.

It was a balmy spring afternoon and we should have been
home 'cause the Mysteries Solved office was closed, it being
a Saturday, with no investigations that were big enough for
us to work through the weekend. This spy business was a different matter, though. Our minds weren't on our usual cases
at all. We were all caught up by thoughts of the war that had
already blighted us for several years and, stuck there in that
gloomy hall of broken things, my mind drifted. I recalled
the years I'd spent on the street, scavenging to stay alive—
remembered the nights sleeping rough under Rook's Bridge
and shining shoes on the corner of Bunson Street. I was
thinking about the time I first met Michael when, staggering
in, a figure trailing blood across the floor jolted me from my
memories. Never mind the missing button, I knew at once it

was the spy. The gunner's jacket was enough—that and the bloody wound in his back.

'Michael!' I ran to the stricken man, who half collapsed into my arms and half over a cabinet of dusty trinkets. 'Michael! He's here!'

Michael came running and took hold of the spy, easing him carefully down onto the floor. He crouched to listen as the spy spoke his last, words both urgent and quiet. They were important words. I didn't know it then, but they were words that would alter the course of my life. And nodding and committing them to memory, Michael collected them all.

I leave the corpse alone, free another barrel and roll it out. Soon all twelve are on the beach below the halker, and I hike off to fetch a rock from the other side of the dunes where stones lie scattered. My third strike cracks a stave of the lid and pressing down in the middle forces an end to pop up. I lever out the stave. The smell of fish hits me and with dubious caution I lower my face for a better sniff.

'Ain't too bad. Edible, I'd say.'

Stink looks at me with curious eyes: *If it's food, why ain't we eating?*

I dig out a pale, salted herring and toss it to him. He catches it mid-flight and gulps it down with barely a chomp. Then he's jumping up on his hind legs, fighting to stick his nose into the gap in the lid. I pull out another herring and throw it for him, take a third and eat that myself, savouring every morsel, bones and all. It's the first thing I've eaten in two days. I sit down and look out to sea until a *thump* causes me to turn. The barrel is on its side, Stink's muzzle wedged in the gap.

'Hey!' I'm up like a shot.

He darts away with several fish hanging from his jaws.

Before long all twelve barrels are cracked open. Fish, fish and more fish. I tamp the broken staves back into place, sit and think. These need to be hidden somewhere safe or they'll be stolen. I certainly couldn't leave them here. The sea would wash them away or spoil them. It's a puzzle 'cause I'd rather take the whole lot with me. But twelve barrels? Not a hope. Not without a horse and cart or a steam truck—neither of which are an option right now.

After some thought, I recall seeing an old haulage rig back in the steam tug. Tipped on its two wheels, that would take one barrel and I'd be able to pull it. I decide to take one with me and bury the rest on the landward side of the dunes. There's an old tarp in the tug, too, which will protect the barrels a little.

I set to work, returning to the wrecked tug to drag out the iron rig, drop it over the side and toss the canvass tarp after it. The next phase of my plan takes ages. The barrels are big and heavy, and rolling them across the sand is hard work. Pushing them up and over the dunes is tougher still but I persevere as this food could save my life. If I venture inland and find nothing, I can always return to dig them out.

I find a broken board from a ship and use it to dig a deep hole while considering the barrels. They could help others. That's certainly true—and if they're buried, no one else will find them. No one will eat the herrings unless I come back. If I don't—and let's face it, I might not—then they'll all go to waste. Several times I pause, thinking I might just leave them to be found and used, but in the end I carry on.

I carefully roll them in, cover them over with the tarp, weigh that down with rocks, and shovel sand over the top before shoving the broken board into the sand as a marker. Satisfied that the dune looks pretty much as it did before, I load up my one barrel onto the rig, collect my pack and bedroll from the tug and set off, hauling the rig inland with Stink running around me as the cold winter sun begins its slow descent.

Out to the south, a line of cliffs jigger-jags away into a distant haze, the land rising and falling in gentle hills that are green though patched with blackened, scorched earth. There are no settlements in sight and trudging ever further from the coast, I quickly lose the sea. To the west the land flattens and seems to roll on forever. That's where I'm heading. Into forever.

I pause to stock up on pebbles from the path, picking them out with my fingertips and polishing them clean on my sleeve before dropping them into a deep pocket of my Draker long coat.

Fields and hedgerows surround the path that's grown into a gravelled road, and after a mile or two more, a hamlet appears ahead. The half dozen houses seem deserted. I work my way through them, checking for food or other perks. High up at the back of a dusty shelf, I find an old can of hallard—the meat of those giant red crabs with sixteen long, spidery legs—and a jar of pickled eggs. Not the greatest combination, but I ain't complaining. It'll make a change from herring.

The next building looks like a store. Old painted signs in the windows advertise all kinds of goods: canned food, tobacco, boiled sweets, carbolic soap, potatoes... I cup my hands at the dusty glass to see better. The place looks empty, the food and other stuff raided long ago, but I enter anyway to check and make a circuit of the store front until a hiss calls my attention to the six-foot thresher that's ambling out from behind the counter.

I guess you might not know about the dragons, or threshers as we call them. A medium sized thresher is easily stronger and faster than a man: the bigger ones more so. Their jaws can rip an arm clean off with ease and their venomous bites soon kill any who escape injured. There's no antidote to the poison, far as I know.

I back away slowly, find the door and leave the dragon to its small kingdom.

A signpost stands by a crossroads at the heart of the settlement, an arrowed board pointing the way to Louborough.

BEN MEARS

Another tells me Snettings Hill lies opposite. Fordby Sea Town is at my back and Finglesford is ahead. Hoisting my pack higher on my shoulder, I move to set off but then stop. There's something else on the signpost, lower down—something scratched into the wood of the post itself. I tilt my head and squint at the etched symbol: a backwards S with a horizontal line topping the upper end of the letter, and a downward pointing arrow at the base. What does it mean? And who left it there?

The salted herring is a real find but the one I ate straight from the barrel has left me feeling sick. Too much salt on an empty stomach, I guess. I watch Stink as he pads along nearby, nose to the ground, sniffing at who knows what. He ain't fussed, but we better rinse the others before eating them, or better still, soak and cook them. My mouth waters at the thought of hot fish stew, but my canteen's dry.

Water, then. That's next on the list in my head. I view the land through my telescope and fix upon a line of trees that snakes around the foot of a hillside about five miles ahead and off to the right. That could be a river, which would do nicely. Picturing an ideal camp with a fire on the shingles of a modest beach and a bivouac built of branches—moss and leaves as a mattress—I slide my telescope back into my pack and aim for the treeline with quickened pace.

*

It must have been less than an hour since the death of the spy in the green gunner's jacket, whose name I was never to learn, and we were back home at 96 Bunson Street. Michael's strapping business partner, Josiah Mingle, soon called me to the study, so in I limped. The room smelled of beeswax, parchment and ink—scents that were usually comforting, though they did nowt for me that day. The men were wearing their gun belts and rapiers, which was worrying.

THE JICKER MAN

The two had returned from their draft overseas fighting for king 'n' country. We were all hoping that would be an end to it, that the war would be over, and they'd be home for good. But there was a new urgency about Michael. Quill in hand, he stooped over his old desk, scribbling a number of circles on a map in his bright, quick way.

'Ah, there you are, Ebadiah. What I must tell you is of the utmost importance. I'm now certain the gawper Skallagrim is behind this entire wretched war, and that he has plotted the doom of us all.' I watched with interest over his shoulder as he continued. 'The information our brave spy died for leads to but one conclusion—that Skallagrim will seek to hide in one of six lairs, the locations of which are scattered the length of Londaland. I've marked them here. Be assured, our foe is more dangerous now than ever before. He's a threat to all humanity.' Rolling the map, he had thrust it into my hands.

Skallagrim, the Gawper King... His name would become synonymous with the downfall of humankind.

I'd begun to speak. 'Why are you giving—'

'Yes, I know,' said Michael. 'The three of us had planned to pursue this together, but a few minutes ago our summons arrived. If Josiah and I are not at the docks by two o'clock sharp, we'll be hanged as deserters, which really would negate any chance of us finding this fellow.' He had brushed a strand of raven hair from his brow and put on his battered tricorn hat. 'Though perhaps we shall return in good time, yet—I'm sorry—for now our secret mission must fall to you.'

This was all happening a bit too quick for my liking.

'Fall to me?! There must be a trooper who'd do a better job—one who ain't half-blind and who don't limp. Blinders! If the army won't take me, why would you think *I* could do it?'

Michael paused, resting a hand on my shoulder. 'I have the utmost faith in you. You are more resourceful and

street-smart than any trooper I know. And you shan't be
entirely alone...'

I stared at my twisted foot with my one good eye.

Briefly, he lifted my chin with a finger and lowered his
voice. 'You may be young, but you're stronger than you
think, Ebadiah.'

*

Hauling the loaded rig, I notice shoe prints in the
rain-softened dirt of the track. I stoop, unnerved.
They're small, a woman's or a child's, I'd say, but the feeling
don't lift. Birds scatter from bushes like black bullets sweeping up into the blanched sky. Moving on, I pass a tall clump
of dense foliage following a curl in an animal trackway and
come upon the scene quite suddenly. Stink is behind me
somewhere, snuffling in the undergrowth. I was right about
the shingle beach, there's a fine one. A brook babbles around
it in a broad bend while the surrounding trees dapple it in
shade from the winter sun.

I stop dead in my tracks.

A slender girl, around eighteen years old, is kneeling at
the water's edge and bowing low, about to drink from the
stream. She is like a doe in a clearing. Nearby, her shoulder
bag sits on the ground, a bound roll of fur strapped across
the top. I check for others but she's alone. Her lips sink
nearer to the rippling surface.

'Don't!' I blurt.

2. THE GIRL

Startled, she scrambles back from me, brandishes a knife from a sheath on her belt, though I'm nowhere near her—around fifteen feet away—and posing no threat. To be honest, I've just saved her from making a big mistake. I wonder at her naivety and the fear and suspicion on her face, a rather pretty one though it is: slim with fair features and delicately curving lips, framed by a head of blonde curls.

She stares at me.

I stare at her.

'It ain't safe. You should boil it first.'

'Who are *you?*' she asks in a haughty voice, focusing upon my occluded eye. The corners of her mouth twist as though she's repulsed. 'Are you alone?' There's a northern twang to her accent, though she's well-spoken. Sounds like a silker to me—born to money and influence.

Stink arrives at my side, pausing to watch her. He tenses, so I stroke his head. 'It's alright, boy.'

He offers the usual growl, but it soon peters away as he decides she ain't dangerous. Still, he glowers at her distrustfully.

'Just the dog and me,' I say. 'You?'

'My family and a few others are beyond the trees.' She nods towards the woodland over her shoulder. 'One shout and they'll come running.'

'Call 'em if you want. We won't hurt you.' I gesture to the barrel on the rig. 'I got fish. Want some?'

Tentatively, she nods.

'It's salted but we can wash it in the river and boil it up. There's a can in my pack and we can make a fire.'

'You can make fire?' she asks, looking hopeful, but then she quickly looks away as though she's revealed too much. She lowers the knife.

'You're alone, ain't you?'

She looks scared. 'What if I am? I can look after myself.' She raises the blade again.

'Alright. You seem frightened. I'll just leave some fish and go.' I lever up the broken stave from the barrel lid, pick out a herring and throw it onto the stones at her feet. I toss her another two before turning to leave. 'Oh, if you don't mind, I'd like to get some water from the stream first.'

'Alright then, but no artifices.'

I look at her blankly.

'No tricks.' She takes several paces away from the water's edge while tracking me at knifepoint and when Stink sniffs his way closer she seems scared, sweeping the blade towards him.

'It's alright, boy.' I slip the pack from my shoulders and delve inside to find my canteen, take it to the stream and submerge it until it's filled with icy water before corking it. I fill my cooking can, too, collect my rig and turn to leave. It's a shame 'cause the shingle beach would make a neat camp and I'd have a good supply of water in the morning, but never mind. There'll be other places further upstream. I haul the rig about five feet before she calls after me.

'There's something wrong with you, boy. Are you ill?'

Been a while since anybody called me boy. This girl's irritating.

'Listen. I have a blind eye and a limp from a long ago beating. I've just one friend in this wretched world: a dog called Stink—and Bear Dog, when he's being cute—but mostly it's Stink. My name is Ebadiah and I seek the Gawper King.'

That's shut her up. She gawks at me as I turn again to leave.

'Wait. Can you really make fire?'

Looks like I'm staying after all. I ask if she'd like me to make a campfire and she nods. A while later we have a workable camp arranged and I blow flames to life. Tucking my fire kit back into my bag, I ask, 'What's your name?'

'Della Mae Eliza Cordington-Blithe. You may call me Miss Della if you wish, but only because Miss Cordington-Blithe takes too long to say. You said Ebadiah but you didn't say your other names?'

'Ebadiah Joseph.'

'Is that it? You must have other names. Everyone has *at least* three.'

'They're all the names I got, though some used to call me Shoe Shine.'

'Ebadiah Joseph Shoe Shine? How funny!'

Stink whines, pawing at my arm: *Feed me?*

I give him a scratch behind the ears.

'You don't know much about threaders, do you? No fancy names. I was a street boy before...' The words choke in my throat. As I gaze into the flames, the memory of what I've lost overwhelms me.

Michael was serious. 'Now, this can't go through the official channels, Ebadiah. The government doesn't know what we know, and they wouldn't believe us if we told them. Other than Josiah and me, you're the only soul in Londaland who understands the true extent of Skallagrim's handiwork—and who has half a chance of locating him—the only one we can trust. But *you* must trust no one. Understand?'

I nodded and tried to swallow a great lump that had snuck up into my throat.

Michael crossed to a bureau from which he took documents, throwing them into his travel bag. He tossed in a bottle of ink, some writing paper, a few new parchments and grudgingly added several exquisite quills. 'Carry the skull at all times. Keep it safe. Tell no one about it or the power it holds. On this your life may depend. I can't take it where I'm going. It's in your keeping. You know where it's hidden.'

I knew about the gawper skull. Michael had shown it to me several times, taught me all about it.

'There's a file you should have, too,' he added. 'It may be useful.'

'A file?'

'The gawper file. You'll find it on the shelf over my desk with the case files in the Mysteries Solved office. It contains all I've learned about the gawper kind.' He looked thoughtful. 'If I were you, I'd get out of Camdon as soon as possible.'

'But where should I go?' I'd asked, my mind spinning.

'Head for the countryside,' said Josiah, his voice a low growl. 'Stay away from the cities. They're no longer safe.'

Michael gave me a piercing look.

'Find Skallagrim. Kill him before it's too late.'

The campfire cackles as I feed it with more of the dead branches we've collected and stacked in a pile. There should be enough to see us through the evening, which is settling softly over us as we speak. The green glow over the southern horizon deepens by the minute while in the west, the sun drops behind amber-trimmed clouds. 'I'm a threader.'

'Oh.' Della makes no effort to disguise her disappointment.

'You seem surprised. Ain't it obvious?'

'Nothing seems obvious anymore.'

'I know. You're a silker, right? I mean, you were before the war. You must've been rich and had fancy things an' all. Don't suppose it matters much now.'

'Oh, it still matters,' she says snootily, facing me across the fire. At least her knife's back in its sheath...

Stink steals a fish from the barrel. Della laughs.

'Hey!' I shout.

With the herring dangling from his jaws, he runs to the other end of the beach to eat.

'Little thief,' I say, though without anger. He's just being a dog. Can't help it. 'When I began training him, I used food, having him take it from me. Now he'll snatch whatever I'm holding when told to *take*. But he'll nick anything if you let him.'

Earlier we gathered young shoots of boarwort from along the stream to add to the fish and now we sit on the shingle beach, warming ourselves and waiting for the stew to boil. I've rigged a makeshift tripod from branches and hung the can from its iron handle to heat over the flames. Before that, we built two bivouacs: one tucked in behind the weeping branches of a willow, mostly hidden by undergrowth, and another that's sitting out in the open on the beach. In the latter, I've primed a trip wire across the entrance and rigged it with a brass bell I took from a rich woman's house a while back. If someone enters the decoy bivouac, the ringing will sound to warn us of a visitor in the camp while we are still in the hidden shelter.

To our side, the stream babbles a silvery song. I take my shard of mirror and the cutthroat razor to the water's edge, splash my face and shave while we talk.

'What happened to you?' she asks, and I answer, though I'd rather not say.

'No parents. Grew up on the streets but was taken in by a kind silker who brought me up, gave me a job, an education of sorts.'

'What do you mean?'

'Michael Banyard was his name. A detective, him and another.'

'Well, there's your other name, then. Ebadiah Joseph *Banyard*. Or should it be Ebadiah Joseph Banyard Shoe Shine?' She laughs at me.

I don't mind. It's never bothered me before but hearing her say it is rather pleasing: *Ebadiah Joseph Banyard*. I mouth the words to myself. 'They trained me, taught me the trade, taught me everything. That was when I took the beating that did these.' I gesture to my bad eye and ankle. 'I was out on a job and the rogues we were investigating cornered me.'

'It sounds terribly exciting.'

'It wasn't. I nearly died.'

'Oh. So where are they now, your detective friends?'

'Conscripted.' I think again of the meeting in the study when Michael gave the map to me.

At a gesture from Michael, Josiah took a crystal decanter and glasses from the corner cabinet to pour three measures of rum. Since their return, it was the only spirit I'd seen them touch.

Michael raised a glass. 'To the three of us. Until next we meet!'

They each downed their drinks in one swig. I peered into my glass before replacing it on the desk.

'We *will* meet again, won't we?' I asked.

'I promise you, we will,' Michael said.

'In this life or the next,' added Josiah with a mirthless grin.

It wasn't that I didn't like rum—I just didn't want them to leave. Didn't want this moment to end 'cause when it did, I knew they'd go.

Michael flipped open his pocket watch to peer at its polished dial. 'I'm sorry, we're out of time.' Shouldering his pack, he hurried out of the room, Josiah close behind. 'You must take every precaution, my friend,' said Michael over his shoulder.

'Blinders...' I muttered and, full of questions, I followed them to the front door of the house that for five years had been my adopted home. 'But how will I do it?'

There on the step, Michael had clasped my hands in a gesture of warmth.

'You must find a way.'

No pressure, then.

Their horses were already saddled and tethered outside, awaiting them—Michael's a black gelding, Josiah's a dappled grey mare. For they, too, were bound for war. I watched the men loose the tethers and mount up.

'Godspeed, Shoe Shine,' said Josiah from his saddle, with a tip of his hat. I was touched that Joe had used my old street name—but then, he'd never let that go.

'Godspeed, Ebadiah,' said Michael. 'I do believe the world's future rests in your hands!' Turning the horses about, they set off for the docks.

'Godspeed!' I called after them as my heart sank. I made the sacred sign, tracing a ring on my brow before touching the shirt over my heart. 'And come home soon!'

And just like that, my mentors, teachers, heroes and friends, were gone.

As their mounted figures receded down the bustling street, I was left with a single goal: to find and kill Skallagrim the Gawper King, for that had been our plan even before the spy had delivered confirmation of our fears. The odds were against me—I knew that much even then. But with a gawper skull? Well, that could make a difference. Using the skull I could communicate with the gawpers—with a few good ones at least—the ones who might help.

I climbed the stairs in a hurry and found it under Michael's bed, snug inside an old hat box. Lifting it out, I removed its oilcloth covering to peer into the empty eye sockets of a creature long-dead.

The skull was like a human's, only a little larger and longer. Of its teeth, the canines were biggest, being lengthier than the rest. All in all, it looked like something from one of Josiah's penny dreadfuls. I wrapped it with the cloth before shoving it into my bag.

When most people encounter a gawper it's the last thing they ever see. But that didn't worry me. I'd seen them before: eyes like white fire, their tall, dark shapes, swathed in long, ragged cloaks of the black weed. And Michael had told me all about them.

'They are powerful beings, once human,' he'd said. 'Dwelling in the caves of Mors Zonam, they hid themselves from humanity and over countless years, developed abilities that set them apart from us. Be in no doubt, Ebadiah, that gawpers can speak to each other through their thoughts alone. They can move objects with their minds and can travel without ever leaving their lairs.'

This and more, Michael had taught me.

Ain't no doubt about it, gawpers were deadly. And they were our enemies.

Mostly.

I felt numb. Who was I to take on such a ridiculous mission? A nobody. Less that a nobody. Not a soldier nor a spy, nor even a whole person. I was merely an assistant to a private detective. And with Michael gone, I wasn't even that anymore.

I was nothing.

I must have looked as though I was going to continue because Della was watching me expectantly.

'Last I saw of 'em, they were leaving for a gunship, in His Majesty's Fifteenth Regiment. Bound for Morracib to

strengthen the front. Who knows what's become of them?'
The fire spits. The flames dance. I finish shaving and put my
things away. 'This poxy war's taken everything from me.'

'Me too,' Della sighs.

'Yeah?'

'You were right about my family and the others I mentioned. They're all gone and I'm alone. Hopelessly so. I'm
afraid I don't know much about surviving in whatever this
is—this pile of rubble we used to call a country. I didn't know
I should boil the water. I can't start a fire without matches. In
all honesty, I struggle to light a fire *with* matches. I haven't
eaten in four days and most of the time I feel as though I
might faint.'

'You need food. You probably ain't drank enough, either.
Let's hope you ain't caught nothing from the water. Here, the
stew's ready.'

She fetches a copper cup from her bag, the sort folk used
to drink black bean soup from, back when there was black
bean soup to drink.

I take the cup and dip it into the stew, let it fill to around
two thirds, making sure to capture a good few lumps of the
flaking boiled herring before passing it to her.

'Careful. It's hot.' I must sound like an idiot. Of course,
it's hot. But then, she *was* about to drink water that's likely
fouled form corpses floating upstream, so...

Cradling the cup in her hands, she blows at her steaming
stew as I find my cup and scoop a portion for myself.

We gaze into the fire, silent for some minutes as the stew
cools.

'You said something about the Gawper King...'

I nod keenly. 'I'm looking for him. And when I find him,
I'm gonna kill him.'

'Why?'

''Cause all this is *his* fault. He started the war.'

'But I thought the war began when Urthia quarrelled with
Amorphia.'

'It did, but it was the Gawper King and his followers who rigged it. He wants the human race gone. He has judged us all, and his verdict is death. We were investigating before the war. Learned all about it with the help of some rebel gawpers.'

'You spoke with gawpers?' Della seems doubtful.

'We did, but that doesn't matter. Skallagrim could have stopped it all but he wanted it to happen. Worked at it until he had men spilling blood.'

'How?'

'Don't you know? When a gawper has you in its gaze, it can look right into your soul. That's how they judge you. Skallagrim and his followers influenced the minds of men. They lied and manipu... Manipu...'

'Manipulated?'

'That's the one. Now he plans to take over all Londaland while it's in disarray and then he'll look to the whole world. Did you know they can talk to each other with only their minds?'

'No.'

'When he was done meddling, he vanished like a ghost in the mist. The coward! Now it's time for him to pay.' I cast my good eye over a bulge at the base of my backpack where the gawper skull is nestled.

'Skallagrim? What a funny name.'

'Gawpers take their names from ancient writings. They think the written word sacred. Skallagrim's the Gawper King. He used to be alright but he changed. Turned bad. Now there ain't nothing good about him.'

'You do realise that's a double negative...'

'What?'

'*Ain't nothing*—a double negative. What that means is *there isn't nothing*, which means *there is everything*. So, what you're actually saying is, in fact, that this gawper, Skallagrim, is really rather wonderful.'

'Blinders! I told you! I grew up on the street. I talk better than I did, but some habits are hard to kick. Anyway, you know well enough what I meant.'

She nods and sips her stew. 'This is good!' Blowing keenly, she cools it further and dips her fingers in to pick out pieces of the milky white meat, chewing them with delight before little by little draining the cup.

'More?'

She nods quickly.

'Help yourself.'

She refills her cup and blows the stew. 'How will you know this Gawper King when you find him? My father said all gawpers look the same. Tall, hooded, no face, ragged cloak of black weed...'

'Not this one. I'm told he has eyes that burn with a red fire.'

'My father didn't believe in gawpers, not until the *gawper dawn*.' She's referring to an event when Skallagrim's gawper army made itself known, proving once and for all that gawpers ain't ghosts or visions of the drunken or deluded. Gawpers are real. I knew it then and I know it now. Gawpers are all *too* real.

I laugh dryly. 'There were a lot like your father.' The stew *is* good. Way better than the salty, dry fish straight from the barrel. The little water we added to the pot has become sweet with the juices from the flesh. I down a few mouthfuls and feel its warmth spreading through my aching insides. 'What happened to your family? You don't have to say if you'd rather not.'

'We lived in Loncaster, in a big house in the city. Father was a cloth merchant—silks mainly. He was set to work in the fields in the countryside to the north when things became tight during the war. We were all moved out there to help. A place called Frammington. It's not far from here.'

'I think I passed through it a while back,' I say. 'Why was your father not called up?'

36

'The army wouldn't have him. He fell from a horse when he was younger and has suffered a troubled knee ever since.' These last words are said with distance and dismay.

'He's dead?'

She nods and turns away to watch Stink who's now stretched out between the trackway and the fire, basking in the warmth of the flames. 'Here you are, boy.' I offer him some cooling flakes of fish and his tail thumps the ground as he gulps them down. He watches me quizzically, his eyes flashing gold in the flickering light: *That all?*

I spoon some more of the flesh aside to cool for him and tell him, 'Wait.'

Della continues. 'The Urthians pushed north and overran the town. My father was shot in the chest while defending us. He never made it out. Mother and I escaped but she took an arrow in the shoulder. The wound became infected and we couldn't find anyone to help. No surgeons. No one. We dodged another band of Urthian warriors then, but she grew feverish when we were hiding out at an old watermill down that way.' She points upstream. 'I tried everything I could. Couldn't save her. She fell into a stupor and never woke. That was two weeks ago. Two weeks today, in fact.'

'Brothers? Sisters?'

'Only child. Spoiled little rich girl, I suppose you're thinking.'

I am but don't say it. 'I can show you how to start a fire if you like, but you'll have to find your own flint and steel.'

'Alright.' She pauses. 'How will you find him—what's-his-name—the Gawper King?'

'I have a map. There are six sites that could be his lair. I've been to one already. Found it abandoned.'

A distant animal cry drifts to us across the stream. It sounds like a wounded war bird. Stink scrambles to his feet at the water's edge, points his nose and barks into the gathering dusk. Della peers towards the trees and edges closer to me around the fireside. 'Are you armed?' she asks.

I pull my slingshot from a long coat pocket. 'Just this, unless you count my razor. Lost a good knife a week ago. You?'

'I have my knife.' She rests a hand on the pommel at her belt and nods towards my slingshot. 'Will that thing take down a dragon lizard? You've seen the dragons, haven't you?'

'I've seen them. Killed one with a brick a while back. A lucky shot, right between the eyes.'

'Do you have any bricks?'

'No, but it's better to avoid the dragons anyway.' I glance up at trees that line the bank on our side of the water, beyond the beach. 'We could make spears. You know, just in case.' I set about snapping off the longest of the straight branches I can reach. 'Lend me your knife.'

Della takes her knife from its sheath and passes it. I strip bark from the shafts, four in all—one spear each and two spares—and shave points at their ends. With the night quiet once more and our spears stacked to one side, I take my place by the fire again. Stink begs while we eat. We leave some more to cool for him and when it's all gone, he licks the pan clean.

'Won't he give us away, barking like that?' Della asks.

'Not particularly. There're lots of strays now. Who's to say anyone is with the dog they can hear barking in the night?' I watch Stink study the opposite bank. 'Dogs can see fewer colours than us. Did you know? But they can see better than us in the dark.'

'You know a lot about dogs.'

'Their hearing is amazing, too. And their sense of smell. Having him with me means I know something's coming long before it arrives—way before I would otherwise notice. I swear he's saved my life more times than I can say. It's definitely safer with him, though sometimes he'll stand there barking into the night and I know he's sensing something out there but don't know what.'

'Alright. I suppose we should keep him then.' She moves again to sit by me, seeming unnerved by our surroundings.

'*We?*'

'Yes, we. Us. I feel safer with you than I do alone. As a threader, it's your duty to protect your betters.'

'Well, if you think I'm gonna serve you like a slave, you can think again.'

'Just keep me safe, please, or I'll die out here.'

'I'd do that if I were a threader *or* a silker. That would just be the decent thing to do.'

Other animal sounds reach us: a gibbering off to our right, a squawking to our left, and again that wounded cry from far across the stream. She looks out into the shadows, shuffles tight to my side and threads an arm through the crook of mine.

'I'm awfully tired. Do you mind if I sleep?'

'Not at all.' For a moment I think she's gonna sleep right here leaning against my shoulder but yawning, she rises and takes herself off to the hidden shelter.

Stink pads over to me, murmurs softly and nuzzles in against my neck.

'Hey, Bear Dog. Time for bed.' I give his ears a rub and go to the stream to rinse out my cup and can. I wash my hands and face, fill the can with water and douse the fire. It's better not to advertise our presence while sleeping.

Della is already wrapped in a thick fur from her pack, her head resting on her bag, and she don't stir when I enter the shelter to lean the spears against the sloping, conical wall. I lay my bedroll close by. With my pack to one side of the folded blanket that I use as a pillow, I lie quietly down and huddle beneath my coat. It ain't long before Stink pads in and noses his way under the coat to curl in against me. I feel the warmth of his sleek body, close my eyes and listen to the sounds of the night: the wind rustling the willow leaves, the trickling stream, the hoots of owls in the trees, and Stink's breathing as it slows and deepens into slumber.

Before long, I sense Della stirring in the shadows. Her fur-covered form closes against my other side, sandwiching me between her and the dog.

'Do you mind?' she whispers. 'I feel safer over here.'

I fall asleep, warmer than I've been in a long time.

*

Something wakes me in the night. I'm startled, unnerved and in near darkness. A sound has disturbed my sleep, but what made it? I glance to my side. Stink's gone. To my other side I sense the rise and fall of Della's breathing beneath her blanket of fur. Beyond the branches of the shelter, the sound rises again: Stink's low growl, closely followed by the tinkling of the alarm bell. Throwing on my coat, I rise, creep to the opening and peer into the cold night where the moon casts the world in ghostly tones that shimmer beneath thin drifts of cloud. Stink stands poised, ridged in the space between the shelters, his nose pointing to the bivouac out on the beach. I spot movement in its shadowed opening and stare, trying to make out what's inside. Digging the slingshot from my pocket, I slip a smooth pebble into its leather pouch.

The dog holds his ground as I tread cautiously past him. The crunch of small stones is low beneath the chatter of the stream. He barks a warning, continues his growl.

Fixing upon the beach shelter, I edge nearer.

'Hello? Is somebody there?'

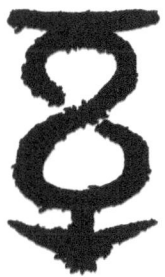

3. THE THRESHER

Slowly, Stink retreats a step, his eyes locked onto the shelter. That's a bad sign.

A scuffling sound comes from inside: the something—whatever it is—moving around. I think if it were a person, my question would have been answered in some way. So, then, it's a creature of sorts.

Please let it be a fox. A fox, I can deal with. Better still, a plump chicken!

I listen hard, trying to pick apart what I hear, to separate the sounds of movement from the tumble of running water. Failing, I approach anyway, duck low at the entrance and peer inside. A sudden lurching form makes me recoil. Tripping and falling backwards, I scramble away, shingles flying as I scrabble for grip. The thresher lizard is a giant—around ten feet long—and fast. Its jigger-jag run swings its tail left and right as it thrusts its red, serpent-like head towards me. It's on me in a blink, jaws yawning wide.

Stink darts in, biting at its ribs. The thresher twists away from me, turning on the dog. I drag myself away while Stink narrowly avoids those monstrous teeth. He runs to join me

41

ahead of the thresher as it releases a long hiss. I struggle to my feet and hurry to load another stone into my slingshot. The first is lost somewhere on the beach.

On the dragon comes: muscular legs, long, scimitar claws swiping, left, right, left, right. Moonlight glints with a blue sheen on several plates of steel armour that remain strapped over its broad head, neck and back. It must have shaken the rest loose and lost them somewhere along the way.

I draw the slingshot and release the missile, only to hear it rebound from the peaked armour plate on the monster's brow. As though in response, the beast hisses vengefully.

'Della!' I cry. 'Run!' I'm on my feet now, sprinting back towards our hidden refuge where the spears lean. 'Thresher! Run!' Reaching the shelter, I tear inside and grab a spear before racing outside again to thrust its point at the face of the oncoming reptile.

Della takes a spear and slips out behind me, stopping further up the beach, with me between her and the dragon. Stink comes to my side, barking his face off and baring his teeth. He shifts stance in a show of threat, hackles raised. I'm glad he's here.

The thresher pauses as though weighing the situation. I jab with my spear again to ward it off as we hold it at bay.

'Cross the stream!' I shout to Della. 'They hate water. It won't follow us there.'

'Can't you kill it?' she calls back to me.

She's beyond my restricted view. Not daring to disengage with the thresher for a second, I wonder what's she doing— keep my good eye locked onto it. It pads around to our left, probing our defences before switching back to our right. Its long, forked tongue flicks out to taste our fear. Its razored claws clicker-clack against stones.

'Cross the stream! Tell me when you reach the other side,' I shout.

A scream pierces the night. 'Della!' I lunge at the beast and risk a glance over my shoulder. There, a second thresher has

Della by the thigh, its jaws clamped tight. It drags her along.
Her back ploughs shingle, her arms flail.

'Della!'

I whip around to see the thresher before me make a run
at Stink, its mouth stretching wide to strike. I thrust the spear
hard and fast into the beast's exposed side, feel the point pop
sickeningly between its scales, and drive deep into flesh. The
creature releases a hideous rattle, writhing as Stink sinks his
teeth into its throat, tearing, ripping. I lean in with all my
weight to pin it to the ground and when it finally stills, pull
my spear free, turn and run for Della, only to find the beach
empty except for her abandoned spear. Blood seeps away
between pebbles, slick and black in the moonlight. There is
so much blood.

Too much.

'Della!' I sweep foliage aside with the tip of my spear
as Stink joins me, and sound a double click, crouching to
follow the bloody trail into the trees. Stink stays close as
we weave through undergrowth, tracking, keeping low.
He sniffs at the ground. We press through bushes until we
reach a small clearing and there we stop dead. Before us, the
thresher feasts upon the remains of Della Mae Eliza Cordington-Blithe. Her ribcage is open, what's left of her body
unmoving. I retreat, throwing Stink a signal, an upturned
palm: *No*.

When we're far enough away from the thresher to feel
safer, I mutter. 'You should've crossed the stream, Della.'

My bag needs little packing. I ain't staying here. Not now.
The thresher may return to the beach with the scent of blood
all around, and that ideal campsite ain't ideal no more. I collect the bell, roll and stow my bed, and grab the best of the
spears. I hoist my pack onto my back, tip the rig and leave
the way I came with Stink trotting behind me. *It's a shame
about Della*, I think to myself. I was just starting to like her,
but there's a limit to how much I can allow myself to care
when it seems everyone I love is always taken from me.

THE JICKER MAN

*

At dawn I pause to rest on the forest path. I let down my pack and slide the map from the inside pocket of my long coat, holding the paper up to study it in the mottled light. It's frayed and tattered in places, and worn through along two of the folds. Six sites are marked by circles of red ink. The map is of Londaland, before the war, so in some ways unreliable now.

One circle has a cross scratched through it in charcoal. That's Hick's Gate, the one I've already visited. The next closest one to me is forty or so miles to the west at a place called Fenlock. That's two days hard hiking, which I ain't about to try with my twisted foot. Factor in time searching buildings for perks along the way, and I'll be doing well to reach it within a week. If it still exists.

From there I'll head directly north for two more sites before bending north-east and crossing into the wilds of Scolanda for the fifth. The final site is down south, labelled *Caverns of Magwitch*. That's way out in the toxic desert of Mors Zonam. I decided a while back to try that last, if all else fails. It ain't a place I want to be.

Bird song surrounds me in these unspoiled woods. Water drips from naked branches, run off from the recent shower. The trees sprawl and climb: ashblack, willow and syculumn, like back there along the stream, but other species also abound; spiniker, oak, stonewoods, borrowstout, beetlebay, holly, birch and... sweet chestnut. I spend a while scavenging beneath the branches for old chestnuts that may still be edible, wrapped in their leathery, spiked shells, find a handful that don't smell too mouldy, and pocket them to roast later.

My breath fogs like steam in the cold forest air. A person could sit here forever, unaware that the country has fallen into chaos, that towns and cities lie in ruins and the population has been scythed to a fraction of its former toll.

Della was the first person I'd seen for a week, and the first potential girlfriend I'd seen for around three months. Sure, she was haughty, but she was alright. I fantasise about what might have been, of Della and me finding somewhere good to settle, somewhere we could defend and make safe, and who knows where that might have led? But terrified, she had clung to me for safety. And I'd failed her.

Stink's disappeared into the trees, hunting no doubt, though I ain't worried. He does that often and always finds his way back to me. But I was here when he went, so here I wait.

Michael showed me how to take bearings from a pocket watch using the position of the sun in the sky and the time of day. I search out the sun, though with the trees all around it's hard to find and I've no master clock with which to set my watches. I simply make an estimate for that, usually noting the point when the sun seems highest in the sky and setting the time on each watch to twelve and, after that, comparing the various times to confirm they're all functioning. It's worked alright so far.

Aligning the hour hand to point at the sun, I hold the gold watch flat to the ground and imagine a line halving the angle between the hour and the twelve o'clock mark. The end of this line—the one furthest from the hour hand—is north, which tells me I'm still heading due west. There are limits to the method. It's confusing to try around six o'clock, but by then I'm usually seeking shelter or building one, and in the winter there's no sun that late in the day anyway.

When Stink returns, he bounds over to nuzzle me, his tail whipping to and fro. I give the hair on his neck a ruffle.

'Hey, Bear Dog.'

He gives me this look, as though I'm the one who's been holding us up: *Well, what are we waiting for?*

I throw the pack onto my back, tip the rig and walk on as he resumes his usual routine, padding around twenty feet ahead. He likes to do this whenever we're on a clear path.

45

When our way is less obvious he tends to hang back, staying closer. We reach a decline where the path narrows to drop into a valley, before opening out again and bending right onto another tight stretch that follows the lower edge of the hill. All the while I watch for movement on the slope that rises to my right. Tall trees sway and creak in the wind overhead. The forest has twisted trees, too, some fallen and lying at odd angles. There are others that, with the right play of light, look like a figure when glimpsed from afar. At least, they do when you only have one good eye. It's harder to judge distances, too.

The forest seems alive sometimes, with a cunning of its own creation. Numerous times I stop and whistle a rising note that sounds like a bird call to tell Stink to wait. Then I creep closer to get a better look and check we're not being watched or hunted. It almost always turns out to be the trunk of a tree that's in shadow or catching glances of sunlight, or a meeting of branches that happens to mimic human or animal features.

Slippery with mud and decaying, wet leaves, the path climbs before meeting another track that slopes down from the hillside to lead right again. Even so, I'm quite sure we're still heading in a generally westward direction. We've just skirted part of the hill, that's all.

Soon I stop, statue-still, fixing upon a tall gawper-like shape that catches in the corner of my eye—a figure in crisp silhouette. My mind screams, *RUN!* But turning, I see it's nothing more than a large gatepost formed from a single standing stone. The gate is long gone. Its partner looms opposite, partially submerged by undergrowth. The old gateway sits on a rise in the track. Beyond, the sky between the trees is bright through a thin veil of branches and twigs and I can't see what's waiting for us over the ridge. We walk on anyway.

Our way drifts through the woods and we come to a rocky gully that cuts into the slope at an angle from the path, an

incline flanking one side, a steep decline on the other. Thinking a clear view of the land ahead would be useful, I call to
Stink and clamber up.

There's a path between trees, crossed here and there by
jutting roots that writhe up out of the leafy soil like thick
brown snakes, only to dive back underground. Occasionally
it's a trunk or branch that curves in my way and I'm forced
to duck low to scramble beneath, or else find another way
through. Eventually the woods thin and I exit onto the foot
of a sloping meadow, the top of which crests the hill.

There, I stop before a scatter of bones—both animal and
human. Some have slivers of old yellowed flesh still adhering, and beyond is a large nest set in the tall, wild grasses.
A dozen or so threshers idle around a clutch of round, pale
eggs. I drop low in the grass. Stink halts and throws me a
questioning look. Perhaps this is the home of our night
visitors. The dragons ain't seen us yet, so I back away slowly
and Stink follows my lead, sniffing at the air. For once he
don't bark and I'm glad of it. When I'm confident that we're
hidden by the woods once more, I up the pace to put some
decent ground between us and the deadly thunder. It's no
use trying to climb past them to a viewing point. Ain't worth
the risk.

We descend the hillside and before long, leave the
woods and their phantoms behind, and a hamlet appears
as the landscape broadens. Houses straggle along the track
which firms into a cobbled road. The settlement looks as yet
undamaged by war, though apparently abandoned. There
could be frightened survivors cowering in cellars or watching
me from attic windows as I pass through. I really wouldn't
know. Not if they hid well enough.

A cursory search of the houses and barns turns up nothing and I'm about to leave when I stop before the second of
the hamlet's two watch-lamps. They ain't lit, of course. They
would have burned with blue flames but the gas ran out long
ago. I see that sign again: the backwards S, a horizontal line

topping the character, a downward arrow at the base. This time it's painted on the iron post with crimson gloop. *Is that blood? What does it mean?* I find my map and sketch the symbol in one corner with the nub of charcoal I keep in a pocket. How I wish Michael was here! *He* would know. *He* would tell me.

Looking back at the empty buildings, I'm tempted to stay for a night. One of them could make a comfortable stop-over—hidden dangers aside—but it ain't even midday and I should push on. Weary, I trudge the stony road.

*

Up ahead, Stink stops, his nose pointing at a bulky shape in the distance that's tipped up at an odd angle by the verge. Some sort of vehicle, most likely. From here it's impossible to tell, though I stop and squint. Corn fields span either side of the road, last year's crop still wasting, rippling tall in the wind. The road runs level along higher ground, traversing a long ridge. The thought of scavenged ears of corn, ground and baked into a loaf, makes my mouth water. We walk on, closing on the vehicle. It's a clockwork car, crashed or run off the road and sitting half in a ditch.

Stink runs a ring around it and pees against a rear wheel before I even reach it. Thinking the car could be occupied, I dump my pack and pitch the rig to investigate, but it's empty. Not even a corpse at the steering wheel. One of its iron-rimmed wheels is missing from a front corner and it reminds me of a time I found a similar model, a Gear and Cog *Thunder Strike*, though one more serviceable. Back then I had dragged the bullet-riddled corpse of a finely dressed silker gent from the driving seat and laid him on the pavement out front of Yorkson's Bank, leaving his silken topper on his chest. I managed to force the hood open and crank the spinny enough for the car to start before loading it with my meagre belongings. I drove northwards from the ruins of Camdon City, stopping to crank the spinny as needed, until it finally broke down near Loncaster. All that morning I tried to fix it but eventually abandoned it, choosing instead to plunder the mechanism for parts with which to make my slingshot.

Stink barks at me 'cause I've been stood still, staring at the car. I blink the memories away.

Using my spear, I lever up the hood of the three-wheeled wreck until it pops open and taking out my pocketknife, stoop to slice out the rubber lines from the winch drive to use as slingshot spares. Finding nothing else of use, I move on.

Wind rustles the cornfield, a sound like the whispers of a thousand lost souls. The thought of entering the corn is unnerving. The stalks are around eight feet tall—way taller than me—although great swathes lie broken and flattened by the wind. The best chance of finding edible grain is from those still standing, so in I go, swallowed horribly by the grey forest of tattling stems. It soon becomes clear that there's no grain left that ain't shrivelled and blackened. Stink's in here somewhere but I've lost him, along with any sense of direction.

'Stink?' Peering heavenwards, I stop, trying to work out where the road lies. 'Stink?' I'm lost. A sense of panic rises in my chest. 'Stink! Stink! Where are you?'

Somewhere in the distance, he barks.

I run, forging a path through the corn, my head awash with fear, my hands and face battered by the rough stems. Stink is in trouble; or someone is taking my gear, or *I'm* in trouble and I just don't know it yet. Anything could be hiding in this field and I wouldn't see it until I ran right into it! What a fool I am!

Reaching a break in the corn, I glimpse the road and turn for it as Stink emerges from the field opposite. He seems alright. I begin to relax. My gear's untouched. All is well. Panic over. I take a breath.

Get a grip!

Pack shouldered. Rig tipped. Walk on.

The wrecked car is no longer in sight when I see before me another ghost town, this one larger and more sprawling. Wondering what I might find, I drop off the edge of the road to skirt a cautious approach through a patch of thin woodland. Someone is here. I sense it. There must be someone here 'cause the place is surely too big to be completely deserted. At least, that's my gut feeling.

Edging down the first of the streets, I test the theory. Loading a pebble into my slingshot, I draw back the rubber to let fly at an iron sign that hangs from the shop front of an apothecary near a crossroads further on. The stone strikes, sounding a loud gong-like note that echoes around the empty roads to announce my arrival.

I wait, watching from the shadows of a butcher's shop. An animal cry comes back to me from deeper in.

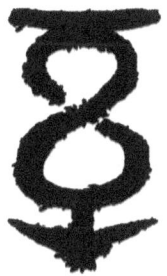

4. ROACH IS ENOUGH

Stink's ears twitch towards the sound and he's off, running. 'Stink!' I call him back but he ain't listening. He's heard a creature and he's keen to investigate, perhaps hoping it's something he can kill and eat. He ain't concerned that it might be an armoured thresher or some other monster.

Idiot hound.

I hide the rig in a ruined garden, covering it with a front door that's been blown from its hinges. Then following at a distance, I try not to lose Stink as he bounds along the barren streets.

Skeletal bodies clutter the pavements and doorways. There are more in the houses. I glimpse their drawn faces, and cover my nose with my scarf against the stench of decay. It's clear that some were shot or cut down in battle. Others are in pieces and lie scattered about, as though animals have torn them apart, while a few appear to have died in their homes, perhaps from battle wounds, illness or starvation in the weeks that followed the violence.

Making the sacred sign, I pass swiftly on after the dog, stopping only when I leave a narrow alley that opens onto the town square. In other times it might have been quaint. There are fine houses with thatched roofs and the town's most splendid buildings: a turreted courthouse, a trade hall and several grand taverns. All are now ruined by explosions, bullet-ridden and in disarray. At the centre is an old stone-built well, topped with a conical tiled roof that's supported by timbers and next to it stands the source of the noise: a sorry looking mule, tethered to a post. The poor animal seems terrified as Stink postures before it, barking intensely. The mule rears, whinnies and brays, pulling at its tether. It's odd to find it unattended so I'm instantly wary. A trap, perhaps, meant to lure victims in, making them vulnerable while they try to steal the mule? Still, I consider it. Standing nearby, I study the many doorways and windows of the surrounding buildings yet see no one lying in wait.

'Stink!' I whistle repeatedly to call him off, relieved when he eventually obeys. The mule begins to calm, its hooves clattering on the cobbles. Although now that things have quietened, I can hear a voice, one that sounds close and yet echoing strangely. Walking to the circular wall, I peer over into the deep shaft from where the voice rises.

'Hello! You, up there!'

'Hello?' I reply.

'Good afternoon.' The voice sounds frail and decrepit but remarkably hopeful.

I squint skyward. The cold sun has passed its zenith. I glance down into the shaft, trying to see who's talking in the deep shadows.

'Are you stuck?' I ask, quickly checking around to be sure there are no attackers closing in on me before looking back down into the hole.

'Of course I'm stuck!'

My eyes adjust to make out the craggy features of a grey-bearded man with a hawkish face, peering up at me.

'How did you get down there? Is this a trap?' Leaning my spear against the well, I load a pebble into my slingshot and hold it ready.

'I'm old, infirm... I was trying to draw water but lost my balance, toppled over the pail, tumbled down.'

'That's quite a fall. If that's true, you must be hurt.'

'No, no. I'm not hurt. I clung to the bucket and the crank slowed my fall. You'll see the mechanism on the side there. Anyway, I landed in water.'

I look for the hand crank that's used to raise or lower the pail and see that he's right. There's a wooden handle and a system of cogs to help winch up the large pail when it's heavy with water.

'Are you armed?' I ask.

'No.'

'So, I guess I can bring you up if you hold onto the pail.'

'I'd be mighty grateful.'

'Take a hold, then, and if you've been lying, know you'll regret it.' I stuff my slingshot into a coat pocket, grasp the crankshaft and set to work winching, all the while eyeing the surrounding square with suspicion. It's hard work 'cause the mechanism is ancient. Under strain, its rusted cogs jitter on their axles but it holds and, little by little, I see the top of the pail growing nearer and the dark shape of the old-timer clinging on for all he's worth. When he's a few feet from the top, I pause, as though to catch my breath, but truly I just want to take a good look at him, make sure he ain't dangerous. Satisfied he's no threat—to the contrary, he's rather pathetic looking—I haul him the rest of the way and help him from the pail and over the wall to safety, an awkward procedure that leaves him breathless.

'I'm much obliged, young sir,' he says between puffs. His voice is worn and rasping. He looks down at his tatty, sodden clothes as a pool of water collects beneath him before he peers at me. 'There's plenty of water if you've come for a drink.'

'Think I'll pass.'

He nods, takes a canteen from his belt and fills it from the bucket. 'Well, I'd best water Dorothy. She's been here for hours.'

Stink pads around as though stung 'cause we won't be eating Dorothy.

'Ain't you cold?' I ask the stranger. 'The water must be icy.'

'Oh, I'm alright. Hardy stock, you know.' He winks and I'm astounded he's survived the ordeal. He seems remarkably well, considering. Although he walks slowly and with a stoop, I reckon he was like that before he fell in. Half feeling his way around, he fetches a smaller pail from one of the leather bags that are slung across the mule's back and collects well water. He places it on the cobbles and Dorothy lowers her head to drink. 'There you are, old girl.' He strokes the mule's shaggy neck.

'Is anyone else alive in the town?' I continue to scan the bleak buildings and streets.

'None, far as I know. All dead or gone. I'm just passing through. You?'

'Same. I'll be on my way soon enough.'

He nods. His eyes, which are cloudy, travel the length of me before settling upon my battered boots. He leans closer as though struggling to focus and nods towards them. 'You should find a better pair on one of the fallen. They don't need them anymore.' He gestures to the surrounding square where a dozen or so bodies lie rotting in the wind.

It don't take me long. There are Urthian warriors among our own fallen men. I avoid them. Londaland troopers wear stout leather riding boots, far superior to the primitive shoes of our enemies. With my face muffled against the putrid smell, I pull boots from the feet of dead soldiers to try on. The fifth pair I find are a good fit and have some miles left in them. No holes. Good. They'll do.

'Who are you?' I ask the old man, wondering if he's now expecting me to journey with him. I hope not. He looks like he needs looking after. Like he'd be slow on the road and hard work. He seems half blind but then so am I, only in a different way.

'The name's Roach.'

'Just Roach?'

'Roach is enough. You?'

'Ebadiah.'

He nods and throws on a long and faded travel cloak that I imagine was once black. He loosens the mule's tether and with considerable effort, mounts up. 'Well, Ebadiah, I'd best be moving on.' He draws up the hood of his cloak to shadow his face.

'Where are you going?'

'I can't tell you. Be safe on your way.'

'Why can't you say?' I ask, though I hadn't cared until now.

'You wouldn't understand.'

'How do you know?'

'I suppose I don't, but I'm not telling you anyway. Where are *you* headed?'

I feel suddenly secretive about my mission. 'That's *my* business.'

He smiles wryly.

Thinking I might find a good bed in one of the houses, I watch him turn the mule about to ride out. I circle the well, studying the buildings, and picture myself alone again. *Perhaps a little company might be a good thing, even if it is with a decrepit old drifter. He seems harmless after all...*

'Wait up!' I call. 'What's the hurry?'

*

The house we choose for shelter is an end of terrace, not far from the middle of the town, which Roach tells me is Hamsford. Once inside, I find it on my map, disappointed to learn I've only covered some fifteen miles over the last two days, but then I am dragging the rig and my old boots didn't help. And, of course, I do have a permanent limp, so there they are: all my excuses, true in one way or another. I wish I had a good horse to ride but most were taken for the war overseas and shipped out for the cavalry—a fate I was refused. I'm a fair rider, having ridden Michael's horse many times. It sets me thinking about when the war began.

'What were you doing when the first bombs fell?' asks Roach when he returns from an upper room, having changed into dry clothes that are just as threadbare as the wet ones. For a breath, I wonder if he's reading my mind, but that's impossible. Ain't it? I put it down to chance.

'When my friends were sent to war, word got out and I was set to work in a print shop for the Camdon Herald. I ran a Rundlebridge Steam Press, churning out Hapgood's propaganda for distribution across Londaland, reports of the war, that kind of thing. It was a sweltering, hard job.' I was planning to leave town, like Michael and Joe had said, but I was taking my time about it. 'I spent most of the time wishing I'd been allowed to go with the soldiers. Last time I saw that machine, it was blown to pieces, gears scattered across Bunson Street with most of the press office. You?'

'Travelling.' He stoops over the fireplace in the little front room and soon flames flicker to life in the hearth. I ain't sure how he lights the fire. Ain't no sign of matches, nor kindling nor flint and steel, and at first, I don't care. It's not important how the fire's lit. What matters is that we ain't gonna freeze to death. Half of the windows have been blown out of the front wall by some battle blast, so the place is like an icehouse, but it's better than a lot of them. We risk being noticed as we stuff bundles of old clothes, newspapers and cushions that we find lying around into the holes of broken panes, and draw the tatty curtains shut to help hide the fire-light and keep out the draught.

A headline on one of the old newspapers catches my eye.

12th Trimoon 1796

URTHIA DECLARES WAR ON

LONDALAND

Chivers Hapgood announces war as Urthian troops invade Porgula, a country of the allied nations. In a rousing speech given before the crowded Old Town Square of Camdon's inner city, the Prime Minister commented that the invasion is tantamount to an assault upon Londaland itself and must therefore be repelled at any cost.

The article spans the entire front page and continues inside, but I don't read any more. Instead, I ball it up hard, cram it into a hole in the glass and brood on my hatred of Skallagrim.

By nine o'clock in the evening we've each eaten a few mouldering, roasted chestnuts and bowls of hot fish stew— *Oh, how quickly I've tired of salted fish, boiled or not!*—and I sit back in a bomb-damaged chair, forever surprised at the old man as he produces a tin of roasted and ground black beans from his saddle bags. He's housed Dorothy in the kitchen for safety during the night, along with my reclaimed barrel and rig. While Stink curls up by the fire, Roach simmers water in a pan and tips in some of the grinds to stew the black bean soup. It's been a while since I've tasted it, so I watch keenly and when it's ready, accept a cup of the hot, bitter brew gratefully.

It's then I begin to wonder about him. How did he truly survive his fall into the well, so uninjured and in such apparent good health? If he'd been down there for a while, why wasn't he half-frozen to death when I brought him up? Why does he seem so unconcerned about his shoddy circumstances? And then there was the fire lighting and the black beans. He sits quietly on a wooden bench near the hearth, looking unreasonably contented.

'You could collect some better clothes,' I suggest. 'Like I did with the boots.'

'I dress the way I want to dress,' he says, peering into his cup. 'Look the way it suits me to look.'

'What do you mean? You look like a beggar, if you don't mind me saying. No one wants to look like a beggar.'

'Picture this. Two men walk a road, one is dressed in finery with gold rings on his fingers, new silks, bright and clean, in obvious wealth. The other is grey, in rags with nothing of perceived value. Who is the most likely to slip by the gang of rogues who lie in wait up ahead?'

'The man in rags, I suppose. Nothing worth stealing.'

He nods and shrugs. 'As I say, I look the way I want. When I appear to be no one of consequence, I usually find there are consequences for no one.'

'And *are* you no one of consequence?'

'Not at all. In fact, I consider myself to be rather important.'

'Why?'

'It's just who I am.'

'And who is that? Who are you really?'

'I'm Roach. Roach is enough.' He sips his soup and we sit in silence for a time, after which he says, 'You seem like a gentleman. We can travel a way together if you like.'

Stink's waiting to lick out our empty cups. He pads around Roach, wagging his tail. The old man gives the dog's neck a scratch. Stink beats his tail faster and leans in.

'I don't mind,' I say. 'Maybe.' It's not that I don't trust him, but there sure is something odd about him. Something hidden. I don't know what. Still, Stink seems to think he's alright.

Draining my cup, I climb the stairs, seeking a bed for the night, Stink shadowing my every step. I throw myself onto a stranger's mattress in the first room I come to and try to sleep, but it's useless. Every time my eyes close, I expect to feel a cold blade slide across my throat. Stink has no such fears. While he snores away for hours, curled into my side and occasionally kicking me in his dreams, I lie watching clouds drift slowly across the inky heavens through the shattered windows.

In frustration, I rise to dig out the gawper skull from the bottom of my pack and unwrap it from folds of oil cloth. Perched on the edge of the bed, I press the skull against mine, brow to brow.

Magwitch. In thought, I call the gawper by name.

There's no immediate reply. I try again and then a third time, and wait, surprised when he finally makes contact.

Ebadiah, Magwitch hears you.

His gravelly voice echoes in my head and I only need think a word for him to receive it. I get straight to the point while our connection holds. It ain't easy these days. There are often disruptions on the planes.

Do you have news of Skallagrim? I ask.

He's quick to respond. *Magwitch has tried to track him. Skallagrim has many followers, more than the rebels. We are few in number. His followers are hiding him, fogging the planes, spying and laying false trails. We know they are using the roads, lurking on the outskirts of your human settlements. Magwitch will continue the hunt.*

He ain't at Hick's Gate, though I found a lair, I tell him. *He may have hidden there.*

This is truth. Magwitch, too, believes Skallagrim may have been there. Does this one still carry the map?

I have it. The map is safe.

Show it to no one. Trust no one. There are...

His words stutter away into a static emptiness as our connection falters. Returning, his thoughts are distant and thin, and I'm aware I've missed something.

THE JICKER MAN

...are taking the west, moving northwards. Beware the Darklings of Brae.

And just like that, we're cut off.

I recall my visit to Hick's Gate and the search of the town, finding the gawper lair in woodlands on the outskirts. The grizzled heads of their human enemies were mounted on bloody poles as a warning to intruders. The entrance was a roughly carved hole, no taller than me and dug into a steep, mossy bank, hidden behind a thicket of firs. I waited a while, watching for any sign of occupation but seeing none, made a fire on the damp earth and fashioned a torch to light my way. I snapped a green branch from one of the trees and split the end into quarters before winding a nest at one end with wire from my bag, packing pine bark, needles and melted resin into the gaps.

The guttering torchlight lit marks in the earth where large gawper claws had sculpted the lair. I had to be sure Skallagrim was not there. With my breath held, I crept, ears straining for any small sound that might give away a gawper's presence. The tunnel led me past a bend to the left and one to the right before broadening out into a single cavern, shored up with the broken trunks of trees, and with a small hole for a chimney. No other entrance or exit. Empty.

I stooped to examine the remains of a central fireplace, smelt the acrid scent of ash mingled with a dank earthiness and an animal taint. Nearby I collected a fragment of the black weed with which the gawpers weave their hooded cloaks.

*

I must have fallen asleep at some point 'cause I wake in the cold upper room and, feeling reasonably refreshed, look around for Stink. There are ways he can leave the house: the broken windows and a damaged back door with a missing

60

corner large enough for him to squeeze through. This makes me think he's probably gone hunting again. Ever since finding him in that Draker's home among his dead siblings, I've told myself he ain't my dog. He's with me but he don't belong to me. Aye, I may have saved him but he's a free spirit and he can come and go as he pleases. It's a rule I live by. I never trap him in. Never force him into anything. And anyway, if I were to try, he'd probably go for me and that ain't gonna end well.

I get up and descend the stairs to find Roach crouching over the fire in the front room, turning a skinned and skewered morgue rat carcass over the flames. Stink's there, too, crunching eagerly upon the decapitated head of the huge rat.

Roach turns at my footsteps. 'Ah, there you are. Your dog has kindly caught us some breakfast.'

'He ain't mine,' I mutter.

'Well, do you want some?'

I nod and sit down to wind my pocket watches. 'I suppose.'

We eat roasted rat meat, picking off every last morsel of flesh with our teeth and sucking the bones clean, and I make sure Stink gets his share. Morgue rats are four times the size of the common rat and this one's large, so there's enough for us all to have a little. The problem comes in trying to keep it down when you start thinking about what it likely grew fat on.

Soon after, we pack our things and wind our way out from the town, Roach riding Dorothy, Stink scouting ahead as usual while I haul the rig. The barrel grows lighter daily and I got to face it: like it or not, before too long I'll run out of fish and will have to seek out something else substantial or else starve. I ain't sure I could stomach another morgue rat. And I sure ain't going back for those other barrels now. The sand can keep 'em.

We follow a road through open countryside and Roach seems happy enough with our bearing.

'West is as good as anywhere,' he says, when I question him. He don't appear to have much of a plan other than to keep moving. 'Where are you going in the west?'

I'm guarded about telling him much 'cause of his odd nature, but he didn't garrotte me in the night, so I give him the name of the next location on my list.

'Fenlock. Do you know it?'

He nods sagely and glances at me sideways from his saddle. 'I've seen the place, a long time ago. A town by the sea.' There's a glint of recognition in those cloudy eyes, which leads me to believe it has meaning for him. In that moment I decide to tell him no more—not until I know more about him. I'm wary and deeply suspicious of his motives for wanting to travel with me. My mind flits back and forth between arguments: he's harmless, a poor old man, down on his luck and lonely on the road; or is he a stealthy killer, merely waiting for the right moment to bludgeon me and steal my fish?

He's crafty, but in a good or a bad way? It's too soon to tell.

Five miles or so pass slowly beneath us. The mule is old and sluggish but Roach don't goad or harry her. He ain't in a hurry.

'We'd better stop and rest Dorothy,' he says when the sun is about as high in the sky as it's gonna get. Frustrated by our plodding headway, I begrudgingly agree while promising myself, *Tomorrow, I'll leave him behind.*

The afternoon warms a little and for a while we travel in relative comfort, ambling along, dry 'cause it ain't rained all day. We remove our scarves and hoods in the shimmer of the pale sun, though the temperature soon starts to plummet. By five o'clock we've lost the light and we're stuck out in the wilds, not a house or barn in sight.

'We'd best get off the road for the night,' says Roach. 'For safety.'

I peer into a fringe of trees that we've been approaching for several miles now. 'We can shelter in the woods, make a fire.'

BEN MEARS

Nodding, he steers the mule off the road and ten minutes later, we're setting camp beneath a soft, green canopy
of pines where the ground is spongy beneath our feet. Our
chosen site is deep enough in to be well hidden from the
road. It's the firelight that might give us away, that and the
smoke, but the wind is drawing off the road towards us, so
that shouldn't be such a problem.

Roach dismounts while Stink disappears into the trees
and, moments later, the old man has a small fire started and
crouches over the flames, feeding it with pine needles and
twigs that crackle and spark. We brew pine needle tea and I
hunt around for fallen wood to keep the fire throughout the
night 'cause it's too late to build much of a shelter. Instead,
we sit with our backs against the trunks of towering trees,
warming ourselves in the glow of the flames and sipping our
tea. And quite without meaning to, I fall into a deep sleep.

*

Past midnight, something shakes me awake. I open my
eyes to see Roach stooping over me, brandishing a knife
in the glimmer of a dying campfire. I back up against the tree
as his blade swings closer.

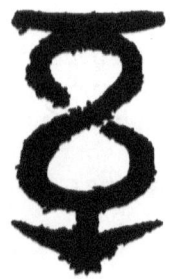

5. JICKERY–POKERY

'**H**ush!' hisses Roach. 'Someone's in trouble.'
Too right! I think. *Me!*

But Roach holds a finger to his lips: *Quiet!* We listen. Nearby, Stink growls a warning. A woman's shrill scream pierces the night somewhere further into the woods. The moon has risen to throw enough light for us to see by, though it's dulled beneath the pines.

Roach sheaths his knife. 'Sounds like she needs help. Are you coming?' He sets off at a pace too spritely for his age. Hesitating, I grab my spear and follow. Stink runs at my side.

'Over here.' Roach gestures in the gloom, weaving nimbly between trunks, and I think it strange that he can move this quickly when it suits him.

We head towards the noise and hearing whimpers that resonate strangely, adjust our path. Bending towards the desperate sounds, we track closer, pausing when flickering lights appear some fifty yards on, dancing like fireflies. We stop, watching the flames of torches move through the trees.

'They're hunting her!' says Roach. 'Hurry!'

'Who are they?' I ask. 'Who is she?'

'I don't know.'

On we go. The forest thins as we reach open ground where a sprawling sawmill lies like a monster steeped in shadow. There, trapped in the dead-end of a roofless, ruined wood store stands a woman, willowy and panicked in a torn white shirt and dark breeches. Five ragged men armed with pitch torches, knives and clubs, close in on her, pausing only when they see our approach.

'Leave her be!' shouts Roach in a voice so strong and commanding that I gawk, wondering if it didn't come from someone else.

'Well, ain't that a stroke o'luck? Fresh meat!' says a pony-tailed man in a black leather journeyman's coat. The men behind him snigger. 'Are you and your boy gonna stop us, old man?'

Roach hurries to plant himself between the woman and the men, slipping into the old storehouse where more of the wall's boards are missing than not. Without thinking, I do the same, Stink close on my heels. The dog overtakes me then, to bark and growl threateningly at the strangers. Ponytail takes several steps back as the dog advances.

Roach faces up to them as the others look us over. 'What business do you have with this woman?'

'Don't worry about me, darlin',' says the woman behind us. I glance back as she pulls a knife from her belt. '*You's* the ones in trouble. Make it quick, boys!'

Strangely, Roach just stands there, seeming unconcerned about the coming attack. His eyes remain fixed on the others.

Ponytail advances. 'You better call off your hound before I spike him.'

'He's not my dog,' says Roach.

'What's this?' asks Ponytail, eyeing the stripes on my long coat. 'You don't look like no Draker t'me.'

'That's 'cause I ain't no Draker,' I say.

Stink lurches, leaping up to clamp his jaws around the man's arm as he makes a failed attempt to strike. Of the two, Stink is the faster.

Hearing the woman approach, I turn to fend her off with the tip of my spear, jabbing at her as she tries to shank me in the ribs. Stink sounds vicious, snarling away. I parry a lunge from the blade, jab at the woman's hands and arms—whichever part of her comes into range. I hear scuffling and fighting behind me, but I need to deal with the woman before I can join Roach and Stink. I fear Roach may have already been overpowered. Stabbed to death, most likely.

Stink snarls. Ponytail yelps.

The woman charges. I slip my spear through the air to clash against her knuckles. The impact breaks her grip and her knife flies, landing among the fallen boards. She glances after it briefly but sensing it's lost, turns to scarper.

I round on the others, fully expecting them to be already upon me. Of the remaining four, two are lying near the edges of the floor, unconscious or dead—I ain't sure which—while Roach holds Ponytail, one arm bent up behind his back. Roach also has Ponytail's other arm in a lock, the man's own knife poised at his throat. Giving up, Ponytail winces. Stink and Roach stand their ground, watching the remaining goon: a ratty, bristle-faced youth holding a long club. I level up with them, spear first. The youth drops his weapon, preferring to run.

'Go!' says Roach, releasing his captive and thrusting him after the fleeing youth.

'Blinders! What just happened?' I peer at Roach and glance at Stink to see if he's hurt. He seems fine.

Roach shrugs. 'We beat them.'

'What?' I ask, disbelieving.

'We beat them. They attacked. We won.'

I look at him sideways with my one good eye. 'You and a dog beat five men in a fight?'

He shrugs again. 'It wasn't much of a fight and he *is* a *very* good dog.' Roach bends to stroke Stink's head. The dog wags his tail. 'Anyway, they were more like boys, really.'

'Sure, you're a strange kind of drifter.'

I hunt for the woman's knife, find and claim it. It's a good one, long and heavy enough to hack at a branch like a short sword.

Roach glances at the blade dubiously.

'It'll be useful for chopping wood,' I say, ignoring the old man as I slip it into my belt. We head back to our camp, Stink trotting with his tail high, proud of himself.

'Do you think we're safe? They could come after us.'

Roach shakes his head. 'They're long gone. We'll not see them again.'

We add broken branches to build up the dwindling fire. When I settle down again, I sleep fitfully for the rest of the night, dreaming of the bombs.

*

When the first bombs fell, Londaland didn't know what had hit it. The Urthians came at night in their katta-langs and bombahdahs, flying so high in the stratosphere that no sky lamps could reach them. They came in their thousands to drop a deadly hail. That night was when it all began for us Londalanders, who were left behind. For many, it was the beginning and the end. There came no warning. No word from our spies, nor even from the lookouts stationed in the watchtowers or the sea-bound storm brakers, set every mile or so along Londaland's jagged coast.

Ill-prepared, the people fled their homes in the dead of dark, desperate and exposed, their flesh blasted to pieces, children made orphans and mothers bereft. The few remaining men ran like the rest, died like the rest. What else could they do?

THE JICKER MAN

The memory lies like a scar across a great swathe of my mind, a blemish that will never fade. The scenes repeat in my dreams as I sleep, trouble me when I wake. I hear the whistles of the falling bombs, see again the print shop explode into rubble and dust, parts of the Rundlebridge Steam Press fly across Bunson Street as I dodge and weave the giant bounding cogs. My home, a matter of a few houses away, took a direct hit just moments after I scampered outside to stare heavenward and, feeling the tremors of other detonations rising through the soles of my feet, I ran.

I ran and ran until the terrible dawn broke upon the horizon.

*

I sense light and warmth hitting my face. Opening my eyes, I squint up at the rays of sun that stream in through a break in the firs. Roach sits before me, tending a pot over the fire. Then I remember what happened at the sawmill during the night.

'You'd best get ready to move,' he says, without taking his gaze from the flames. 'Looks like a storm's heading our way. We should find some proper shelter.'

I consider asking how he knows. Perhaps he's taken a walk back to the road and seen clouds on the horizon. From where I sit there's only blue sky beyond the high-reaching treetops.

'Here.' He passes a cup of steaming pine needle tea that he's brewed.

I drink the hot, aromatic liquid and take out my map to study the route.

'What's that?' asks Roach, glancing at me. 'A map?'

'Nothing.' I fold it and tuck it away in a pocket of my long coat. 'Last night, how did you do that?'

'Do what?'

'You know what. How did you beat all those men? It was impossible.'

'And yet it happened.'

'And how did you light the fire? Where did you get the black beans? I haven't seen any for a year. How did you know we wouldn't see those rogues again? How did you survive the well? And how the blinders do you know there's a storm coming?!'

He shrugs. 'I am what I am.'

'Well, you ain't what you seem, that's for sure. Wait a minute,' I say with sudden realisation. 'You're one of those jickers. You're a *jicker man!*'

Roach shrugs again and nods acceptingly. 'Some would say.'

I'm shocked that I didn't see it before. 'I didn't know there were any left. Didn't even know they were real. I thought they were only in stories.' I say this as much to myself as to Roach.

'Oh, we're real, alright. At least, we used to be. We're as real as the Old People were.'

'What do you know of the Old People?'

'Plenty. Look, we need to move.' He slings out the dregs of his tea to dampen the fire and hoists his bags over the back of the mule. 'We can talk later when we're safe from the storm.'

I realise he don't use a saddle. That's just the way a jicker man would ride. When everyone else was using a saddle, they would see no need for one. Their ways were somehow different—simpler, and always somehow more effective. In the stories, anyway.

As we thread our way through the trees and back to the road, I try to recall everything I ever heard about the jicker men, or majickers, as they were also known. Most of it comes from folktales and bedtime stories, those told to me by the kindly old widow who used to live with us in our house on Bunson Street—and sometimes recounted by my surrogate mother, Sarah Banyard. Most of those stories began with words like 'Long ago' or 'Back in olden days' and occasionally 'When the Old People ruled the world', and I suppose that's why I thought the jicker men no longer existed. They were as fabled as the Old People who flew ships to the moon and mined the planets. I ain't ever heard of a *real* story, nothing in the papers or such, but one thing's for sure: in every single tale, a mysterious man would turn up to become a hero: the jicker man. He would step from the shadows when no one knew he was there, or swing down from the trees, swim across vast oceans or perform other daring nigh-on impossible feats—and all to save the day in some unexpected and marvellous way. How I loved those stories! Snug beneath the soft blankets of my bed, a cup of warm milk cradled in my hand, I would beg for more as the tallow candle at my bedside was snuffed, and the widow or Sarah would tell me, 'That's all for tonight,' and 'It's time to go to sleep now'. Then I would lie awake for hours, picturing everything that had happened in the latest saga and if I was lucky, dream about it too. The memory brings back the scent of candle grease, the silky feel and taste of warm milk on my tongue, and a deep sense of comfort and security. I loved the widow and Sarah for all that. And I felt loved, too. It was as far as could be from my life before, sleeping on the streets, huddling under Rook's Bridge with holes in my shoes, alongside the other freezing, homeless, threader urchins.

It's funny how—now that I find myself in a saga of my own and alongside a real, live jicker man—I have a longing for those old times in the safety of that warm home. I'd much rather be there, cosied-up in my bed, listening to the tale I'm in.

Roach was right about the storm. Right about everything. As we plod along the barren road, clouds roll in, dark and heavy across the sky. We travel a while without speaking and I wonder, *How does a jicker man know these things?* Roach seems to be driving Dorothy as fast as he dares, which ain't fast at all, so I'm fairly sure the coming squall must be a bad one.

The majickers in the stories were powerful and mysterious, always quietly spoken and composed. They left me in awe. Glancing up at the old man hunched in the saddle, I wonder if I'm mistaken. He looks a little sad and lonely, certainly poor, and weary in his ragged clothes. Perhaps he ain't a jicker man after all. Perhaps he's just mad or deluded, and thinks he knows things that he really don't. Well, if that's true, he's had a blinder of a run!

*

When the storm hits around mid-morning, we're sheltering in a barn about four hundred yards from the road. For a while I watch from the doorway but spy no one on the stretch beyond the fields, beneath the torrential rain that hammers over all I can see. The barn is not much to speak of but it's free of the dead and mostly dry, and sometimes that counts for a lot. I bury myself in the dusty remains of a hay store to keep warm and watch through a small window as the sky darkens ominously. Stink paces back and forth, frustrated by the delay. I feel his pain but my thoughts of moving on without Roach have become clouded. If I'm right about him and he really is a jicker man—quite possibly the last jicker man alive—I'd be crazy not to stick with him.

Tired from another disturbed, uncomfortable night, I find myself drifting into sleep, but not before noticing that Roach is also nodding off. I keep myself awake, then, waiting and checking my pocket watches for something to do, holding one after the other up to my ear to hear them tick. Winding each crown in turn, I feel the tension of their inner springs tighten like the tension in my mind.

The mule settles down at one end of the barn and Stink eventually lies against me to doze. Once I'm sure Roach

71

is sound asleep, I dig out the gawper skull from my bag, unwrap its oil cloth covering and, holding its forehead against mine, call for Magwitch in my mind.

There's a moment of transferred thoughts and feelings like a barrage of incoming information, though it's garbled and confused. It clears to reveal Magwitch's gravelly voice inside my head.

Any news? I think.

Skallagrim's Darklings are moving by night, creeping north. He will seek a wilderness where none can find him. We hear rumour he has split his forces. We do not know if he is with them or if he travels alone.

I realise that with their telepathy, which seems unaffected by distance, the gawpers don't need to be together in order to work as one. Skallagrim could scatter his Dagomite army across the world—let alone Londaland—and still direct their every move.

Magwitch continues. *Our numbers grow. The Lotharians are fighting wherever possible, but Skallagrim is cunning. He sneaks and crawls into hidden domains like a hell snake. He must be stopped at any cost before he gathers his masses.*

I imagine a hell snake is something that lives out in the toxic deserts of Mors Zonam. I've never seen one and I don't wish to, either.

Lotharians?

We Dagomites who refuse to follow Skallagrim are known as Lotharians. Lothar was a rebel who brought down a terrible Dagomite king more than two thousand years ago.

I will find and kill Skallagrim. I think the words to him.

This one should not pursue Skallagrim. Leave it to the Lotharians. The task is too treacherous for a human child.

I ain't a child and I'm gonna do it anyway. You see if I don't.

This one must step down and seek him no more. It will bring only death.

If you won't help me to find him, I'll talk to Deadlock. Is he there? Deadlock? Deadlock?

I sense Magwitch reluctantly retreat into the foggy edges of my perception. As his mind gate eases closed, another opens. Deadlock's severe tone enters my head.

Ebadiah, Deadlock hears you.

Help me to find Skallagrim and I will kill him.

Skallagrim will not be easily found, nor softly slain. The task will be dangerous.

Don't matter. I don't care if I die trying. Just help me!

There's a pause and I think Deadlock and Magwitch may be talking beyond my hearing.

Deadlock will help this one, though this one knows everything there is to know about Skallagrim's movements. We Lotharians also seek him, and his captain, Tacitus.

Tacitus?

Skallagrim's most loyal supporter.

Promise me you will tell me when you learn something new.

Deadlock will tell this one.

What are the Darklings of Brae? I ask.

Our communication is disrupted by a sudden rush of interference: another confusion of thoughts and emotions. I sense a stab of hatred, glimpse the shadowed, black-masked faces of gawpers, and hear shrieks of pain and terror. Somewhere, Skallagrim's gawpers are killing. For the next few minutes, I try to reconnect my mind gate with Deadlock but get nowhere. Giving up, I carefully wrap the skull in its oil cloth and slip it back into my pack.

I turn at a movement across the barn. Roach is wide awake and watching me with interest.

6. QUESTIONS

'The Darklings of Brae,' says Roach. 'I can tell you who they are.'

I'm startled and unnerved. He wasn't supposed to witness my communication with Magwitch, but now that he has, it changes things. I feel vulnerable and foolish, and angry with myself for letting it happen. Michael's face flashes in my memory.

Keep it safe. Tell no one about it or the power it holds. On this your life may depend.

'So, you commune with gawpers. Are you an enemy of humankind?' asks Roach, getting up and delving into one of his bags for a pan and a canteen of water. He collects odd-ments of wood that lie scattered about on the dirt floor with which to make a fire. 'Should I fear you, Ebadiah?'

His half-smile tells me he don't fear me at all.

'Ain't no reason to.' I watch him snap twigs from an old withy broom he finds in a corner to use as kindling. 'And not all gawpers are bad.'

'Is that so? I suppose that was a *good* one you were just talking with?'

'How do you even know what I was doing?'

'I'm not entirely blind, nor deaf.'

'What do *you* know about it?' Clutching my pack to my chest, there's a defensive edge to my voice.

'Don't worry, lad. I'll not take it from you.'

'You couldn't if you tried, old man.'

'Oh, couldn't I?' Now he says it, I'm not so sure. 'That's a rare thing you carry. I'm curious as to how you came by it.'

'Ain't none of your business.'

He kneels to arrange the kindling and wood on a broken millstone as, outside, thunder roils across the heavens. Its booms and cackles—like the sounds of war—cause me to start. A rumble resonates throughout the barn and has me glancing up at the roof, hoping it will hold. The downpour is heavy and constant. A furious wind pummels at the walls, quivering the weathered boards, wailing mournfully. Here and there, water seeps through the roof shingles to drip.

'Well?'

'Well, what?' he asks.

'Who *are* the Darklings of Brae? Wait. Have you been reading my mind? How did you know what I was thinking?'

Roach looks unsure for a moment. 'You were mumbling the odd word. There's an art to mind-walking. Boy, you've a lot to learn.'

'*Mind-walking*—so that's what it's called. Don't call me *boy*.'

'The Darklings of Brae are a particularly pernicious tribe of gawpers, who dwell in the mountains of Scolanda. They're taller than other gawpers and friends to none.' Roach crouches by his little steeple of wood. His hands dart about and a moment later, a small flame springs to life, licking up at the base of the twigs. 'You want to stay clear of the Darklings. They're a bad lot.'

At last, Magwitch's words make sense. He was trying to warn me of the Darklings 'cause my route will take me into their domain—if I ever get that far. I wonder, are they sheltering Skallagrim? They sound like his type.

'Are you truly a jicker man?' I ask.

'There are different names for what I am. Jicker is but one.'

'But you know things others don't? Can control things?'

'Control things? If you mean manipulate people, no, that's not what I'm about.'

'But you manipulated those rogues back there at the saw-mill. Didn't you?

'I didn't make them do anything, if that's what you mean. I didn't use *ma-jick*.'

'Then what?'

'Boy, you ask too many questions.'

'I ain't a boy no more, an' I was taught that asking questions was a good thing.'

'And it is, but not too many all at once. I've answered enough for now. Why don't you tell me how you came by that gawper skull of yours?' He rigs an iron hanger from one of his bags and pours water into the pan, suspending it over the growing flames.

I consider telling him about the skull and watch to see if he's making black bean soup or pine needle tea. I hope it's the soup. If he really is a jicker it must be safe to talk. 'I'll tell you for a cup of black bean soup.'

Roach pauses, a handful of pine needles hovering over the pan. 'No need to barter for soup.' He returns the needles to a pocket of his scruffy coat and delves into a bag again for his tin of ground black beans.

'How do you know about the gawpers—about the Dark-lings?' I ask.

'Questions, questions...' He tips the ground beans into the warming water to let them steep.

'I was always told you should only put the grounds into boiling water.'

'There's more than one way to make black bean soup, Ebadiah. None are right or wrong. They're just different. Now, are you going to talk or not? The skull?'

'I was given it by a man who took me in from the streets. I was sleeping rough before that.' I tell him all about the private detectives Michael Banyard and Josiah Mingle, who looked after me and gave me a profession, one other than shining shoes on the corner or running errands for the shipbuilders down Dockside. I mention the widow and Michael's mother Sarah, who schooled me. 'Michael kept a case file on the gawpers—one his father began to compile before him. In it are records of sightings and reports going back years. They include accounts of his own encounters, which were many. It was he who passed the skull to me and taught me its use.'

'And where did this Michael find it?' Roach stirs the soup with a bent spoon.

'A gawper gave it to him so they could talk. That was in Mors Zonam.'

'Michael went to Mors Zonam? Willingly?'

'Aye.'

'That's hard to believe.'

'It's true. Anyway, why do you want to know?'

'I've only ever seen one gawper skull before. They can be dangerous. You should be careful with it.'

'I *am* careful with it. Though not careful enough, it seems. Is it ready yet?'

'No. Be patient. A decent stew takes time.'

'Why do you say they're dangerous?'

'Well, I suppose it's not the skull that's dangerous. It's more about the gawper at the other end of it.'

'I know these gawpers. They were Michael's friends. They ain't dangerous to me.'

Roach nods. 'If you say so. You can get some rest if you like, when you've had your soup. The storm will blow for an hour or two. No use setting out 'til it's past. I'm rested. I can keep watch.' He takes a set of wooden pipes from his bag and raising it to his lips, plays a slow melody that I find strangely soothing. I listen, captivated and yet again, surprised by him.

'Didn't you know?' he says, sensing my reaction and pausing for a moment. 'Every jicker man makes music.'

'Why?'

'Because music has a big old ma-jick all of its own. It can reach down through any plane to find parts of your soul long buried.' He plays some more and I begin to feel drowsy.

He stops to give the soup another stir and I pass him my cup which he dips into the pan before passing it back to me. He takes a cupful and makes himself comfortable by the fire, blowing at the steam.

I guess I'm safe with Stink sleeping at my side. He always wakes at the slightest sound and is ready to fight in a blink. So, settling down in the hay, I drink and before long, I close my eyes and drift into slumber to the sound of the pipes.

*

After the bombs fell, I returned to the ruins of Camdon, as did others, to look for survivors. They were few. The able-bodied among us worked to dig the injured from the rubble, hauling away bricks and vast chunks of masonry to uncover and drag out the dead. The men hunted for armaments in the houses that remained standing, and gathering them up, shared out guns and blades and mortars to those who knew how to use them. At the junction of Bunson Street and Brittling Street a huge steam truck carrying munitions lay on its side, its load spilled across the road. I approached, meaning to take a carbine and a share of ammunition.

'Not you, boy,' said the self-appointed captain of arms, pushing me aside. With his clothes coated in dust and grime from the rubble, he looked like a coal miner.

I didn't argue—had heard it already more times than I cared to remember. 'Blind in one eye, lame in one leg... Sorry, son. You'll have to make yourself useful elsewhere.'

Turning away, I began bandaging the wounds of the injured using any fabric I could find. I climbed to the crest of a high rubble heap that used to be a silker's fine home, and scanned the devastation, saw bodies scattered on the surrounding streets as far as my view allowed. And then a distant high movement drew my gaze eastward over the sea, and I squinted at the sky above the isles of Myrh where a crimson glow still hung in the air. There, a multitude of dots peppered the horizon.

'Sir!' I called down to the captain. 'Look there!'

He glanced, saw the oncoming threat.

A shout arose from a nearby street and others began peering skyward, wondering.

'What are they? Airships?'

'Not airships. Too small.'

'That one looks like an airship.'

'Too fast for airships.'

'They're coming!'

I descended the heap.

'Arm yourselves!' shouted the captain and relenting, he tossed a carbine and an ammunition sling into my arms. We readied ourselves as best we could as the dots grew larger in the sky, rushing in from the ocean to blight the heavens. There were small, fast airships among them, though they were drawn by huge, red-feathered birds, each carrying a painted warrior. Other giant birds flew freely, swooping down upon us, their riders launching grenades, spears and shooting arrows. The winged giants snatched our people from the ground to climb back up into the sky, only to drop their victims to their deaths. They clawed and gouged with their huge talons and stabbed with powerful beaks.

Red is their colour and red their banner. The colour of the war birds' wings, the colour of their fiery arrows... the colour of newly spilled blood. There were few guns among their number, most preferring more primitive weapons. Though I did not know at the time, this was a choice driven by cultural belief. Urthian warriors considered firearms a cowardly choice. At least they did at the start. The survivors ain't so fussy these days.

The Urthians fell upon us from the heavens, their tattooed faces leering, a wildness in their eyes. They rained arrows and spears, diving and dashing through the air in a terrible display.

We had never seen the like.

*

'Wake up, Ebadiah. The storm's through.'

I open my eyes, bring Roach into focus as he stands over me. Across the barn Stink sniffs around the fire.

'Thought you might want to see this.' He nods towards the end of the building where a large set of double doors stand open and a grey, wet light seeps in. He heads out.

Getting up to follow, I ask, 'What is it?'

'Oh, you'll see.' He leaves the barn to lead me down a dirt path and through a scatter of tall, dense firs that still drip from the rain. We come to a stop before a sudden hulking form, which by its shape must be a vehicle of some kind, though it's hidden beneath a huge green canvas that covers all. Roach grabs a corner and hauls it away to reveal a polished steam truck. Across the vast grill the words *Clansly Haulage* gleam in silvered letters. Four round headlamps glint in the daylight.

'Fancy a ride?' He tugs the last stretch of tarp aside. 'I used to drive these in the army.'

My jaw drops. 'Blinders! You? In the army?'

'In my misspent youth. Is that so unlikely?'

'I just don't see it.'

'I was an engineer. I'll teach you to drive if you like.'

'Blinders!' I say again.

80

We spend the next half hour searching the site. There's a big old house on a ridge behind the truck but it looks like nobody's been home for a while. We look the truck over, top up the boiler with water, test the engine, check the wheels and tyres, light the firebox and load up a supply of coal from a bunker at the back of the house using a shovel from the cabin. We even grease the jibes using a can we find in the back. There are ropes in there, too.

Roach seems to know his way around the machine. He teaches me the basics, pointing to each part in turn.

'The firebox heats the boiler. The steam pressure in the tank drives the jibes. The jibes power the turbines and they turn the gears. The gears drive the axles. It's easy, really. See these valves here? With these you can change the pressure, take it faster or slower. You change gear accordingly.'

Up front there's a splendid array of levers, controls and dials set in a broad dashboard, all polished metal and glass. The wind shield is a squat split-screen, angled to help cut the air. Before all this is mounted a large brass steering wheel.

While the engine warms up and the steam pressure builds, we fetch our gear from the barn, dowse the campfire, and coax the mule up the tailgate and into the back along with my barrel and rig. Stink will ride in the cabin with Roach and me.

When the tailgate is raised and locked off, and we're all aboard, Roach squints at the main gauge, tapping at it with a grimy fingernail. 'That'll do. Look.' He points to a canister wedged between the seats that's labelled *Old Fisher's Wick Grease*. 'Oil for the lamps. We can even drive at night!'

I lean out of the open cabin door and call to Stink.

'Well, are you coming or not?'

He don't seem to get that we're leaving in the truck, but he eventually bounds up into the cabin and onto the bench next to me, where he slobbers my ear. I swing the door closed and glance at Roach doubtfully.

'You sure you've driven one of these before?'

'Of course. Look, these are the gears. That's the throttle. This is the brake.' He sweeps the gear levers back and forth until settling on one as a loud *clunk* comes from the engine.

Sliding open a side window, I think of his struggling eyesight. 'Perhaps I should—'

He draws up the throttle, releases the brake and with a judder and a roar, we lurch forwards.

'Hold on, Dorothy!' he cries with delight. Stink seems to like it too. He sticks his head out of the window, his tongue lolling in the wind as we track around to re-join the big road.

'West, you say? To Fenlock?'

'Aye. Just as fast as you like!'

With the swaying of the truck, I'm soon sleepy again, but it don't matter. It's been this way ever since the bombs. You grab sleep when you can. The nights are cold and usually uncomfortable, often disturbed. You make it work. You get by.

*

Bombs. War birds. The invasion by sky was but one part of a larger, well-planned attack: a strategy we were to later learn was tried and tested on the shores of Porgula, Cett and Latatia before rolling out across Londaland with devastating effect.

What came next were the dragons. Not flying or fire-breathing, like in storybooks. Real dragons: huge musclebound lizards that can outrun a man. The threshers were bred in eastern lands for the purpose of killing. They appeared from a fleet of numerous ships, vessels smaller than our proud galleons, but lighter and swifter, and sitting low in the water with men at the oars and sails full of easterly winds. They drove ashore under fire from gun and cannon, yet so many were they, that they engulfed our beaches and coves, and killing as they spread, they spilled over every defence.

I glimpsed their advance, saw the sun glinting from their blue-steel plate armour and their skin, scaled in rusty tones of orange and red. The reptiles were held on long chains, two to a man, wreaking chaos whenever they turned, and the dragon masters were big men, every one of them bulging with muscle.

Dockside was harder to take. There our homelanders hunkered down, fighting from warships, blockading the quay and bombarding with cannon, grenade and musket shot. They made an admirable stand, though one that would ultimately fail.

I witnessed the threshers tearing men apart, chasing down women and children to rip at their soft flesh. They would turn on their masters, too, and where the handlers had fallen in battle, the beasts ran loose, killing at will, their great chains trailing.

The threshers set a new fear into our hearts.

*

We make fine progress with the steam truck, though it ain't the fastest of vehicles and we can't go too far without stopping to refill the water tanks. We use water from rivers and streams, from wells, village pumps, anywhere we can find it. The truck lumbers noisily down the road, chugging smoke, gears whining, but it's much quicker than walking. A worry rides with me with every turn of the wheels: we are too loud and drawing attention—too obvious, too exposed. I'm used to slipping through woodlands or skirting settlements unobserved. Darting from house to house through the shadows in search of food. That ain't happening here. The truck thunders on for around an hour before slowing and then whatever levers and switches Roach throws, it don't help. I clamber into the back of the cabin where the firebox glows hot, use the heavy mitten that hangs on a peg to swing open the chunky iron door, and scoop a shovel full of coal from the bunker.

'No more coal!' he says. I stop. He peers at the steam gauge. 'It's probably the tank. The secret with these engines is to never let them boil dry. I'll get the water.'

'What happens if it boils dry?'

'*Boom!*' Roach mimics an explosion with his hands before topping up the water from the storage tank using a can that's stored on a hook at the rear of the cabin.

A couple of minutes later I'm back on the bench, the needle on the gauge is high, the steam turbines are whirring, and we're trundling at full pelt. Miles pass beneath us as the afternoon wears on.

Around three o'clock, we thread a small town that looks oddly untouched by the war, the houses and stores pristine, all strung out along the road with iron watch-lamps every thirty paces or so. There ain't a bullet hole in sight, nor a corpse to be seen. I get an uncanny feeling in my guts, then, watching the shopfronts go by from the thick windows of the truck. Seems empty too, not a soul anywhere. I usually welcome the chance to scout for perks, but not here. Not now with this feeling sitting like lead in my belly.

Out of need, we stop near the town's well to refill the boiler and storage tank.

Roach watches me taking in the town. 'You want to search the stores?'

I shake my head. 'Something ain't right here. We should go.'

He drives on. I wonder what the place is called and checking my map to see where we are, learn the town's name is Midcarrow, which means we've gone around twenty-five miles in the truck.

We're coming to the end of the town when I see the sign again, daubed on the post of another watch-lamp.

'Stop!' I say.

Roach shifts out of gear and yanks up the brake lever. We lurch to a halt.

He looks at me. 'What is it?'

'Back there. Something painted on a watch-lamp.'

Opening his door, he hobbles down from the truck and I join him outside. Ahead of us, Stink wets the post as we walk back to view it.

'There.' I point. 'A symbol. I've seen it before.'

'I know this sign.' Roach nods.

I look around, nervous of what the ghost town might be hiding. Back there, from a few hundred yards down the street, come's a clattering that sounds like a can rolling across the road. Roach seems to sense my apprehension. 'Let's go. I'll tell you about it in the truck.'

We climb back up into our seats. Roach releases the brake, shifts into gear, and we're away again, trundling out of the town and into open countryside that's grey beneath a bleak sky.

'So, what's that sign all about?' I ask.

'It's a gawper symbol. They call it the planum horis. Represents the four planes. You know about the four planes, right?'

'Michael taught me a little.' I lean out of the window to look behind at the streets, fancy I glimpse a tall, dark figure peering back at me from a shadowed doorway. We jolt over a bump in the road and when I refocus, the figure—if it was ever there—has gone.

'Well, you just used the second plane back there with the skull. There are four planes or horizons. The first is where you do your basic thinking.' He taps his head while keeping one hand on the wheel. 'Like the thinking you hardly need to think about. That's the downward-pointing arrow.' He marks an arrow in the fine layer of dust on the wind shield. 'It's like the part of your thinking that's closest to your body. The second plane is where all the mind-walking happens, telepathy.

85

That's the shape that looks like a broken figure eight.' He adds the figure to the drawing. 'But there are two further planes, also. The third is dominated by your higher thoughts and feelings, all the basic everyday kind'a stuff—happiness, jealousy, pleasure...' Now he adds a vertical line, joining the bottom of the figure to the arrowhead.

'And the fourth?'

'The fourth is where you feel extreme emotions—love, hate and so on. It's by using a glitch in the fourth plane that gawpers can move objects with their minds alone. It's the same with their conjuring.' He marks a curved line in the dust across the top of the figure.

'Michael told me about that part. About how they appear to move from place to place using only their minds, but really they're conjuring the places into their presence.'

'That's a fine way to say it.'

'But why on the watch-lamps? Have the gawpers been there?'

Roach nods. 'Skallagrim is marking his territory.'

'Like a dog, you mean?'

'Aye. Just like a dog.'

I think back to all the times I've seen the planum horis on watch-lamps, and shiver. Was someone observing me all that time? Are we, even now, being watched?

BEN MEARS

7. FENLOCK

Our journey takes us onto higher ground that leads into the hills and I'm glad of good old *Clansly*, hauling us up there. It grows colder and windier the further we climb but we're snug in the cab with the firebox blazing. Roach shows me again which levers do what and I begin to get an idea of how to drive.

We come to a house built of stone that looks as ancient as the surrounding hills and there, in the shadow of a rocky peak, Roach slows the truck, eases on the brake and with a hiss of steam we roll to a stop.

'Best see if there's coal to be had. Don't want to get stuck up here in bad weather.'

'What is this place?' I peer out at the old house with its windows all dark and dreary. 'Is anyone home, do you think?'

'My guess is it's empty.' Roach stretches and climbs down from the truck.

Stink leaps from the window before I can open my door and he's on the house in a trice, sniffing around the door and circling the walls and its broken wattle fence. He don't bark or get overly excited, which likely means Roach is right again—ain't no one home. What's more, at the back there's a bunker full of coal. Roach drives the truck over and with a squawk of gears, reverses it up. We lower the tailgate and take turns shovelling until the truck's hopper is full before loading the rest into sacks and hefting them up into the back alongside the lazing mule.

'What about the people who live here? Shouldn't we leave them some?'

Looking exhausted, Roach leads the mule carefully down the ramp.

'They won't return from where they've gone. Dorothy needs water and a break from the truck. I'll check the boiler. Why don't you see what's in the kitchen?' He guides her over to a scraggy patch of grass and she chomps away. Stink laps from an icy puddle at the side of the road.

I glance into the back of the truck at a pile of mule dung. 'You want me to clear that out first?'

'That there's good fuel.'

'Alright.' I nod and head back to the house.

He calls after me. 'Ebadiah, be sure to check behind the icebox.'

I throw him a puzzled look. *That's very specific.* 'You been here before?'

'I don't think so.' He frowns briefly as though trying to recall. 'Stay sharp. This is morh-beast country.'

I creep in through the back door, wondering if the house truly is abandoned. Don't want no surprises. The kitchen's ordered but most of the cupboards and shelves are bare. The owners must have used everything up or taken it with them when they moved on, or else the place has been raided before. That's usually the case these days.

I find a jar of homemade pickles dated five years old and three cans of dog food. Stink's gonna love this! He pads around nearby and follows his nose out through a door, investigating further into the house. Bagging my finds, I follow and call for him to come back, but he ain't listening.

Roach might be at ease with this place, but I sure ain't. I feel the hairs on the back of my neck stand tall.

When I catch up with the dog, he's standing in a doorway, looking into a dim bedroom where the owners, presumably, are resting in bed. Most of their bodies are covered by blankets. Looks like they've been lying there for a good six months or more. A musty smell of decay hits my nose. I call Stink out and close the door.

I've had it with this place now. Want to go. Heading for the back door, I pass through the kitchen again, stopping by the icebox. Looks like nothing's there. Like the box is sitting snug against the wall with no hope of there being anything behind, but I look anyway, 'cause Roach said to. I slide the box aside and there it is—a deep cubby hole—and stashed inside, a sack of oats and another of roasted black beans.

Once more I'm forced to ask myself, *how does the old man do it?*

Back at the truck I head for the passenger door but find he's already sitting on the bench inside. He nods towards the empty driver's seat.

'Might as well start now if you want to learn. I've stoked the firebox, filled the boiler.'

Stink runs ahead and leaps in before me. I climb up into the cabin to check the gauges.

'The pressure's good.'

I select the lowest gear, release the brake and grab the wheel. The truck jolts and lumbers forwards. The steering is heavy, though it gets easier the faster we go and before long I'm hitting the higher gears and we're chugging along at a fair speed. I feel a thrill at controlling the powerful machine and from then on, we share the driving.

*

Roach is at the wheel again when Fenlock appears in the fading daylight between the crook of two wooded hills. It's a sprawling town skirting the southern sweep of a broad bay. I spy on it through the telescope, watch for a good while, but it seems quiet. No battles raging, at least. Beyond, the sea is leaden, grey and broken by a scatter of low islands.

I don't know where the gawper lair is, or if there even is one—ain't sure why Michael marked the town on the map, but he must've had a reason. There were reasons for everything he did and even when I didn't see them right away, the chances were they'd soon become clear. I wish I could slap my head against the skull and ask him, but it don't work that way. The skull's just for reaching gawpers. I've already asked Magwitch and Deadlock, and they don't know.

So I watch the town grow larger as we roll in on that big old road and think and wonder all the time where to start looking. It won't be an obvious place. Gawpers are too cunning for that. It'll be a hole clawed out beneath the ground or in a secluded cave or twisting cavern, or maybe in the town itself, craftily hidden between buildings in such a way that no one suspects it's there. The gawpers have their ways... It could be anywhere really.

As we near the first building, other details become clear. A tall spire aims skyward, the highest point in the town. It belongs to an ancient stone church, fenced in and visited by sightseers before the war. There's a sign outside telling you all about it. We pass it as we roll by. The church has survived the bombs better than many of the other buildings. Rubble lies scattered about the streets. Great, jagged walls remain standing in defiance. The glass from a thousand leaded windows glistens across the cobbled roads, catching in the light of the waning sun. Here and there stand makeshift shelters, oddly shaped and patched together from the remnants of other buildings: bits of iron, boards, doors, and canvass flapping in the wind. They look like drifts of rubbish. People are here still, though most are hiding. Smoke rises from their fires to streak the heavens.

The air is salty in my nose. Way out in the sea, stone and iron-built towers stand proud, relics of a time before, all constructed by the Old People before the waters rose. A marvel catches my eye: a stretch of ancient road climbs from the water suspended by pillars of concrete. It levels and loops around before ending in a broken wound over the ocean. I glimpse the faded white lines that mark its centre.

We thread our way between abandoned vehicles that clutter the town to find a street with a market of sorts. Townsfolk sell wares from barrows and carts: fish caught down in the cove, homespun clothes, coats made from rags and furs, bits and pieces that people have gleaned along the way, hoping that someone will buy or barter. There's no money changing hands. Coin's no good now. You can't eat it, wear it or burn it to keep warm—so what use is it?

Roach keeps the truck rumbling on through and the grimy people stop to stare as we pass.

'Best if we don't settle too near other folk,' says Roach. 'That just leads to trouble. If we really think it's safe, we can always return to see what we might swap.'

'I've no appetite for salted fish anymore, so we could trade what's left.'

We slow in a dead-looking part of town and draw up off the road into an overgrown courtyard between two tall buildings, parts of which are still standing. This way the truck is mostly hidden.

'You think the Gawper King is hiding here?' asks Roach.

I wonder if he's taunting me. 'Could be. I'm gonna look anyway.'

'Big place. Could take a while.'

'Don't matter. Ain't nothing better to do. Stay here if you want.'

'You're going now?'

'Aye. Why not?'

'Because night's closing in.'

'I'll be back before it's fully dark.'

I'm two blocks away before the feeling kicks in that I've been stupid. Roach could just drive out of here in the Clansly with everything we've gathered. But then I tell myself, it don't matter. My pack's on my shoulders and Stink's running ahead as usual. I managed like that before and I can manage just the same again.

Stink has a good nose and I've done a fair bit of scent training with him. He can sniff out a morgue rat at sixty paces and I made sure he took a good long sniff around the lair back at Hick's Gate. I reckon he could hunt out a gawper lair here pretty well, if there is one. I hold the gawper weed for him to smell.

'Find.'

He sets his nose to the ground and we move off.

We work though five or six more blocks, poking around broken houses, workshops and papermills before circling around and returning to the truck. It's wise to know what's around you in any case, so I feel easier about the thought of bedding down as we pick our way back.

The sun's sinking over the islands and filling the horizon with a hot glow when the shriek goes up. It's a familiar sound. Someone about to die who don't wanna die—just like that woman at the sawmill, except she was faking. I think, *maybe this one's faking, too.* But I don't know. A scream's a scream, after all. Ain't no way to know it's real.

Roach's head pops up over a pile of rubble that lies between me and the Clansly and then he walks out across the street to join me.

'Someone's in trouble,' he says. 'Want to go see?'

I nod. Stink whimpers at my side but soon runs off to find out what's going on for himself. We follow and I have that odd feeling like when you've been somewhere or done a thing before but can't quite place it. It's probably just that

Stink's run off a thousand times already, and mostly I've followed to see why.

There are other noises now, a desperate sobbing, running footfalls, a metallic creaking and banging... more screams.

We hurry, with Stink way out front, bounding along a street strewn with battered clockwork cars and steam trucks, some crashed, others simply forsaken, their windows and lamps smashed, or hubs propped open, or wheels missing. Some are burned out and riddled with bullet holes and red-feathered arrows. There are broken carts here and there, tilting at angles, and a carriage complete with two skele-tonised horses, their bones bleaching on the road.

'Stink! Stink!'

Turning a corner, we enter another street and stop. Stink runs on, ignoring my calls. Ain't nothing gonna stop that dog when he wants to go somewhere.

Before us, a shaggy creature lurches up on its long front legs, taller than Roach or me. It's huge and real quick, with a wolfish head, though it ain't no wolf. It's maned with long hair about its neck and hunched shoulders. Its haunches and legs bulge with muscle. Its teeth and hooked claws are primed to rend flesh. Yellow eyes fix upon us from the shad-ows of a black face.

Stink stops before it, posturing, snarling.

'Blinders!'

'A morh-beast!' Roach sounds amazed and steps back. 'Down from the hills.'

Another scream comes from a girl who cowers in a burnt-out clockwork car. The vehicle's smashed windows offer little protection. The beast circles, testing each opening in turn. It's too large to fit its torso through but with its long reach it's only a matter of time before it hooks her out like a winkle from a shell.

'She's trapped!'

'We should help,' says Roach.

'Wait! This could be a trick like last time. She could be bait!' I check around but see no one else.

'Or she's truly in trouble. What are we going to do against a morh-beast?'

'That's the biggest I've ever seen.' I gawp while Stink barks and gets crazy, his hackles up. He don't know what to do either.

'I'll draw it off! You help the girl,' says Roach.

'Are you mad? It'll kill you!'

'Then, what?' Roach throws out his arms.

I don't have any better ideas right this moment, but a flicker of orange light draws my eye, way off to one side. Some of the survivors must have been warming themselves around a fire in the street, and scarpered when the beast arrived. Ain't no one there now, just a barrel of flames.

'Fire!' I run for the barrel while Roach hobbles after me. It looks as though they've been breaking up wooden chairs to burn 'cause there are spindles and legs and broken panels all heaped in the barrel, the flames peaking at the centre. I snatch at the unburnt ends of two spindles and with one in each hand, turn back for the car.

Roach follows my lead with his own branches. We approach from the rear of the car as the beast thrusts a long foreleg in through the back window, clawing at the girl. Backing up, she shrieks, inches from its grasp. The beast roars. We run closer. It turns towards us but seeing the flames, backs up towards the front end as we wave the brands to ward it away. It advances then, choosing to fight for its supper, but when it lunges, we press in, waving our flames at its face. A patch of its mane catches alight and then it's the morh's turn to shriek and scream. It fears the fire, bounds away to lope into the labyrinthine streets of the fallen city. We listen to its patter as it flees over cars and ruins, howling in defeat.

The sounds fade and I open a side door of the burnt-out car to peer in at the bedraggled girl. Her large, almond-shaped eyes peer back at me from a dirt-smudged face that comes to a smooth point at the chin. Her hair is lank and greasy looking.

'It's alright. The morh's gone,' I say.

She retreats into a corner of the car's rear bench, cowering. 'Keep away! What do you want with me?!'

'Nowt.'

She stares, her eyes darkly ringed with grime and exhaustion. She's wrapped in two old, badly-fitting coats, and her trousers—blue-grey with a used-to-be white, military stripe—look like they've been snagged from a dead trooper. They're bloodied and torn on one leg.

'Are you alright, *Two Coats*?'

'I'm alright.'

'Well, are you coming out? We have food...'

Roach joins me at the open door. 'We'll not harm you. I give you my word.'

'Your *word*? What about the dog?' she asks, nodding towards Stink who's snuffling at the ground where the morhbeast had stood. 'He giving me his word?'

'He's alright. I won't let him hurt you.'

'Promise?'

'Promise.'

She edges slowly out of the car as we back up to give her space and then, as though thinking better of it, she dashes away into the ruins of a nearby building. In a moment she's gone.

'Huh,' I say, shrugging. 'Guess she wasn't hungry. We'd best get back to the truck.'

Roach peers after the girl, looking bemused, but he turns to follow and we leave.

At the truck, we set about feeding the fire and scavenging enough wood from the surrounding wreckage to see us through the night. Our gear seems untouched. As the last light of the day dissolves about us, a distant, bestial howl echoes across the town.

The fire Roach started while I was out searching is now little more than embers. He blows it back to life and we heat water in a pan and drop in a few salted herrings, some pine needles and some wilted greens that Roach foraged in the hills. He even found a few onions in an old vegetable plot by the stone house, so he cuts one into shreds and adds them, too. Half an hour later, there's a mouth-watering smell wafting up from that pot and Roach dips his cup under the bubbling surface to collect a share.

When it's cooled he takes a sip. ''S'good,' he says, with a slurp.

Stink gets up to stand between us and the truck, staring into the murk beyond reach of the firelight. He seems unsettled, letting out a low growl. Something's out there. I tense, and think of that great morh-beast prowling the night.

8. THE FILE

A hooded face rises from behind a rear fender of the truck. It's the girl. She's found us—has followed the smell of fish stew, I suppose. I nudge Roach and tip my head towards her.

'Thought she'd be back,' he says with a half-smile.

I dip my cup into the stew and wait for it to cool a little before tasting it, all the while conscious of the girl watching from her hiding place. I must admit, it's the best we've ever made, even if I *am* utterly bored of fish.

I call out. 'Ain't no point hiding, Two Coats. Might as well come eat.' And we sit there by the fire, like we don't care if she comes or not. Stink growls on. I pour some stew onto a large flat stone for him and tell him, 'Stop your noise.' He loses interest in the newcomer to lap up the food.

A few minutes later, she edges out from behind the truck to creep closer, pausing midway to the fire. 'I ain't got no cup or bowl,' she says. Must be a threader, talking like that.

'You can borrow mine when I'm done,' I offer, trying to finish my fish stew quickly, and she cautiously comes over to join us.

'Sit down,' says Roach. 'Warm yourself. Have you come far?'

The girl settles nearby. 'I came down from Longhaven, looking for somewhere to hold up. It's bad up there. No food. People dying.'

'Starving?' I ask.

She nods.

'Do you have a name?' asks Roach.

'Jade Garaday. You?'

'Call me Roach.'

'I'm Ebadiah.' I watch her eyes flit nervously from Roach to me and back again. 'Are you gonna rob us, Jade Garaday?'

'I ain't no thief! Just cold and hungry, that's all. An' your stew smells fine.'

I drain my cup dry and refill it before passing it to her. 'Keep it. I got a spare somewhere.'

She takes it and sniffs at the steam, cradling the cup to warm her hands.

We don't speak much then. She watches us, sips at the cooling stew. When she seems to have warmed through, she peels back the hoods of her coats. We get to see her face properly then, though it's blackened with filth. Even so, it's clear she's a looker. We let her finish the rest of the stew as she seems half-starved.

Stink sniffs at her but I call him off and grumbling, he slinks away into the shadows, probably to hunt for rats.

We don't bother Jade with questions after that. She looks drained and before long she curls up in her coats to one side of the fire and closes her eyes.

'You think she's safe?' I ask Roach when I think she's asleep.

'She's safe,' he says, as though it's fact.

I've been thinking about just how old she may be and reckon on eighteen or so. Same sort of age as me, though maybe younger.

'She's pretty,' says Roach, peering at me. 'Beneath all the filth.'

I laugh. 'Ain't no way she's falling for you, old man.'

Roach scowls. 'Not for me, you fool. For *you!* She could be good for you. You could be good for each other...'

'Or she could stab us both in our sleep.'

'You don't trust anyone, do you?'

'I don't even know her.'

'That can be remedied.'

He's talking like he knows things again—things he's no business knowing. I get to thinking about him being a jicker man, and all my questions come bubbling back up.

'What *were* you doing down that well? I bet you could have climbed out any time you wanted. You ain't as blind or rickety as you made out.'

He feeds the fire another slither of wood. 'I saw you coming down the road from three miles away. Wanted to know what you were made of.'

'I could have taken your mule.'

'Then I'd have learned you were a thief.'

'But you would've lost Dorothy.'

'That's what *you* say.'

'You'd have taken her back?'

Roach shrugs. 'And known you'd have made a lousy companion. Known it was best to leave you behind.'

'Canny,' I say. 'But why take the risk? Why bother? You could have just avoided me altogether.'

'The Great Elder Light.'

'What?'

'The Great Elder Light tells me what to do and how to do it.'

'What's the Great Elder Light?'

'It's like a voice, up here.' Roach taps the side of his head. 'A whisper. All you have to do is listen.'

'And the voice told you to get down that well? Some voice... What, to test me?'

'You were tested, were you not?'

'How do you mean?'

'You considered taking Dorothy.'

'Suppose it crossed my mind.'

'Well, there you are.'

'What if the voice in your head was wrong?'

'It's never wrong. If it was, I wouldn't be a wind-strómer.'

'A what?'

'A wind-strómer, a sangolorum, a follower of the broken sword, ma-jicker, a jicker man... A traveller of the Way.. There are many names for my kind.'

'My head hurts. I'm going to sleep.' It's true. My head does ache. But I also feel the need to distance myself from Roach. I guess it's a trust thing. I turn to find my pack.

'Before you do, listen up. It's no coincidence that we met at the well. It was meant to be. Our paths were meant to join.'

'What are you talking about?' Irritably, I give my pocket watches a wind, one after another.

'The Great Elder Light made it happen.'

'You're serious?'

He nods. 'And there's a reason. I heard what you were saying to your gawper friend back there.'

'They call themselves Dagomites.'

'In Amorphia they're the Witchety Nava. In Urthia, the Gankatan. In the eastern lands of Icta they're known as the Barrow-morty. The point is, I'm also looking for Skallagrim. Well, not for him, exactly, but for something in his possession.'

I'm surprised and drowning in a sea of questions, but the one I ask is, 'What?'

'It's a book. A very old one. One that's important to someone like me.'

'Is it a book of ma-jicker spells?'

'Not exactly, but it does contain knowledge of an ancient ma-jick. Not really ma-jick but something that existed even before the world was ever born.'

'Sounds pretty deep.'

'It is. Most people wouldn't understand it.'

'Does Skallagrim understand it?'

'I don't know. The writings might be unreadable to him. It is written from cover to cover in an ancient tongue. It would appear as an indecipherable code to most people.'

'But a jicker man could read it and understand it.'

'He might. Without having the book, it's hard to say.'

'So, you've never seen it?'

'No.'

'I used to think the gawpers were just in stories—that the Gawper King was a fable.'

'So did many. Now they know different.'

I think for a minute, my mind in turmoil. 'Like I said, I'm going to sleep now. Goodnight, Roach.'

I roll out my bed mat near the fire and lie down, huddling beneath my Draker coat and blanket. Stink returns to slip in beneath, where he curls up, warm against me and drifting close to slumber, I think back to the old stories of the jicker men, which leads me to recall the bomb-broken home I left behind on Bunson Street, in Camdon City:

The dragons and their masters had crawled across the land, passing through the ruins like a plague. I'd returned to what was left, thinking the Mysteries Solved office might have survived, and had planned to take the gawper file as Michael had said to do. But I was too late and the office was gone, reduced to rubble. Around the wreckage, charred papers fluttered in the wind: the remains of our old case files. I gathered pages up, though realising it was useless, quickly abandoned them. The gawper file was no more.

Despondently, I backtracked down the battered road to where number ninety-six used to stand. I poked around in the debris, not knowing what I was looking for, yet searching all the same.

THE JICKER MAN

Something half buried between the fallen stones caught my eye. Sunlight glinted from a yellowish metal. I moved a stone aside to find an old brass telescope, dented yet still in working order. I remembered playing with it in those early years soon after Michael took me in from the streets and gave me a home. I used to spy on the neighbours, pretend I was a proper detective on an important case. I recalled my fascination with the polished brass tubes that extended and collapsed so cleverly within each other. For a boy from the streets, the way the glossy lenses made things appear larger was like a sort of ma-jick.

Fondly, I rubbed the telescope clean with a sleeve of my coat and slid it into my pack. Stooping to reach again into the gap, I plucked out a diary and blew dust from its pages, saw that it was Michael's, and began to read.

Over the following months, I read about Michael's daily life, his hopes and thoughts, and still I felt ill-prepared for a journey to confront and kill the Gawper King. If only I had taken the gawper file from the office before the bombs fell. For without that file and the information it contained, I felt bound to fail.

Rather than set out for the first of the lairs, I simply tried to survive. I scavenged food, dodged threshers and rider-less warbirds, hid from Urthian warriors and sheltered in deserted ruins on the outskirts of the city. From time to time, I'd venture back in towards the city centre to search the surviving houses for food or warm clothing, risking many dangers. I found Stink and carried him in my pack for much of the time, feeding him until he was big enough to keep up with me.

During the nights, I'd read Michael's diary by candlelight and recalled the times before the world turned up-side-down. I heard his words alive in my head as I turned the pages. Listened to him talk about when he and the other agents from Mysteries Solved tracked me down to a shipyard to question me about a case. I was in awe of the detectives from the start, though I tried not to show it. They took me for black bean soup and cake, and that was the start of it. Before long I was running errands, delivering notes and generally spying for them from the streets.

I flipped forwards through the pages to the day of my beating. Read his account of the trial he and the others attended while I lay half dying on the cobbles of Bunson Street. I was moved when I saw how sorry he was about the event, how it wounded him and how furiously he had set out for vengeance, storming from the courthouse when he'd heard the news.

And one day, huddled in a dank corner of an abandoned town house where I was reading the diary, I came upon an entry that changed everything.

Elventide Day 1795

Today was a good day. The most challenging case we have faced so far is now concluded and what's more, my cousin became engaged to the city coroner!

Josiah seems more contented than I thought he might be. His sweetheart has moved to Camdon City and it's likely I won't be able to delay their engagement for much longer. Oh well. Good luck to him!

Our neighbour, Jinkers, is also in good cheer, since I have presented him with a copy of the gawper file as an Elventide gift. He is obsessed with the beings and—I am quite sure—at this very minute, thumbing keenly through the documents, which contain almost everything I've learned about the Dagomite kind.

I read and reread the last two sentences. Jinkers had a copy of the gawper file! But where was he? I tried to recall the state of our neighbour's house after the bombing. Was it still standing? Half standing? Levelled? I didn't know. The entire landscape was changed and our neighbour's house was of little interest.

I made a special trip back into Crowlands, found Bunson Street once more and stood peering up at Jinkers' old home. It had survived. Mostly.

Feeling odd to be following such forgotten civilities, I stood at his front door and knocked. I knocked again and then, when no answer came, tried the handle to find it locked. A short way into the garden at the back of the house was a patch of disturbed soil. A small grave. The name Mr Kaylock was scratched into a large rock that had been used as a headstone. I found a broken window and called into the house.

'Mr Jinkers?'

Silence.

Smashing out the remains of the leaded glass with an elbow, I heaved myself over the sill and into the kitchen. From there I worked my way through the musty old house, following the stench of death, until I found Mr Jinkers curled up beneath the blankets of his bed, hugging a thick file of papers to his chest. It seemed to me that he'd given up trying to survive after the death of his beloved cat and, perhaps too frightened to leave the house, had preferred to starve.

I prised the file from his stiffened arms and drew a blanket up to cover his face.

9. FUEL

Jade's gone when I wake the next day. Roach stirs pine needle tea over the fire and seems lost in thought. In the pale
morning light, I squint around at our camp: a small, enclosed
space between the truck and the remnants of buildings. Ain't
nothing missing, far as I can tell, except for Stink, who's off
hunting again. Dorothy stands nearby, endlessly chewing,
her velveteen nose nuzzling a small pile of oats that Roach
has poured out for her.

'Where's the girl?' I dig out my watches, check the time
and give them each a winding. It's around nine o'clock.

'I don't know,' says Roach with a shrug. 'She left before I
woke. Thought I might walk back to the market. See what's
what.'

'I'll stay. Take the fish if you want. See if there's any bacon.
Eggs would be good.' The thought of smoked meat and rich,
yellow eggs makes my mouth water.

'We should keep some of the fish. It's preserved. It will
keep better than a lot of things.'

'Fine. Trade half. I'll watch our stuff.' I find my spare cup,
swill it clean with water from my canteen and take some tea.

A few minutes later, Roach readies himself and sets off, two dozen fishes in a bag slung on his back and soon, Stink returns with the carcass of a dogfish in his mouth. He must have found it washed up on the beach. It smells too far gone for me but he ain't worried.

'Here, boy.' Thinking I should roast it for him on the fire, I try to take it but he growls and drags it further away. Ain't no way you're gonna take food from a Draker dog when it's trying to eat.

'Suit yourself.'

He chomps away, pinning the fish to the ground with his front paws and tearing the soft flesh apart with his teeth.

I climb up onto the roof of the Clansly to take in the town—get a pretty good view from up there—and try to think like a gawper might. I see the islands, the broken road and the light bouncing blue-green off the sea, and then that old dogfish draws my eye back to the ground.

Caves! I bet there are caves down there!

I don't want to leave the truck and our gear unguarded, but once Roach is back with a bag full of trades, I set off pretty sharp. There's a string of coves joined together by rocky cliffs and it ain't long before I spot some caves low down near the waterline. I head for them, crossing a broad beach, and Stink races about on the wide flats of wave-rippled sand. He tries to eat a mop of seaweed but soon drops it.

I was right about the caves. Gawpers love 'em. And they've been here. I can tell before we even enter 'cause Stink picks something up that's in the air. He stands in the entrance, peering in, releasing a low, rumbling growl. There's even a planum horis high up on the ceiling of a cavern, fifty yards or so in under the cliffs. The symbol is daubed onto the rock in black paint, or maybe it's dried blood. In the dimness of the cave, it's hard to say. I figure that's the cavern they used for a lair and spend some time exploring it, searching for any evidence they may have left. There are remains of several campfires: charcoal and charred wood mixed in with the sand, rocks and pebbles. I find another fragment of the black weed the gawpers use so much.

'They were here,' I tell Stink.

Perhaps it was Skallagrim. Perhaps not.

Part way down a narrow channel in the cavern, Stink stops again. He growls and barks into the darkness beyond, refusing to go further. I pause to make a torch from a stick of driftwood and some supplies from my bag, strike my flint to light the brand.

I got to leave Stink behind if I'm going deeper.

'Wait here, boy.'

Uneasy, he turns circles but then settles on the stone floor to watch me go.

At the end of the channel, I reach the final chamber and sweep my torch around to light empty eye sockets staring back at me. A pile of human skulls sits on a ledge and, above them on the wall of the cave, are daubed nine symbols. I don't recognise them.

My torch burns out. The place gives me a proper dread deep down in my guts then, so I leave real quick, glad to find Stink in the channel and to get back out into the daylight.

*

B ack at the camp, I take a piece of cold charcoal from the edge of the fire and sketch out the symbols on a slab of fallen masonry.

'You say these were written on a cave wall over a pile of human skulls?' asks Roach, studying the drawings.

'Aye. All in a line. What do they mean?'

'Nothing good, Ebadiah. It is a sacred vow to destroy all humankind. This last symbol, here,' he points, 'is the Dagomite emblem for the name of Skallagrim.'

*

Around midday, the Clansly chugs to life with a belch of black smoke. I finish shovelling dried dung into the fire-box and close the iron door. Roach releases the brake and we drive out through Fenlock, weaving northwards on a street scattered with abandoned vehicles. Bodies lie in the road, their flesh withered, their clothes fluttering rags. Hills loom in the mid distance and at the edge of the town, I glance back to see a slight figure standing there, watching us go. I blink and look again.

'It's the girl.'

'What now?' asks Roach.

'She's back there on the road.'

Slowing to a stop, he leans out of his window to glance behind. 'That's her, alright. Do you want to talk to her or should I?'

'I'll go,' I say, one foot already out of the truck.

She watches me approach.

'You want a ride?' I ask. She nods.

I sling her shoulder bag into the back and for the next fifty miles or so, we sit bunched up in the front of the truck: Roach, Stink, Jade and me. She's wary of the dog so I sit between them. She don't talk much, just sitting there all tense and, when we stop to let Dorothy and Stink out for a while, she takes herself off to stand away from us, just staring out over the misty hills. I wonder who she is. What she's been through.

Roach drives for another hour until we hit a road edging a stream, high up on a heathery tor.

'Looks like a good place to camp for the night,' he says. 'The water's good 'n' fresh up here. Hey, girl, you should wash up a bit. Looks like you could use it.'

Jade scowls.

Dorothy wanders a grassy path, chewing at the tips of the heather. Stink bolts away, disappearing over a rise. There are often rabbits on hills like these.

A few minutes later, Jade's down at the stream, splashing water over her face and rubbing away at layers of dirt. When she returns to the Clansly, I'm struck by the delicate nature of her newly revealed features.

'Is there some place I can bathe? Ain't strippin' for you and the old man, but I want to get proper clean.'

I walk with her back to the stream's edge and take in the lie of the land. The water dances past us and down through a gully in the rocks where it disappears for a short way.

'Down there.' I point. 'We won't see you if you're beyond the rocks.' I take a towel from my pack and pass her my spear. 'Take these. Keep a lookout for morh-beasts. Do you have clean clothes?'

'In my bag.' She fetches her bag from the truck and with the towel under her arm and the spear over her shoulder, follows the stream. While she's bathing and Roach is off poking around in the heather, I get a fire started on the sheltered side of the Clansly and put some water on to boil.

When Jade returns, she looks different again, not like the street girl I took her for. She smells better, too. She's run a comb through her long chestnut hair, which falls damp around her shoulders. She seems glad to warm herself as she drops her wet clothes by the fire, throws my towel back to me and plants my spear into the ground.

'Thanks,' she says. 'I needed that.'

Roach joins us, emptying his pockets into my hands. I stare at the heather tips he's collected.

'What's this for?'

'Tea,' he says, frowning at me. 'You never had heather tea?'

I shake my head. Jade laughs. She takes the harvested tips from me to drop them into the simmering water.

We gather branches of deadwood from the low, wind-blown trees and prop up the towel and Jade's washed clothes to dry around the fire. We drink heather tea, which is less bitter than the pine needles, so I prefer it, and cook up a pot of stew with bacon and dried beans that Roach traded back in

Fenlock. He adds a chopped onion and stirs in some ground corn to thicken it. Stink returns with a decapitated rabbit and settles down nearby, crunching bones.

Later, when we're full of food and the others are sleeping, I dig out the gawper skull, hold it to my brow and call for Deadlock. I wonder if he'll be able to reach me up here in the hills but he soon responds. Our mind gates meet and I hear his thoughts.

Skallagrim is not in Mors Zonam, he tells me. *The Lotharians have searched every cavern with a source of water. None can survive Mors Zonam without water.*

The news is welcome. *He's gone north, then? Like you said.*

It seems likely. Skallagrim will seek a remote place that is hard to reach, harder to find, somewhere he can defend. Our spies have learned he is trying to gather his forces, but they cannot tell us where. He must be stopped or all is lost.

He ain't at Fenlock, though I found the lair.

Where is this one now? He means me.

We're in the hills, somewhere between Fenlock and Threadmoor. We?

I'm with two friends and a dog.

Trust no one.

Our connection blinks out and with a shooting pain in my head, he's gone. Dazed, I take out my map and put a cross through Fenlock and Mors Zonam. That leaves only three sites left. Feeling like I'm getting somewhere at last, I fold and pocket the map and stow the skull away in my pack. But the feeling don't last long. Over the next few days, we stop at several homesteads in the hills, hoping to stock up on coal, but there's none to be had.

'What does it matter?' asks Jade when my face drops at the latest empty coalhouse we find.

'I got to get to Threadmoor. Other places too.' I stare at the black dust lining the floor of the bunker.

'You got folks there?'

'I don't have any folks but you and Roach.'

That makes her smile. Her face seems to shine when she smiles. 'Are we your folks, now?' She glances across an orchard of apple trees at Roach, who's dozing in the truck out on the road.

'I don't know. Maybe.'

'If it ain't for folks, then why go?'

'There's something I gotta do. You wouldn't understand.'

The smile's gone now. 'Try me.' She pins me with a stony look.

I tell her about Michael and show her the map. Explain about Jinkers' file and Skallagrim's warmongering. I say that Skallagrim is to blame for the entire war. 'So, you see, I got to kill the Gawper King. And I must do it before he digs in so deep he can never be found. Ain't no choice, see. I got to do it. He's taken everyone and everything I ever had.'

'Then, you should let us help. Does *he* know about it?' She tilts her head towards Roach in the Clansly.

'Aye, he knows. He's coming with me. It'll be dangerous though. And I'll probably die trying to kill Skallagrim. Ain't no easy task.'

'You'll need all the help you can get, then.' When I look away, she adds, 'I lost people, too, you know. Lost my folks in the war.'

'I'm sorry.' After a moment I add, 'It'll be dangerous. That's all I'm saying.' I turn back for the truck but hear her voice, angry behind me.

'You think a girl can't fight? I can fight! How do you think I made it this far?!'

'I ain't saying that. Blinders! You can help if you want.' I head back to the truck and bang on the door to wake Roach. 'How are we gonna make it to Threadmoor on half a tug of coal?'

He blinks, looks around, still half asleep. 'I don't know. I don't have all the answers.'

'Oh? I thought you did.' I've had enough, angry at nobody and everyone all at once. With what fuel we have left we'll make it halfway through the mountains before we get stuck. Then we'll be walking again. The thought's painful.

I hear Roach's footsteps following me. 'Wait! What's wrong with you?'

'I need to get this done. With every day that passes, Skallagrim strengthens his position.'

'We'll find him. Don't you worry.'

'Not without coal, we won't.'

Jade joins us, arms crossed and frowning. 'Where I come from, they burn peat. Dig it straight from the ground. Dry it out. Any reason we couldn't use that for the truck?'

'She's resourceful, this one.' Roach leans close to whisper in my ear. 'I told you she'd be good for you.'

*

Jinkers' death hit me like a punch in the gut. Michael had called him miserable, but I'd always found him merry. There ain't no explaining some folk. Whatever the truth, Jinkers would always smile when he saw me and he'd often given me a cheery wink. But the grim find of his body triggered something deep inside of me, a loneliness that felt like it would go on forever. A fear that I might be alone for the rest of my drab and luckless life.

Consoling myself in the gawper file, I read and reread it from cover to cover. I learnt about gawpers, about how they conjure places into their midst. About their judgement of humankind. About their deadly abilities. And about how Skallagrim turned away from the gawper traditions of *shrivening* individuals. This is the term they use for what they do to people: peering into their souls to judge them worthy or not. And for those found unworthy, death came quickly. No, Skallagrim decided that was a waste of time. Better to condemn the entire human race and be sure none escape.

BEN MEARS

Skallagrim—I found the name and read about the time
Michael had ventured into Mors Zonam to come face to face
with Magwitch and soon after, the Gawper King himself.

*Skallagrim is taller than any other and is the only gawper I have
ever seen who has red eyes. Yes, Mr Jinkers, you were right about
that! Skallagrim has a cruel way about him and he rules over his
kind with an iron-clad authority. I felt his gaze upon me and shud-
dered with dread.*

*

A gale is building by the time our last shovel of coal burns
out a day later. The dung's all used up, too—until the
mule makes more, of course. There's not a home in sight
as the Clansly grinds to a halt on the crest of a ridge. Roach
clamps on the brake and we climb down from the truck, our
boots crunching gravel. Hugging our coats tight against a
cruel wind, we squint into the rolling landscape: a patchwork
of grasslands and forest, broken by lines of dry stone walls,
trackways and distant roads. The world is grey today, heavy
and grim beneath a slab of darkly brooding sky.

'There's another storm coming,' says Roach. 'They'll be
snow. We'd better make ready.'

'I don't suppose we can cut peat and get ourselves off this
wind top?'

'There's no time for peat to dry before the storm hits
but, if we can get the truck moving, we might roll it to lower
ground for shelter.'

'We can sit out the storm down there,' says Jade, pointing to a deep valley below, where our road dips to disappear
beneath a thick forest. 'And they'll be plenty of wood to
burn.'

'The girl has a plan.' Roach raises an eyebrow. He releases
the brake and shifts a lever to put the Clansly out of gear.

THE JICKER MAN

It takes all three of us to get the truck rolling. Dorothy stands in the back while we push. At first it seems an impossibly dead weight, but then we feel it shift and a moment later it rolls forwards an inch. We try again and gain another inch or two. Shoving with all out might, we get it moving. Then it's down to me to run around to the front and jump in before it gains too much speed, for even with my limp I'm faster than Roach, and Jade can't drive. Not yet. I steer with the Clansly's big wheel and brake on the downward slope to let Roach and Jade board. They ride up front with me while Stink keeps pace outside.

We reach the forest and slow where the road levels for thirty yards or so before climbing again. The Clansly rolls to a stop surrounded by woods and not before time, for the wind is howling hard and the first flurries of snow rush through the trees like down from a wounded bird. We hurry to gather fallen branches from the forest before it's all dampened afresh by the new snowfall, but it's already moist and it don't want to burn when we break it up and add it to the embers in the firebox. Jade and Roach stack wood in the cabin to dry while I walk the woods, gathering more. We'll need a lot to get us through the night 'cause it's turned so cold that I'm more worried about freezing to death than attracting unwanted visitors. There are pines, rowans, wych elm, ash and hazel. Soon I've gathered all the fallen branches from around the truck and must go further into the woods, the trees creaking and clacking in the wind overhead. I get to thinking about the morh-beast back in Fenlock, and can't help imagining there are more roaming these woods. Peering deeper through the trees, I fancy I hear them rustling through the leaves and head back to the truck in a trice, though perhaps I'm hearing wolves.

As I dump my collection of wood into the rear of the Clansly, Stink passes me, his hackles rising, his gaze intent upon the forest. He slips away, as sleek as quicksilver, while the snow sets in heavy. I call after him.

'Stink!'

If morhs or wolves are out there, they could rip him to shreds.

'Stink!' Grabbing my spear, I run into the darkening woods.

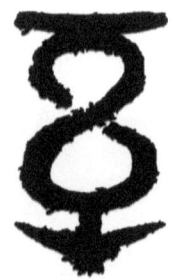

10. STINK

Beneath a canopy of tall boughs, I scan the forest floor for signs of the dog. The blizzard blows in from the side, flashing pale streaks through the trees. I'm scrutinising the shadows when a sudden hand on my shoulder startles me.

'Easy!' says Jade, finding herself at the tip of my spear.

'Two Coats...'

'Thought you might need help looking for your dog.'

'He ain't my dog.'

'Alright. But you *are* looking for him?'

I nod, nervous of what might lie beyond my limited view. 'Reckon there's a big old pack of morh-beasts out here. He probably smelt 'em.' I draw the long knife from my belt. 'You'd better take this.'

She weighs the blade in her hand, glances uneasily at me and then into the woods. Now armed, she looks braver than that timid girl we first met, cowering in the back of a burned-out car.

'You sure?' I ask. 'You can go back to the truck if you want.'

Her knuckles whiten around the knife's haft. 'I'm sure.'

We walk deeper in and I think a spear would be better than a blade, so I pass mine to Jade and take back my knife to reach up and hack down a long straight pine branch. It's good and strong and already has a kind of point at one end where I lopped it from the tree. With a few swift strokes I shave off the twigs, sharpen up the tip and slide the blade back into my belt.

From the murk comes a growl too deep to be Stink. Must be a wolf or a morh-beast. There's nothing to tell us which. Then a movement stirs the leaf litter under the trees. Shadows dash, and roar. In the darkness an animal yelps.

'Stink!' I rush forwards as a dozen or so morh-beasts slip into view, their eyes gleaming in the half-light. Some are larger than others. All of them are tall on their lengthy front legs, lethal looking, their long, pointed ears pricking. As one they turn towards us. Behind the pack, Stink hangs limp in the jaws of a massive male that has blood streaming from his throat. The big morh's ears twitch. Seeing us, he drops the dog to join the pack, but then stumbles and flops to the forest floor to move no more.

'Yah!' I shout and lunge with my spear at the nearest oncoming morh—another huge male, whose amber eyes are locked onto me with deadly intent. I reckon he's the alpha. Black, slavering lips reveal curving teeth twice the length of a wolf's. Its high shoulders roll beneath its mane as it stalks closer, rumbling a guttural growl. I sense Jade at my side, glimpse her outstretched spear.

'There're too many!' I hear panic in my voice. 'Yah! Yah!'

Jade takes up the cry. 'Yah! Yah!'

Trying to hold our ground, we thrust up at them with our spears, but on they come, towering over us, their narrowed eyes searching for opportunity. I cast around for some cover, find nothing but the trunk of a tree that's marginally broader than the rest.

'Over here!' Closing on the tree, we set our backs against the trunk, and not too soon. The morhs encircle us. Keenly, they watch our spears.

And all at once they advance. I've missed some subtle signal from the alpha. They press in, lurching to test us: leaping, snarling and roaring, growing braver the closer they get, the alpha barely two feet from my spear. He takes a swipe at the tip to knock it aside. I whip it back in line, retaliating with a jab that impacts his shoulder. Howling, he withdraws to pad back and forth before me. He directs his snarls at me. The others follow his lead as though awaiting a further sign.

'Wait!' I reach for my slingshot but can't load and fire it while holding the spear. 'Take this!' I pass my spear. 'Hold them off!'

Jade adjusts her grip, a spear in each hand, a shaft tucked under each arm.

In a moment, I have a pebble loaded up and draw the rubber back to take aim. Morhs don't have hard armour or scales like the threshers. Under their thick fur, they're just flesh and bone.

Thwack! My first shot catches the alpha on his flank. He roars and turns for me. I hurriedly reload, smelling smoke on the air. *Thwack!* This stone impacts his skull. The great morh staggers and falls sideways to lie twitching on the ground.

A flaming brand off to my side dips into view.

'It's Roach!' says Jade.

Roach has two fire brands extended towards the beasts. They round on the new threat, unsettled by his arrival and the loss of their fallen leader.

Thwack! I loose another stone to hit a morh that's closing on Jade. The wounded beast flees, bolting into the forest.

'Yah!' Jade shouts, striking out to stab with a spear and sending a second morh running.

Roach sweeps a burning brand in towards a line of them, the wind tearing at the lamp oiled flames. They smell the smoke and cower, the fire flashing in their eyes. They snap and growl, but leaderless, retreat.

'Best be sure.' I reclaim my spear and plunge it down between the fallen alpha's ribs with all my strength before running to Stink's side. His breathing's shallow. From what I can see, he's wounded badly, though the blood around his mouth is from the large morh he mortally wounded, not from him. From the way the morh-beast had him in its jaws, he looked dead.

'He must have broken ribs, if not his neck,' I say.

Jade joins me, laying a hand gently on Stink's bloodied flank.

'He needs help or he could die. My Ma taught me healing. She had the gift.' Jade runs her fingers down Stink's neck, tracing his spine, feeling for the line of bones.

'Let's get him back to the truck,' I say.

I feel her hand on mine. 'He'll be alright, you know. He's still breathing. His neck and back ain't broke.'

I meet her eyes, then, wanting to believe every word. Just hoping.

Sensing another presence beyond her in the depths of the forest, I refocus upon the fiery white eyes of a watching figure. There, a gawper hangs in a blur of snow. Did it somehow manipulate the morhs to hunt us? With a sweep of its cloak, it vanishes, the air seeming to close around it.

'They know,' I say over the howl of the wind as Roach approaches. 'Skallagrim knows we come for him. I think I may have just seen his captain, Tacitus.' I feel my jaw clenching.

'Then our task will be all the harder,' says Roach, eyeing the space where the gawper had been.

Stink whimpers as I slide my arms gently beneath his body. I carry him to the Clansly, where I nod towards my bedroll that's in the back. 'There, use that.'

Jade unrolls the thin mattress and I lay the dog carefully down. His fur's matted with blood where the morh's teeth scraped and pierced him.

'I'll clean his wounds.' Jade cups her hands into a patch of unblemished snow and uses handfuls of it to wipe the raw gashes. Stink whines softly at her touch.

Roach calls to me from the woods. 'Ebadiah, lend a hand.'

I find him beneath the trees, struggling to drag the body of the big morh that Stink killed. It weighs way more than he does. Nearby lies the other fallen beast. 'Treat these right and we'll have meat for months.'

'How?' I grab a leg and start pulling.

'You cut the flesh real thin. Smoke it dry over a fire.'

'I've never eaten Morh-beast.'

'I imagine it's tough.' Roach puffs, heaving the body. 'Though it will sustain us.'

We work our way backwards to the truck, leaving channels in the snow—one carcass at a time—and then hoist the dead morhs up the tailgate and into the rear by their gangling front legs. The mule starts at their feral smell.

'They'll return when they've worked out a new leader,' says Roach. 'Morh-beasts are vengeful creatures. We should move out of the forest. The sooner the better.'

'But the fuel...'

'Yes,' he nods regrettably. 'We're stuck here for the night.'

'Will the wood power the truck?'

'Not like coal, but yes. When it's dry, it should work. We'll be slower, though. It won't burn as hot or as long.'

'What if they come back in the night?'

'We'll get a fire going with the little dry wood we have. Dry more. Cook some of this meat. Eat. If they come for us, we must be ready.' He peers out into the shadows, the outline of his hawkish face dark against the squall.

We rig up the tarp to make a shelter in the lee of the truck. With help from a little of the lamp oil, we set a campfire and stack branches around it to dry in the fading twilight.

Roach butchers a hind leg from the big morh, burns off the hair and hangs it over the flames to roast. Taking a few rags and some wire from my pack, I wrap strips of cloth around a half dozen branches to use as torches. I collect grease from the dripping meat, add that and a few drops of lamp oil to the cloth, and bind up the brands with wire.

Skallagrim's gonna pay for hurting Stink. I'm gonna find him and mount his stupid head on a spike. This I solemnly promise myself, glaring into the trees where the gawper appeared.

Silently, we watch the surrounding woods for movement as smoke and cinders gust and eddy with the heavy snow-flakes. Jade fusses over Stink, cleaning and binding his chest with strips of linen she tears from one of her shirts. She brings him water in a bowl from her bag. I huddle on the Clansly's tailgate, stroking Stink's head and warming myself in the glow of the struggling fire.

'You're good at that,' I tell her.

Questions buzz like bugs trapped in my head. Will the morh-beasts return to take revenge? Will we face more of them next time? What was the gawper doing back there? Has he travelled to the forest or is he elsewhere, conjuring the forest into his presence? I got to know for sure and I ain't gonna find out sitting here, moping.

'Build up the fire,' I tell Roach. 'I'm going back into the woods.' But there's a fire already built deep inside me, a blazing bonfire that's out of control. I stand and glance at Stink's unmoving form while my inner fury boils. Perhaps I'll stumble upon another morh-beast and kill it. If I find the gawper, I will kill that, too. Pretty much whatever I find, it's gonna die—unless it kills me first.

'It's not safe,' says Roach, snapping another branch across his knee and throwing the pieces into the flames. Though from his expression I guess he knows I'm off, whatever he says. 'At least eat something before you go. Here.' He cuts a hunk from the sizzling joint with a knife and passes it before working on the raw flesh of the carcass, slicing it into ribbons.

I sit down. Chew on the gamy meat. I ain't hungry on account of my bellyful of rage, so don't eat much. I'm soon ready to go. Collecting my spear and lighting a torch in the fire, I slope off into the trees.

'Don't go!'

I turn.

Jade stands at the edge of our camp, looking cold and scared. She seems small in the deepening shadows as snowflakes catch in her hair.

'Stay. We need you.'

'Sorry. It's just something I got to do. Look after the others.' I trudge on and the next time I look back, the truck and the camp are swallowed by the billowing storm.

I try to track my way back to the place where the morhbeasts attacked, but it's useless. The snow falls thick and fast, quilting the forest floor in all but the densest areas. Any signs are long-buried. My mind turns instead to the gawper and its potential lair. I traipse for an hour—my boots biting shindeep into the thick white crust—and reaching the foot of an open knoll, stop. There, fresh footprints leave the shelter of the trees. They can only have been made recently. I follow them up onto the mound where they end, the snow flattened and disturbed. By what? I wonder. I can't say but I've a notion, and shout at the sky.

'Skallagrim! I know you're out there, hiding like a coward. I know this is you. Skallagrim, I'm coming for you!' My words swirl into the ether, weightless and empty. He's not here.

I scan the surrounding woods, now black against the night-washed blizzard, but see only trees. Then something in the snow catches my eye. Stooping, I collect the red feather of a war bird.

BEN MEARS

*

I found something noteworthy towards the end of the gawper file. Michael had written concerning words that Magwitch had spoken to him while mind-walking:

'It seems to me that the gawpers do not truly have a weakness, though Magwitch perhaps gave away more than he meant when questioned about their peculiar abilities. I had asked, *If you can conjure a place into your presence, why then would any Dagomite ever walk or go anywhere by other means? Surely you have no need to do so.*

Magwitch replied as a voice in my head.

Dagomites cannot survive by moving through the fourth plane alone. The effort is too great and cannot be made without end. Dagomites must still walk like your kind.

I had asked, *You have legs, then, underneath all those robes of weed?!*

Magwitch had laughed at that.

Dagomites have legs, indeed, though they are thin and weak. Thousands of years of conjuring have made it so. Dagomites cannot travel far without rest, unless carried by another creature.'

The note had left me thinking. So, Skallagrim was likely riding a creature of some sort that was powerful enough to bear him. That may help me to track his journey. And feeling better prepared, I had set out for Hick's Gate the very next day.

*

We leave the forest with a meagre supply of fuel, which allows us a further two days of travel.

123

'That's the last of the wood.' With a mittened hand, I close the iron door of the firebox and watch Roach tip another pail of snow, which hisses and pops, into the steam trap.

He clamps the trap shut.

'You never know. We might find more coal around the bend.'

I grasp at the notion, wondering if it's one of his mystical insights, but decide despondently that it ain't. He's just being hopeful.

'If not, it's peat when this has burnt through, or we walk,' he adds.

'But Stink...'

The dog has barely moved since I laid him down in the back of the truck.

'Dorothy can carry him. I'll use my feet.' Roach sits at the wheel.

'How long does it take for peat to dry?' I ask Jade, who watches us from the bench up front in the truck.

'Oh, we cut it in the summer, leave it to dry in the sun for three days. Then it's stacked in the barn. We burn it the following winter.'

'You mean over a year later?' I'm dismayed at the prospect.

'Yes, but it's probably usable long before that.'

'How long?'

'I don't know. It's winter, so a couple of months, maybe.'

'But we have nowhere to dry it and I ain't got a couple of months!'

'Take a seat,' says Roach.

I sit with Jade and Roach releases the brake. The Clansly lurches sluggishly on through the rolling, white landscape. The road is a vast curve dipping down a colossal vale and up into foothills beyond. The trees are mostly behind us. Now we're into the highland moors. Above and to the north, east and west of us rise purple mountains, steeped in mist.

We pass a large standing stone carved with weather-worn, ancient symbols.

I sit by Jade and grapple with the reality of our fuel problem. Ain't no getting round it: without coal progress is slow. The wood don't burn as hot. I suppose peat won't be any better, but we got to try, even if it means camping on the moors for several months.

'Is there even peat here to dig?' I ask. 'How would we know?'

'We won't know until we try,' says Jade. 'But there's a sort you find in uplands. They call it blanket bog.' She takes in the long sweep of the landscape. 'Must be rabbits up here. Hares, maybe.' She ain't keen on morh-beast meat.

The speed ain't the only issue with the wood-fuel. It don't last as long as coal, either, like Roach said. Half an hour later, the firebox is all burned out and the Clansly chugs to a stop. Ain't a tree or house in sight.

We make camp. I check my map, climb up onto the roof of the truck to turn about, scanning the horizon. I reckon we're not far from Threadmoor. My pocket watches and the position of the Sun tell me the truck's pointing north. I use the telescope. See a column of smoke rising way off in the distance, grey in the air. Looks like a whole town's gone up in flames. I glimpse the silhouettes of war birds circling high, their vast wings outstretched.

When I climb down Jade is sitting in the rear of the truck, nursing Stink and stroking his neck. 'Look!' she says. 'He's eating!'

He laps slivers of the dry-smoked morh-beast's flesh from her fingertips, his head flat against the bedroll.

'It's a good sign.' Jade grins. 'He's going to be alright. I told you he would.'

I lean down to nuzzle into him, rest my head on his and whisper. 'You got to get well, Bear Dog. You just got to.'

In response, he offers a lazy flick of his tail. Roach walks his mule off the road to clear snow from the grass so she can nibble at the icy green tips.

'Here, you should eat, too.' Jade drops a handful of the cured morh-beast flesh into my hands.

I gaze at the mountains and chew on the smoky, tough meat.

'Suppose it's time to dig for peat. Wish we had a spade.'

'It could be worse,' she says. 'At least we have the shovel.'

11. DEAF

'Tighter!' cries Roach.

'That's as tight as it will go,' I tell him.

As the rain begins to fall, Roach hammers the final wooden peg into the ground to secure the tarp of our make-shift shelter. I release the corner and duck inside. Jade and Roach are quick to join me.

'This could slow us down,' I say, peering out at the down-pour.

'We must be patient,' says Roach. He sits, and taking out his pipes, he begins a softly rolling tune.

Jade builds a small campfire near the entrance. Shrubs dot the surrounding wilderness: gorse and heather and ferns. We've already gathered some small branches of dead wood from around our camp to heat water and burn against the cold. Just as well, now that everything's getting a fresh drenching, though it wouldn't be enough to power the steam engine more than a hundred feet.

We tend Stink closely over the following days. Jade cleans and binds his injuries with fresh dressings each morning, washing out the old before hanging them to dry by the meagre campfire. She has a way with him, a gentle touch that tells me she cares but despite her best efforts, his wounds weep and ooze, and a week after the fight with the morhs, his breathing grows weaker and dreadfully shallow. I'm scared that he's dying.

I stay away from him after that. Can't face watching him fade. If that's gonna happen, it'll be without me there. I want to know, though. Want to know what I'll be dealing with, one way or the other, so I find Roach one morning as he's washing out his cooking pot at the bank of the babbling stream that edges our camp.

'Teach me how to hear the Voice. I want to know things, like you do.'

He gives me one of his measuring looks. 'Alright. If you're sure.' But then turning away, he goes back to work on the pot.

'Well?'

'Well, what?'

'Are you gonna teach me or not?'

'If you wish. We can begin tomorrow.' He scrubs and rinses in the icy water.

'Why not now?'

He stops, turning to look me in the eye. 'Because, if you want to hear the Voice, the first thing you're going to have to learn... is patience.'

'Pah!' I leave him and stomp off to be by myself. Patience is the last thing on my mind.

*

At night we take turns to keep watch while the others sleep. The land around us seems quiet and unoccupied but you can never be sure. Desperate people conceal themselves. The monsters stalk in shadows, never stepping into the light. The truth is, we could be surrounded even as we camp in this apparently tranquil vale.

My first lesson begins when Roach calls to me from a track that leads into a nearby stretch of gorse bushes. 'I've found a good place,' he says as I follow. 'The Voice will never force itself upon you, so you much truly listen for it, seek it out. Do you understand?'

'I think so.' We reach the gorse and enter. 'Where are we going?'

'There's a clearing. It's not far. Somewhere with few distractions. Distractions are your enemy when it comes to listening.'

I trudge after him. When we enter the open space, he directs me to sit on the grass, which I do.

'You must clear your mind, Ebadiah. Rid it of anything that may interfere. Do you see?' He sits before me, cross-legged.

'I think so, though I don't know how.'

'Some things you can only learn by trial.'

'And this is one, I suppose.'

'Indeed. Yet there is more to it than that. When you have quietened your mind, you will notice other voices. They will be gentle at first, but when you are more accomplished at listening, they will grow louder. They may even fight for your attention.' His voice grows strong. 'It will sound like an earthquake in your head. Like wind and fire!' He softens. 'Yet it's the whisper you must seek, the quiet, small voice.'

Ain't no quiet voice in *my* head. Just a big old shout at Skallagrim. Just a raging furnace of hate. I try everything he tells me but it's useless. Giving up, I walk away.

*

My second lesson ain't much better. Roach takes me away from camp to a quiet place by the stream, muttering something about *trying a different approach*. We sit on a grassy bank, the water's song underlying our talk.

'Are you ready?' he asks when we've been sitting quietly for several minutes.

'I suppose.' I start to think maybe he could just tell me what'll happen to Stink, but I don't ask. Something tells me he wouldn't say.

'Then close your eyes and let the sound of the brook settle your mind. Listen only to the water. Do you hear it? It is a peaceful sound.'

'I hear the water,' I say, feeling ridiculous. I'm glad Jade ain't here to laugh at me.

'Alright. Now let the water be the only thing you hear. Let it cover every thought. This may take time and requires patience. Allow it to be louder than you.'

I sit tight and listen. The stream sounds good, calming in a way. Although I soon grow bored and my mind wanders back to the realities of life, to Stink's injuries, to Skallagrim and all he took from me. I picture Michael and Josiah departing for war, the house on Bunson Street levelled to the ground by Urthian bombs, Jinkers' corpse, still clutching the gawper file. I see the unliving faces of the widow and my adopted mother, Sarah. And it's not the stream I can hear any more, but a vast cacophony of strife.

'I'm sorry,' I say, opening my eyes to see disappointment on the old man's face. 'I just can't do it.'

*

We take turns to cut slabs of peat from a waterlogged stretch of land alongside the stream, laying them in the sun—when it graces us with its measly presence, which is rarely. At night, we stack the blocks high and pile rocks on top to squeeze out the moisture. When the rain or snow comes, we hurry to gather them into the back of the truck. There's an ever-shifting cycle of sods placed around our campfire. The process is messy, tiresome and long. A month of drying, turning and moving the peat from here to there leaves most of it still too damp to burn.

'It's just not working,' I tell Jade, despondently as we sit around a pathetic fire on a bitterly cold evening.

'It is. Just give it time,' she says, hugging a blanket around her coats, her knees drawn up to her chest.

'How much longer?' I demand.

'I don't know. Everything's so damp here. A month perhaps. It dries quicker in the summer.'

'Another month! Blinders! I can't afford another month!'

She glares at me. 'Well, you don't really have a choice, do you?'

'Can't we speed things up? Heat up all the peat somehow to dry it faster?'

She rolls her eyes. 'If we had the fuel to do that, we wouldn't need the peat.' She's right, of course. I've yet to find that Jade is wrong about anything. She continues, her voice softening. 'You need to relax. I'm pretty sure Skallagrim will still be waiting in another month and, if he ain't, you won't have to worry about him, will you?'

Now I'm frustrated by Skallagrim *and* her. *Why don't she understand?* Springing to my feet, I storm away.

Jade shouts after me. 'Why do you do that?'

I turn. 'Do what?'

'Run away whenever there's a problem?'

'I ain't runnin',' I tell her. 'Anyway, what would you know about it?!' Miserable, I head off, just wanting to get away from everyone.

When I return to camp an hour later, Roach is playing a peaceful tune on his pipes and Jade is contentedly darning a hole in one of her shirts. I'm an odd peg, I realise. I don't fit here. I start to wonder if it wouldn't be better to leave and go my own way. They'd care for Stink if he survives—though I'm sure he won't—so I wouldn't need to worry about him. The thought leaves me hollow, with an empty sick feeling inside. There's only so much I can do. Only so much I can take.

Laying out my bedroll, I lie by the fire with my pack for a pillow but try as I may, I can't rest. Instead, a plan begins to unfold in my mind. I'll need supplies, though I must leave enough food behind for Roach and Jade. I'll take only my fair share: one canteen, one spear and my pack. And when all is ready, I'll leave during the night when they're asleep.

For hours these simple ideas spool over in my head and I can't pin down the reason. The thought is complete, so why does my mind insist on this endless examination. It's as though a part of me is convinced a flaw exists and refuses to stop searching until it's found.

When I awake the following morning, Jade is tending the fire. There's no sign of Roach.

'Tea?' she asks, out of habit. There's boiled water or tea. So, tea always wins, whatever the kind.

I rub at my bleary eyes and look around. The camp's quiet. Dorothy lazes near the truck and the peat is already laid out in the feeble sunlight on a nearby stony bank. Roach must be off foraging.

'Pine or heather?'

'Heather.'

'With a drop of honey.' A joke without cheer.

'Perhaps we'll find some in the next town.' She hands a cupful to me before serving herself. 'Or sugar. Imagine if we found a pound of sugar!'

'That would be good.' I nod, imagining the sweet taste. Recalling my plans of last night, I go quiet. No point in pursuing a relationship that's doomed. My mission to kill Skallagrim is all. I sense my face harden.

'Are you alright?' Jade sounds concerned.

I sidestep her question. 'How's Stink?'

That shuts her up. Clearly, he ain't doing well. And that seals it. I promise myself I'll be gone before he dies. The weight of seeing it would be too much.

We drink in silence.

During the day, I begin to pack away a share of the dried meat. I gather my few possessions from around the camp and the truck. I guess there's enough rope in the back of the Clansly for everyone, so, while the others are busy elsewhere, I toe past Stink's unmoving form, coil up a good length and add it to my pack.

In the afternoon, Roach leads me into the gorse for another lesson. Again we sit cross-legged in the clearing, facing each other on the damp ground surrounded by bird song, but now I'm just doing it to pass the time.

'Close your eyes,' he says, and so I do. 'Remember, the Voice is quiet, just a whisper. You will not hear it if your head is full of noise. So, clear your mind. Empty it, like you would a bag.'

I open my eyes. 'What do you mean? Empty my mind? I can't. I don't have a say about what goes on in there.'

'Yes, you do. You have a choice about everything. You have a say about how you react to each situation, to every thought. Think about it. Control it.'

'I can't control my thoughts. Nobody can.'

'Wrong. If *you're* not controlling your thoughts, then who is?'

I stare at him—his eyes shut, his face serene—and think, *this is going nowhere. I'm wasting time.*

'Close your eyes!' He chides me. 'If you don't focus, *you're* wasting *my* time.'

Again, it seems he's reading me. I close my eyes and gaze at an inner blackness. Thoughts float through my mind. Stink lying, dying in the back of the steam truck. My argument with Jade. Della dragged into the bushes by the thresher. Barrels of fish going to waste, buried in the sand. On they roll as I try in vain to push them away, to suffocate them in darkness. Each has its own noise, its own wretched feel. Each is enough to drown out all else. And I know I'll never hear the whisper over the din.

'It's alright,' I hear Roach say softly. 'These things can take time to master.'

'I don't have time. All I got is purpose.'

'Do you want to do this or not?' he asks.

I open my eyes to find him looking back at me, though he seems strangely calm.

'How do you *do* that?' My voice sounds harsh. 'How are you not angry?!'

'I am listening to the Voice. That's how.'

'Blinders! I'll never hear the Voice! I must be deaf!'

That does it. I'm off, heading back to the camp, kicking at tufts of grass and stones in my path. At the edge of the gorse, I pause to collect a rock and launch it hard into the bushes. A dozen crowlings scatter into the sky. I glance around, suddenly wary. The feeling that someone is watching slides over me and I turn for camp.

*

The fire crackles. Smoke rises to the dark, starless heavens. The peat ain't dry. Stink's ebbing away. I ain't hearing no voice. There's no point staying. Everything's ready. I leave tonight.

I spoon morh-beast stew into my mouth, chew and swallow, watch the others eating. There's a sombre mood hanging over the camp and I wonder if the others sense it, too—if they've guessed my plans. Roach looks tired as the firelight plays shadows with the deep lines of his face, and I can't help but feel I've only caused him more strife since traveling with him. He'll be better off without me, I'm sure. Same goes for Jade, probably.

Slabs of peat stand steaming near the flames. The earthy smell fills the air as Roach offers around the stew. I give a single shake of my head. I want the others to eat well tonight. Need them to have full bellies and a good, deep sleep so I can get quietly away. Jade accepts another helping but takes it off to the truck for Stink. I imagine her sitting with him and failing to rouse any interest from the waning dog. I want to visit him too but just can't face it.

Soon enough, she's back at the fire and settling down for the night with her coats and blankets.

'I'll take first watch,' I say, taking the cooking pot and our bowls to wash them out in the stream while Roach lays out his blankets. We ain't seen a morh-beast since the attack but they could find us any time. I just hope it ain't tonight.

I watch and wait for Jade and Roach to fall asleep. An hour later, even Dorothy is dozing, lying on the ground where she's tethered to the truck. Rising, I add gorse branches to the fire and with a last glance around, grab my spear, shoulder my pack, and pick my way quietly out of the camp. My plan? Trek a mile or two before stopping to consult Deadlock. He may have news that alters my bearings, otherwise I'm heading north. I got my map, my spyglass and my watches. I've been alone before and it didn't kill me. I ain't afraid.

They'll be alright, I tell myself with a pang of guilt at abandoning them. *They'll do fine. They don't need me.*

But walking away, I sense a tug, like my heart is on a line and I'm stretching it tight. I swallow down the feeling and force my feet to plod on. Even then, I find my head turning to look back for one more glimpse. There, in the glow of the fire, I see Jade rising to stand, searching the night about her. I don't know what woke her. I didn't make a sound. Her eyes find me in the gloom and for a moment she stills, like a deer startled in the forest. And then she's moving from the fireside, her silhouette coming after me. Unsure if I should run or return, I stand there, helpless, caught.

'Where are *you* going? You're supposed to be keeping...' She sees my pack. 'You're *leaving*?'

I stare at her blankly while thinking up a lie. 'I was just...'

'You're really leaving?' She's angry now. 'How could you?'

My lie is abandoned before it's complete. 'What do you mean? I can leave if I want.'

'What about him?' She jabs a thumb back towards camp.

'Who? Roach? He'll be fine without me. He's tougher than he looks.'

'Not Roach, you numbskull! I mean Stink!' There's a pause during which she spears me with a dagger-like gaze.

'I don't... I can't...' Looking away, I search for the right words but the night holds no answers. Instead, I'm forced to dig deep for the truth. 'Listen. I can't just sit here and watch him die. It hurts too much. He means too much to me.'

'Who says he's dying?'

'No one, but–'

'Well, he's not dead yet. So, are you really gonna walk out on him when he needs you most?' She pokes me in the chest, stabbing with each word. 'You don't do that.'

I shake my head. 'I don't... I don't know what to do anymore. I'm lost.'

She takes a small step back. I feel the spears withdraw. Throwing her head to the side, she considers me briefly. Then stepping closer again, she reaches up to take my head in her hands and plants a firm kiss on my lips.

'Seems there's a heart deep down in there, after all,' she says, tapping my chest before withdrawing. 'And I had you down as some kind of hard man.' Turning, she heads back to the campfire. 'Come on. You've just been listening to the wrong voices, that's all.'

'You've been talking to the old-timer.'

'People talk, Ebadiah. It's what they do.'

I follow and she leads me up into the back of the truck where Stink lies. 'I'm sure he's missing you. It would probably help him if you were to sit a while and let him know you're still here.'

Now I'm consumed by guilt and shame. I'm glad of the darkness that covers my reddening face as I sit down and stroke a hand gently over the dog's head and neck.

'Talk to him,' she says. 'He'll know your voice, even if he can't see you.'

I lean close. 'I'm here, Bear Dog. I'm right here...' Jade stands over me, watching as I speak. 'And I'm staying with you.'

12. WHEN DARKNESS HAS FALLEN

Several more weeks pass and we move on again. Our work pays off but the new fuel don't last long. One morning Roach steers the Clansly onto the side of the road and lets it roll to a stop. The firebox holds nothing but embers and red peat ash. I close its iron door to clamber out of the cabin and down onto the road. Nearby, a rotting horse carcass stinks up the air, its ribs naked and chalky white. Abandoned clockwork cars, steam trucks and carts clutter the way. Up ahead, Threadmoor lies nestled in the crook between two hills, a river flowing through its centre like a vein.

We gather our gear. I stuff all the food into the barrel, hoist that onto the rig and rope on the spears, then collect my pack. Roach straps his baggage over the mule's back and mounts up. Jade shoulders her bag and we set off, hiking towards the town. A few minutes go by before I turn and glance back at the barren road behind. I wait. Scan the rolling landscape. Then whistle.

A black shape bounds from the rear of the truck, sleek and fast.

'Thought you'd never join us,' I say as Stink catches up. His wounds have healed and he's strong enough to run again. Suppose I have Jade to thank for that. She barely left his side as he lay on the verge of death and when he became cold and unresponsive, we slept huddled around him to warm him with our bodies. Watching her, I allow myself a rare smile.

The road dips and rises over the moors to skirt the peaks of the higher ground. I keep watch for others along the way, reckon most would kill for a barrel of food like ours, so I got to protect it—be ready, should anyone try anything. But we meet no one on this road. In fact, nothing much happens until we reach the town...

*

Roach raises a hand, drawing on Dorothy's reins with the other. We trudge to a stop in the middle of the road, surrounded by the first war-broken buildings on the outskirts of Threadmoor. Roach turns his head, listening to the wind, his eyes glazed as though glimpsing a dream.

'It's a shame about the three sacks,' he says.

'What three sacks?' I ask, because he's making no sense.

'The last three sacks of coal,' he says, as though that explains everything.

'What's he talking about?' asks Jade.

'Don't worry. He does this,' I say. 'Sees things...'

'Hide,' Roach whispers urgently, wagging a finger to his right.

'Why?' asks Jade. 'What's–'

'Shush.' Roach signals again. 'Go!'

Hauling the rig, I grab Jade's hand briefly to lead her into the shadows of a crumbling wall. 'Stink! Come!'

The dog throws a glance at Roach and the mule but then follows us. We tuck our bodies in behind a rubble-strewn breach and watch Roach, who's stood out in the open.

'I must do this alone.' The quiet words reach us though we can no longer see his face. He rides on, the mule clopping slowly between wrecks along the icy road.

'What's he doing?' hisses Jade, peering over an edge of the wall. 'If there's danger, we should protect him. He could be killed!'

'If he says he must go on alone, he means it,' I explain. 'He knows things we don't.' Annoyance gnaws at me for my failure to hear the Voice.

Jade continues to track his movement, fearful for him.

'He'll be alright,' I tell her. 'He's a jicker man.'

We sit and wait, keeping out of sight from the road, wanting to follow and see what's happening, but knowing better.

A huge shadow sweeps over us, passing in a blink.

Cowering, Jade peers heavenwards. 'What was that?'

I risk a glance beyond the wall and spy silhouettes crossing the sky, high over the town. 'War birds.' I point. 'Searching for prey. We should find shelter.'

'I hate those birds. One killed my Ma. It carried her off.'

'I'm sorry.'

The house beyond the wall is empty and half blown apart. At the base of the fallen side a vast bomb crater is patched with dirty snow, an ice puddle glazing the bottom. On the good side there's one room left almost whole. The walls and ceiling look stable. The bitter reek of ash hangs in the air. Slipping in through a ragged hole in the masonry, we find a glassless window facing out over the town, and there we watch for a while. Distant sounds reach us: the shrieks of the giant birds overhead, the rumble of a steam truck somewhere deeper in, the aggressive shouts and cries of desperate people. I have the uncanny feeling that Roach is in trouble, that he's under attack and we're hearing it happen.

Jade's eyes widen with concern. 'Do you think that's him?'

'Could be. Don't worry. He knows what he's doing.' I feel her warm hand slip into mine. 'He'll be alright.'

'Are there dragons this far north?'

'I don't know. I've never been here before.'

'Me neither.'

The howl of a morh-beast rises from the moors behind us. The pack bays in response.

'They're tracking us!'

I imagine they've found the Clansly. 'Aye. We must find coal for the truck or we'll never outrun them. Come on.'

'But the morhs...'

'We'll work something out. Deal with them later.' I head out through a broken doorway and hurry around the side of the half-house, crouching low. It's barren and burned. If it ever had a coal bunker, it was blown to pieces along with the missing side.

The chances of finding coal in a town like this are slim. Unless it's been hidden away, it's likely some stranger will have already found and burnt it. But the town is big, with stone-built holdings that ramble out onto the edges of the moors. Somebody somewhere must surely have hidden away their fuel supply. I can only hope. We begin working through the ruins, staying clear of the big road that slices the settlement in half, and all the while I search for a gawper lair as well as the coal.

The sounds continue: smashing glass, screaming, an explosion. Fires smoke the sky. It's as though the entire place is at war with itself. My heart hammers in my chest. My nerves sharpen my senses.

A short way into the town the river bends inwards to run alongside the road, spanned here and there by low, flat bridges. Mostly they've survived intact. As we near the first, a war bird makes a dive for us. Jade clutches my arm and I haul her down the bank. Slipping and sliding with the rig in tow, we make a dash for the shelter of the dingy, low space under the bridge. Even Stink seems to want to get away from the terrors above. He cowers and circles, peering upwards with dread in his eyes. Scratched into the stonework of the arch is the gawper sign. The great bird swoops by, to climb again into the heights.

I point. 'Look. It's the planum horis.'

'What is it?' asks Jade.

'It's the symbol Skallagrim uses. It probably means he's been here before us. At the very least it means a gawper sheltered here.'

Dashing from the river, we find another house before the war bird can dive again. We hide in a charred front room until we think, hope, the creature has lost interest in us. Darting from one hiding place to another, we work our way deep into the town, sometimes running the riverbank, occasionally dashing across the big road and back into the shadows of the crumbling buildings.

Roach appears ahead of us, beckoning. A cut runs down his left cheek. Blood is slick on his coat.

'This way.' He turns down a narrow alley between two rows of cottages, ending at a courtyard flagged with stones at the rear of a solid looking house. The backyard has been covered overhead with a tarpaulin, nailed to the house timbers and roped tight. The door is open and the mule stands outside, as docile as ever.

Roach waits for us to pass before waving a hand in a fluttering motion at the yard's entrance and I wonder, is he casting a spell? He steps into the house and sets about making a fire in the hearth of the abandoned living room, with wood he must have scavenged from the house or the surrounding ruins. On the dusty windowsill sits a lantern. A few old books lie scattered across the floor.

'No one will bother us here,' he says, shifting his hands in his mysterious way to generate a fire. 'The place is deserted.' A host of small flames leap up at the base of the kindling. Taking a few narrow logs from a pile, he gently lays them across the top.

'What happened?' I gesture to his wound.

'Oh, nothing much. A minor disagreement with some local rogues.' He waves towards the windows at the front of the building. Crossing the room, I look out into a street strewn with a dozen fresh bodies.

'Blinders! You did that?' I ask, staring at the corpses. 'Are they all dead?'

'Not all. I asked them to leave me alone. Gave them plenty of opportunity. Some people just don't listen. Guess they thought me easy prey.'

I study him as he blows at the base of the fire, coaxing the flames higher. 'Is that why you had to go alone? You were protecting us? It was the Voice, telling you?'

He shrugs. 'I heard the whisper. If you had been with me, I believe one of you would have died.'

I'm stunned. 'Who?'

'I don't know. It would depend on other choices you'd have been forced to make, had you refused to leave me. You must realise I cannot know everything.'

'So, you just saved us?' Jade pours water from a canteen into a pot.

'Enough questions.' Roach takes the pot and rigs his iron hanger over the flames. 'Black bean soup?'

I nod.

'First let me clean that cut. You could use a stitch or two.' Jade fusses around Roach until he lets her bathe the wound with boiled water. She takes a needle and thread from her bag and boils them before stitching the cut closed. When that's done, she takes a ribbon of cured morh-flesh from our supplies and settles on the bare floorboards to eat. I spy an opportunity as she holds the meat casually at her side.

I whisper to Stink. 'Take!' And before she knows what's happening, the dog dashes past to steal her food.

'Hey! Not fair!' She laughs. We all laugh then, while Stink chomps contentedly away. And for a few small moments, things don't seem too bad.

THE JICKER MAN

*

When darkness has fallen, I wait, watching Jade and Roach drift off to sleep. I dig the gawper skull from the bottom of my pack, place the cold bone against my brow and call Deadlock to mind. Nothing. No skitter of thoughts, pictures, voices. Only silence. I glance at the skull, wondering if something's broken.

I try again. There comes a rush of panicked feelings: dread, darkness and a sense of falling. Grainy images flash through my head amid a fuzz and blur: mountain tops traced with snow, a cave entrance high up in the rock, a triangular gap where two enormous slabs of stone lean in to meet, and a pair of burning red eyes that flame with wrath. Those eyes stare into the depths of my soul as an insidious voice whispers in my mind.

One Eye...

I feel my heart constrict as a wave of giddiness washes over me. A searing pain flashes behind my eyes and I yank the skull away. At last, my mind gate snaps shut. The skull feels suddenly light in my hands. I open my eyes, breathless and reeling, and quickly stow away the skull in my pack.

Skallagrim is somewhere in the mountains!

While Jade and Roach sleep before the hearth, I take the lantern, grab my spear and head out to search for a gawper lair. I'll be faster without the weight of my pack, so I leave that behind, but in my pockets are my slingshot, ammunition, flint, steel and tinder. It will be a long night's work 'cause of the size of the town, and I won't search it all in one go. I hope to learn something of use.

Stink lopes at my side, intangible in the night. A black shadow, blending with the nocturnal world. There's a clear sky so I work by the glow of the moon. Often, I lose sight of the hound altogether as he scouts around, but then a pair of reflective, glassy eyes catch briefly in the moonlight and I know he's there.

Slipping down unlit backstreets and alleys, we flit our way like shadows out to the settlement's fringes where we poke around an old, rambling ironworks, investigating every nook and corner. From there we skirt the town. The hunt takes hours as we scour each building, farmstead and factory, but then I recognise the hulking iron foundry where we began and know we've come full circle. Weary from the fruitless search, I climb atop a broad dry stone wall and scan the surrounding hills in the moonlight. If there are caves out there, I reckon they must be on higher ground, up on the tors perhaps. I recall the images of the lair, with its triangle of great kissing stones, and reckon it's not around here. It looked higher up, snowy, more mountainous.

To the west, a pair of stone tors slope up towards the mountains. We climb determinedly up to the first and check for caves before crossing the hills to the other. Weathered crags and gullies run through the rocks and there are several small caves, but nothing big enough to shelter a gawper. An hour or so before dawn, we tramp back down through the moors to the town and find our way back.

We slip through the narrow alley to the rear of the house, passing the humped shape of the slumbering mule in the covered yard outside, and I ease open the door to stand in the entrance. Roach and Jade are dusky, unmoving forms, either side of the hearth, the room dimly lit in soft orange tones by the dwindling embers of the fire. I hear Roach's muted snores as Stink pads around. He circles on the spot before curling up between them. Details grow clearer as I step carefully in so as not to wake them: Roach huddled on his side beneath blankets, his baggage piled at his back; a few of his things—a cup, a bowl and spoon—on the floor nearby. A cold breeze blows in from the smashed-out widows. Then I notice that Jade is lying on her back, her arms out at her sides, her legs bent, her head thrown back. I step closer, thinking she must be cold with no blanket, but her unusual posture makes me stop and stare. Something's wrong. My bag is open at her side and the gawper skull sits across the floor, tilting at an angle.

Hurrying to her side, I take her by the shoulders and shake her. She's limp, like a rag doll in my hands. I hear my own voice, stark in the quietness of the early morning.

'No!'

13. THE SKULL

Roach stirs. I let Jade down and gently pillow her head with her bag. She looks delicately serene in the ember glow. Beautiful.

'You're back.' Roach peers across at me through the gloom.

'Something's happened,' I say, looking at Jade and then the gawper skull. 'Something bad.'

Roach peels back his blanket and rubs at his beard, his face hard in the shadows. 'What did you do?'

'Nothing. Did you show her the skull?'

'No,' says Roach. 'Did you?'

'No,' I say. 'She must have found it while I was out.'

'You mean she went through your pack?'

'She must have.' I find her blanket and cover her body to keep her warm.

'Why would she do that? I'd have thought she'd have robbed us by now if she was going to.'

'I don't know. She don't trust anyone. Perhaps she just needed something and didn't think I'd mind. Found the skull and...'

'Something happened.'

'You don't think she tried to use it?' I ask.

'That's exactly what I think. Perhaps she saw you mind-walking and wondered what you were doing.' He collects the skull and warily lifts it to his forehead, holding it there and closing his eyes for a moment. He passes the skull to me before kneeling to rest his brow against Jade's, closing his eyes. He draws away to feel for a pulse at her neck before standing, his face sombre. 'She's been taken. Changed.'

'What do you mean? How?' My gut churns at the thought. 'Is she dead?'

'Skallagrim knows we pursue him. He's been aware of the skull, has sought to use it against you. But instead of finding you, he found Jade. He has entrapped her consciousness somewhere on the fourth plane.'

'What does that mean?'

'She'll remain dormant unless Skallagrim's hold on her can be broken.'

'And if I were to kill him?'

'Then Jade would remain bound like this until she dies.'

My mind spins as the room closes in around me. 'So, it's useless then... There's nothing I can do!'

Roach looks thoughtful, glancing at the skull in my hands. 'Not useless. There may be a way, though it would be difficult. And perhaps more dangerous than any attempt on Skallagrim's life would ever be.'

I want to smash something and there's a big skull sitting in my hands.

'Be careful with that,' says Roach, as though reading my thoughts. 'We're going to need it.' He puts more wood onto the embers of the fire and stoops to blow them into life.

'For what?' I ask.

'If I'm right, there's a ma-jick I can perform to release her and bring her back—an invocation. And if I'm right, the knowledge needed to fulfil this rite may be found within the

ancient book I seek—the one presently in Skallagrim's possession. I already knew I had to find the Tanak Codex–'

'The book?'

'The book. What I didn't know was why, until now. I'll
need the book, the skull and of course, Jade. The rite may
only be performed once. If it doesn't work, there's no second
try.'

'But there's a chance...'

'*If* I'm right.'

'Well, how are we gonna manage all that?!'

He sits cross-legged before the fire, frowning into the
flames with hazy eyes. 'Keep your voice down. There's a war
bird roosting across the street. To answer your question–'
Pensively, he strokes his beard. '–I don't know.'

Some minutes pass as I try to come to terms with it all.
She's just a girl. So why does my stomach knot and my
throat tighten when I think of losing her—of her in peril? I
got to face it: in the few short months we've been together,
she's become dear to me. I'm angry that fate has once more
conspired to take away someone I care about, until I realise
it wasn't fate at all. It was Skallagrim. What would I not give
to stand before him for a few seconds, for a chance to end
his life as I so desire? Though even that is now hopelessly
beyond reach. My loathing for the creature only deepens.

'Before I went out searching, I tried the skull again. I
wanted to speak with Deadlock but I got Skallagrim instead. I
think he's hiding out in the mountains.'

'I warned you the skull was dangerous. Perhaps you
should leave it alone now.'

'Perhaps.'

'How do you know it was him. Did he speak to you?'

'I saw his red eyes, staring at me. He called me *One Eye*.'

'You're lucky he didn't take you.'

'I wish he had. Perhaps then Jade would be alright.' I watch
her breathe, her chest barely moving.

'Skallagrim is scouring the fourth plane for those who wish him harm. He will find you all the faster the more you hate him.'

'But he started the war. There must be thousands who hate him. That's if they ain't all dead.'

'Yet few would try to hunt him like you. Fewer still would know how,' says Roach. I shrug. 'How *will* you do that, incidentally?' he asks. 'Gawpers can see everything through the planes. They're bigger than you. Faster than you. They can conjure your location into their presence like that.' Roach clicks his fingers.

'I don't know how, but I'm gonna try.' I brush aside a strand of hair from Jade's shapely face. 'How long can she survive like this?'

'Hard to say. Maybe thirty days or so, if we can get enough water into her.'

'And how do we do that?'

Taking Jade's cup, Roach pours in a little water from a canteen and kneels to trickle a tiny amount from the cup into the corner of her mouth. 'There. We must do this as often as we can. Give her at least one canteen every day. It's the only chance we have to keep her alive long enough for the journey.'

We build a makeshift bier from curtain poles and old curtains torn down from the house, and stand looking down at it and the small pile of ropes we've gathered on the floor.

'Will it work?' I ask, feeling doubtful.

'It will have to,' says Roach. 'It only needs to get her to the truck.'

'The truck? But there ain't no fuel!'

'That's where you're wrong, Ebadiah. Follow me.' Roach leads me through the house into a dusty hallway where he opens a door beneath a worn staircase. We descend steps into a cellar where a half-ton of coal sits piled against the end wall.

'Blinders! This could get us to Firth Glaggan—all the way to Grim Gore, even!'

'We'll take Jade and a bag of coal back to the truck. Fire it up. Drive it back for the rest.'

'Brilliant!' I feel hope rise in my chest. 'But wait. It would be quicker for me to take a sack alone. You stay here with Jade.'

He nods. 'It would be safer, too, what with all these war birds.'

We lay Jade carefully upon the bier and return to the cellar to bag up the coal. There's a pile of sacks in another corner, which means we can heft the lot into the back of the Clansly with a bit of work. When all is bagged and ready, we're grimy with coal dust, head to foot. I hoist a small sackful onto my back, grab a spear and set out for the truck. Stink tags along, my ever-present shadow padding at my side.

The war birds are fearsome black shapes, soaring high in the pale heavens, scanning the land for food. The dawning sun casts long silhouettes about the town. I scurry from shadow to shadow, like a vole in a field, darting here and there. I flatten myself against a shaded wall and watch the birds, knowing they're not the only danger here. The morhbeasts might have pushed up into the streets, although I doubt the monsters of Mors Zonam have spread this far north. But then again, who knows?

I run most of the way through the town and find my answer when I turn a corner only to face a toxic slink. Five feet high, it rears up before me on its numerous, jointed legs, each tipped with a deadly spike. I recoil as it bears down, its long, segmented body arching. It rattles its tail, a hollow sound that rebounds from the ruins about us as Stink moves around to harry it from the rear. Pincers *snipper-snap* as it lunges, its crooked fangs poised. I dodge to the left. It recoils and strikes again.

Snipper-snap, snipper-snap!

151

THE JICKER MAN

I dart to the right, avoiding its poisonous bite by a mere half inch, before driving my spear upwards. But the sharpened tip only skids over the giant insect's glossy shell. The slink lurches at me. I swing the sack of coal, one-handed, catch the creature's flat head with the full weight, knocking it sideways. The blow carries me with it. I tumble as coal spills across the ground. Towering over me, the slink skitters closer and, as it moves to strike, a vast shadow suddenly blots out the sun. The slink folds and rises away into the air. I glimpse the talons and the broad, beating wings of a monstrous bird as it ascends.

Scooping the spilt coal back into the sack, I hurry along the riverside with Stink, out through the ruins, and find the steam truck waiting on the road. Further on, distant shapes emerge onto the ridge: the morh-beasts on our scent. I don't know if they've already investigated the town or not—perhaps they're too wary to enter—but they see us and one after another, launch into a run. I sprint to reach the Clansly ahead of them, scramble up into the cab with Stink, and close the door, but the pack's fast and a moment later, their impacts rock the truck as they leap up at the windows. Unsure if the thick glass will hold, I hurriedly kindle a fire with tinder in the firebox and add a few lumps of coal as the morhs continue to shudder the truck with their assaults. It's a solid vehicle, mostly metal, though the sides are thin and the morh's claws pucker the iron sheeting and score lines in the glass. Soon, their claws pop through the doors, slicing the iron skin with sickening screeches.

I work the fire, coaxing the small flames as the Clansly gathers wounds.

'Come on! Come on!'

Once it's properly caught, I switch to the system bellows and soon the fire is roaring, an orange glow spreading across the coal, and the pressure gauge rising fast.

A large morh jumps up onto the truck's polished nose. The entire vehicle bobs with his weight. Stink's up on the bench, barking his fury. The beast watches me menacingly through the windshield, mauling at the glass. I check the gauge.

'Good enough!' Heaving off the brake, I clamp the steam valves shut. The truck rolls forwards. I shovel the remaining coal into the firebox. Close the iron door and watch the pressure mount while pumping the bellows hard. When the needle reaches halfway across the dial, I take the wheel as the Clansly gains speed. The morh on the hood rears up to batter down upon the glass. I swing the wheel hard about and send the beast tumbling off to the side.

The machine rattles down the road ever closer to the town, the vibrations shaking our bones. I should release the steam valves but then we'd slow and I know I must outrun the pack and gain enough time to collect Jade and Roach and the coal. We won't have long before the morhs follow the Clansly to the house, so I open the engine up, let it boil and grind away—don't ease up until the house is in view. Only when we're outside the front of the building do I release the valves, take the engine out of gear and crank on the brake. The sudden halt jolts us.

Flinging the door wide, I leap out and run for the house to rush inside where Roach is already stooped at one end of the bier, grasping the poles. While I've been gone, he's brought all the coal up to the entrance hall.

'They're coming!' I gasp for breath. 'The Morhs are coming!'

'Let's go!'

Loaded with our baggage, we carry Jade outside, slide the bier into the back of the Clansly and throw in our bags. The bays of the pack reach us on the wind.

The next few minutes are a rush of activity as we hurry back and forth from the truck to the cellar, loading the barrel and then heavy sacks of coal with the rig. Roach coaxes his mule up the tailgate and into the back and she settles alongside Jade's motionless form. He heaves another sack into the truck.

'Three more to go,' he says, breathless and leaning on his knees.

I turn back for the next sack but hearing the howl of a morh-beast closing in, stop. 'They're almost on us!'

'Leave it! We go!'

I slam the pulley door shut, fold up the tailgate and we climb into the cab. Judging by the jittering needle of the pressure gauge, the steam valves are about fit to burst. Roach releases the brake and shifts the throttle. The battered Clansly lurches forwards as behind us, the furious morhs file into the street. The air grows thick with the steam engine's fug and noise and the calls of the pack, but as the truck gains speed, the beasts' sounds grow more distant. As we leave the town behind, they diminish until we hear them no more. Eventually there's only the rhythmical rumble and thump of the engine, which sounds jiggered.

Roach peers at the steam gauge. 'We need to stop, release the valves before the whole thing blows. Did you check the water levels?'

'There wasn't time.'

'We're lucky it's held.' He pulls the truck over and unclamps the steam valves, which hiss and crackle.

It's a shame about the three sacks...

I mourn their loss, but we've made it out of town, we have coal, and the morhs are behind us.

For now.

*

Boredom sets in over the following days. Roach drives as we hug the coast for some miles before the road leaves the beaches and clifftops to rise through unfamiliar foothills. I shovel coal and the occasional load of dung, riddle the firebox grill, scoop out the ashes, top up the boiler. We bag the mule's fresh dung, cook, eat, sleep. Climbing ever higher into the northern reaches of Londaland, we stop at lochs of shimmering water and gurgling streams to refill our canteens and the truck's water tanks. We pass a circle of standing stones that look as though they were there when the world began.

We've sighted no morh-beasts for several days now, and I'm beginning to believe we may have truly left them behind for good. We pile our clothes on the grassy banks and open the Clansly's doors to let the wind sweep through, strip off and swim ourselves clean in the icy mountain lochs. We carry Jade from the back and lay her in the shallow sunlight, take off her coats, bathe her arms and face with fresh water. I think of going further, of stripping her naked to wash her properly, but it seems ungentlemanly, it being only a few days since she fell under Skallagrim's spell. Perhaps I will wash her fully after a week or so, if necessary, though I'm sure it would still feel like a violation. What would she have me do? I wonder. In the meantime, we trickle water into the side of her mouth—tiny amounts, but often—with the hope of keeping her alive.

I want to tell her how grateful I am that she nursed Stink back to health, that she stopped me from leaving and going my own way. Where would I be now? Who can say? Nowhere good. Already dead, probably. I want to let her know that I think she's wonderful, that she's the loveliest person I've ever met. That she's so gifted and brave and kind and wise, and that I see in her a beauty that exists nowhere else.

And I'm angry with myself for not telling her these things when I had the chance.

Roach leads Dorothy down from the truck to stretch her old legs and graze on grass and heather, although she gets slower every time and I don't see her lasting much longer.

The water's different here, cleaner. The air, too. We pass through untroubled wilds, seemingly endless meadows where sheep roam free, their smell greasy on the breeze, and I think about catching one and roasting it whole over a fire, but then we have plenty of dry-cured morh meat still— partly 'cause Jade ain't eating—and we're in a hurry to find Skallagrim and the sacred book. Ain't no time for chasing sheep around the countryside.

Another day passes and we use the last of the fish. Warming myself by the campfire that night, I've mixed feelings about the herring stew—thickened with a handful of oats—as I spoon it to my lips. I place a hand on Jade's brow, feel her skin, cool against mine, and drag her bier closer to the fire. I throw on a few more staves from the broken barrel to fuel the flames.

Roach tells me we should move Jade around a bit because she can't move herself, so once in a while we lay her on her side, flex her arms and legs to keep the blood moving.

The high peaks to the east are solid, dark forms rising into the deep, mysterious sky. My faded map is yellow in the guttering firelight. I trace a road that winds north from Threadmoor to Firth Glaggan, not knowing exactly where we are upon it. The route skirts mountains and threads valleys. The road splits and joins a network of others that link villages and hamlets scattered throughout the foothills between lochs. During the day, I consult my pocket watches to check we're still heading due north or near enough. Frustrated, I give the watches their daily winding and put them away while watching the shallow rise and fall of Jade's chest.

*

For a day we edge the foothills, but then Roach steers the steam truck up a vast, broad valley that seems to run for miles. Ahead, to the north, the mountains are veiled in mist and I wonder if Skallagrim is up there somewhere. On my map there's no route marked out that don't cross the high ground at some point, so I guess we'll be in the high mountains soon enough. My gut churns at the thought.

Can Skallagrim sense the gawper skull even when I ain't using it? Can he somehow find or track me, like Magwitch and Deadlock? I don't know, but the thought's disturbing.

A foreboding grows within me as the Clansly climbs.

We stop for the night beneath a slope where the road leaves the end of the vale to rise into the hills and highlands. From there on, the truck struggles over the rocky landscape for another week or so. Most days we get stuck. The wheels lodge in crevasses. Boulders grind up into the undercarriage. The heavy truck sinks into snow drifts and icy bogs, its wheels spinning. But we press on, fixing what we can, prising the wheels free, pushing the Clansly or levering her up with thick poles hacked down from the thinning evergreens. And then slowly, we descend to lower ground and the sea.

We spot Firth Glaggan as the sun sets over the hills one evening, a mile or two ahead. To the west the low clouds burn with fiery tones. It's hard to miss the city. It's huge. Roach steers the truck off the road and parks behind a strand of wind-blown trees. Taking the telescope from my pack, I climb down from the cabin to spy as the sounds of war reach us on the wind. My view through the scope is good 'cause we're on the saddle of a hill, the highlands at our backs, the city below.

Fires light the streets. Muskets flare in the gathering dusk. There are distant shrieks and screams. Figures run. Chaos. Vehicles dash as warriors shoot from their smashed-out windows. I spy dragons rampaging loose in the streets. Focusing on a long, low building with a shattered end, I glimpse a dark shape moving there and wait for it to move again so that I might make it out more clearly. It looms into the open space beyond the ruined gable, and I see it in full: a tall, hooded form, cloak sweeping outwards to the ground, burning white eyes peering across at an enemy beyond view. Another tall figure lingers nearby. I pan across to find more of them, these caught up in some sort of skirmish.

'There are gawpers,' I tell Roach, sweeping the scope across the scene and finding more of them battling painted, bronze-skinned men. 'They're fighting the Urthians.'

'Behold, the Darklings of Brae,' says Roach.

'Where's Brae? And what are they doing here?'

'This is Brae. It's an old name for the place.'

'You might have said.'

'Would it have changed anything?'

As I watch, the gawper at the end of the building raises a hand. An orb of fire rises from the ground. With a flick of its arm—and without ever touching it—the gawper sends the missile shooting through the air to explode upon the Urthian lines. I shift focus, watch a half dozen Urthian warriors burning, flailing as the liquid fire spreads. The other warriors retaliate with a volley of musket shots that flare from their barricade. More fireballs follow from the gawper camp. A cursory sweep of the cityscape reveals other similar sights, the western side seething with gawper fighters, while Urthians occupy the eastern flank, their armoured dragons on chains. A fleet of mounted war birds soar in the sky.

'It's a sign,' I say. 'We should keep out of the city and skirt around it.'

Roach squints out over the site, though I doubt he sees much through his cloudy eyes. 'Be careful with your numbo-jumbo.'

'You can talk,' I fire back.

'The Light I follow is real, not numbo-jumbo.' He fetches a shovel load of coals from the firebox to start a campfire and sets about heating water for heather tea. 'Here, give the girl a drop.' He throws a canteen over and I pull the cork to ease a small trickle into the side of Jade's mouth, see her throat move as she swallows on reflex.

'We should go around,' I say again.

'Perhaps you're right. We could cross the water.'

Off to the east, a wide estuary sweeps in from the sea. I draw the scope the length of it, see where it narrows into the city's far side. Following the water's curve as it hooks around to the west, I scrutinise the land beyond. There, campfires glow in the gathering gloom but I see none on the far shoreline.

'The land to the west is occupied. It would be safer to cross the water.'

Roach looks at me soberly. 'We'd have to leave the truck behind.'

'Perhaps there's a boat big enough to take it.'

He snorts. 'There isn't. Sorry.'

'How do you know?'

He looks at me apologetically.

'Ain't no way I'm leaving the truck,' I say.

'We go west, then.'

'Skallagrim's hiding in the Grim Gore mountains. He must be.'

'You may be right.'

'He ain't here. He can't be here.' I watch the city and then glance back at the mountains that appear violet in the shadows. 'He would have found us if he was back there. He wouldn't have let us pass. Would he?'

Roach shrugs. 'I don't know.'

I feel my expression tighten. 'Can't you tell me? Why don't you know?!'

'I'm sorry—it's not my place to know all things.'

'Then what good is it to know anything?!' I stomp off into the deepening night, sweep snow from a rock and sit, looking out over the distant blazing fires.

A while later, Roach finds me, bringing a cup of hot heather tea. 'Drink this. You'll feel better.'

A cold wind blows down from the mountains. The tea is good. I shiver, hug the warm cup in my hands and brood on the problems that lie ahead.

'We should turn westward,' he says. 'Find a good place to pass the camps without trouble.'

'And go miles out of our way. You've seen the map. There ain't enough coal.'

'So, then... We give up. Watch Jade slowly die.' He shrugs.

The pulse throbs in my head. He's right. There's no other way. 'Alright. West it is.'

'Best go soon. No lamps. We stand a better chance of making it through in the dark.'

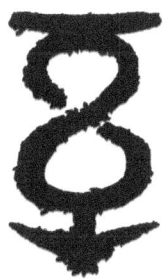

14. CRUSHED

The Clansly trundles down a narrow, pitted road that edges a hillside and drops away into the night. With the headlamps out, we must go slow or risk pitching off the edge, which in this rough terrain could be fatal for the heavy, iron steam truck, not to mention us. I drive 'cause the old man's eyes just ain't up to the job, not in the moonlight. It's hard enough for me. The road's little more than a gravel track that follows an uneven, stony slope. To our left, boulders threaten to snag at the wheels and the vehicle's flank. To the right, the ground undulates wildly, often diving away steeply to the valley below. Ain't no room for mistakes.

For hours we crawl westwards like this, the mountains and Firth Glaggan at our backs, and all the while, a kind of tension builds in me. It's like my head's telling me the more we continue, the more likely we'll take a fall, but I push on just as fast as I dare, driven by that need to reach Grim Gore. We thread forest and heath before slowing to a stop. Before us, a row of tiny white lights glint in the darkness a few hundred yards off. I crank on the brake when I realise they are eyes.

'Gawpers, blocking the way.' Squinting into the night, I make out a barrier of burned-out clockwork cars dumped haphazardly across the road, and glimpse grizzled human heads mounted on poles at either verge, like hideous gate-posts.

'Darklings,' says Roach. 'Quickly, the map!'

I take it from my pocket and pass it over, wonder how he can read it in the feeble moonlight that reaches into the truck. He holds the paper a few inches from his nose and a moment later thrusts it back to me.

'There's a road ahead on the left. Take it.'

I study the map. 'There's nothing marked.'

'Trust me. It's there.'

I crank up the gears and steer us on until he waves to the side.

'There, a track between hedgerows,' he says. 'Take it!'

I make the turn and the Clansly bumps down a rough trail, listing into pits and over rocks. The iron chassis groans. The route leads to a big old house, set in the lee of a hill. I slow down to glance behind from my window, see the glowing specks blinking in the dimness as they follow in our wake.

'They're on to us!'

'How many?' Roaches eyes are wide in the dimness.

'Three. The others must have stayed at the roadblock.'

'Only three. That's not so bad.'

'How on Earthoria ain't that bad?' I grip the wheel hard as we jolt over rocks.

'I was expecting five. Get us to the house.'

I don't bother asking why—nor how he knew of the track that wasn't on the map—just clamp down the steam valves as far as they'll go, ramp up the pressure and shift gear to send us clattering towards that house. Details grow clearer as we approach: a timber-framed building, walled with planks and decked with a veranda.

A sudden, orange glow envelopes us as the whole truck shudders beneath a deafening *boom* that rattles the iron and glass.

'What was that?' I glance at Roach, who's leaning out of the window to look behind.

'They're launching fireballs at us,' he says dryly before drawing himself back inside.

'Can we outrun them?' I ask.

He sounds unsure when he says, 'They're riding morh-beasts.'

'Oh, good.'

A gawper materialises before us, floating mid-air over the track. Cradled in the space between its outstretched claws bobs a globe of flame. Its dark face grimaces in the glow. I heave on the brake as Stink barks like crazy.

'No!' shouts Roach. 'Charge it!'

Releasing the brake, I crank the gears. The truck whines and lurches on, belting straight for the gawper. We're about to slam into it when there's a twirl of its cloak and it's gone. We plough through the fire, flames bursting upon the split-screen, though they quickly fade, leaving us untouched behind the glass as more fireballs hit the rear.

'Jade!'

'She'll be alright,' says Roach. 'The iron won't burn.'

I gawk at the track that ends abruptly at the side of the house.

'Out of road!'

'I'm sorry about the smell,' says Roach.

'What smell?'

'You'll see. Into the house. Hurry!'

'What about Jade?'

'She's safe in the back with Dorothy. They can't sense the unconscious and it's us they want.'

I bring the Clansly to a screeching stop alongside the house and, shouldering my pack, throw the cabin door open to dash out. Stink leaps after me and Roach climbs down as fast as his rickety legs will go. The side door of the house yields at my touch.

'Hello?' I call into the hallway.

'No one's home,' says Roach, pushing past to enter. 'Come on!'

'What's the plan?' I ask, hoping more than ever that he knows something I don't.

A fireball explodes against the house as I slip inside. Flames lick around my ears and heat prickles the back of my neck.

'I'm working on that.' Roach ducks away before me.

I call after him. 'We survive, right? You know that?'

He levels his hand in a wavering motion. 'Well...'

'Great.'

'This way!' He heads deeper into the house. I follow, willing him to move faster or get out of my way. Behind us, the house begins to crackle with heat as the fire takes hold.

In a corridor, he stops dead, then looks around as though lost. Tries a door only to find it locked.

'No. Not that way...' He turns on the spot, searching.

'Where now?' I demand.

'Wait! Give me a minute.' He closes his eyes.

'We don't have time for this!'

'If we don't make time for this, we won't have any time at all. Shush now!'

We stand there, listening to . . . what? The roar of the burning house as flames engulf its timbers.

His eyes flick open. 'Ah! We're nearly there...' He shuffles quickly down a corridor and enters a dusty, neglected parlour. Ghostly tendrils of smoke curl in the air, as though searching for our throats.

'Nearly where?'

'This way!'

The room opens onto a rear landing. Roach hurries across to open a low door set into the wall. Inside is a latrine with a wide, wooden bench, a circular hole cut in the centre.

As smoke thickens around us, he lifts the bench lid and we peer down into a deep recess from which a woeful stench of rotting human waste rises.

'I ain't going down there!'

'Want to live?' he asks, pausing and seeming—quite suddenly—to be in a state of complete calm.

'Aye.'

His spell breaks. 'Then follow me!' he says with a flash of his eyes. With more agility than an old man should own, he leaps over the latrine's edge and disappears into the darkness of the stinking pit below.

Swinging my legs over the side, I take a deep breath and feet first, drop after him.

My fall is quick. The landing stuns me, stealing my breath. There's a distinct crunching sound as my pack takes the full impact. Somehow, I must have turned in the air. The foot or so of reeking sludge at the bottom of the recess does little to cushion the jolt. I know at once that the gawper skull has been smashed. My heart jolts.

Jade!

An outstretched hand appears over me. I grab it and Roach heaves me to my feet.

'The skull! It's crushed!'

'Let's worry about that later.'

Flaming cinders float down to us from above.

'Wait! Where's Stink?!' I peer up at the orifice overhead, now glowing orange from the house fire. 'Stink! Stink! Come boy!'

Roach tugs at my arm. 'No time!'

'Stink! Stink!' I pull free. 'I ain't leaving him!' I try to recall if the dog entered the house with us but can't. I didn't stop to look.

'Stink will fend for himself,' says Roach. 'As must we.' He turns and trudges away into the smoky blackness until he's evident only by the splash of his feet sloshing through the revolting sewage. As my eye adjusts to the gloom I make out the culvert running away beneath the foundations of the house. Behind me, burning debris tumbles from the house to cast a glow along the shaft. I stoop to traverse the low tunnel.

'Where does this go?'

Roach turns briefly, his face lit by hot tones. 'To safety, let us hope.'

The soft glow of night beckons as we near the iron caging of the outflow. Roach stamps at it until it breaks free and crawling down from the culvert's dripping end, we find ourselves edging an open cesspit near a stream that threads the valley. There ain't a gawper in sight. Beyond the hillside, the sky flickers hot. The house is one giant torch, lighting the night.

I make my way down to the stream, drop my pack on the bank and, lying in the water to rinse away the filth, duck my head beneath the surface and scrub at my hair. The water's icy but I don't care. Better to freeze than be coated in rancid muck. Roach clambers in to wash and when we're clean, we drag ourselves out and lie shivering on the bank. I tip out the contents of my pack onto the shingle and gaze despondently at the shattered skull.

'It's ruined. Jade's lost forever.'

Roach comes to my side, peering at the pile of shards. He stoops to dig about in it before straightening and holding up a single, triangular piece of bone. I stare, perplexed. The bone is a rounded triangular shape bearing three pointed lobes, not a broken fragment but something that looks whole.

'All is not lost,' he says, pressing the tri-lobed bone into the palm of my hand.

'What *is* this?'

'It is what the gawpers use to mind-walk. This part is all we need. Keep it safe.'

I take a length of leather twine from my pack and tie it securely about the tri-lobe before knotting a loop to hang it around my neck. I take my empty pack and rinse it clean in the river.

'Do you think they'll have gone by now?' I ask through chattering teeth.

'The gawpers? I imagine so,' says Roach. 'Hopefully, they'll believe we've perished in the fire.'

As I'm rinsing my belongings and repacking my bag, a sound makes me start. I glance up to see the silhouette of a wolf breaking the ridge above me over the stream. I freeze. The spears are in the truck. We have no fire. Backing away, I slowly draw the knife from my belt. The beast leaps. I raise the blade, stumble backwards, topple to the ground and it's on me in a blink, lapping at my face, pawing at my chest. A sleek, black wolf, slobbering all over my ears, my neck and nipping at my jaw. But there ain't no real bites. No mauls. Just a long, pink tongue, slobbering all over me, and those playful nips.

It ain't no wolf...

'Stink!' I cry. 'You found us!' I fight him off to look him over. He seems unharmed although there's a faint smell of singed hair about him. I suppose he must have fled the flames rather than follow us into the house. 'Clever Bear Dog.'

He peers back at me quizzically: *Where'd you go?*

'I'm sorry, boy. I lost you...'

Roach smiles down at us. 'Come on. We have a truck to reclaim.'

*

With our bellies flat to the hillside, we peer down at the burning carcass of the house. Beyond the flames and crumbling timbers, our steam truck is partly visible on the track. We watch and wait.

I grab the telescope from my bag to take a closer look as dawn begins to break, the sky in the east colouring with the first dampened rays of sunlight.

'The truck's taken a beating. Cabin's burnt-out. Glass all gone.'

'It doesn't matter as long as the steam engine still works.'

'What about Jade?'

Roach's silence troubles me.

I scan the road in. Search for signs of the gawpers but find none.

'What if they've set a trap? They could be waiting in the back of the truck.'

'In the truck they torched?' Roach shakes his head. 'I told you, it was us they wanted.' He closes his eyes and remains perfectly still for several moments, as though meditating. When his eyes blink open, he seems decided. 'It's time. Let's go.'

We walk down to the house, keen to warm and dry ourselves near the fire. The burning timbers crackle and collapse as we approach. I hurry to the back of the truck, unclasp and draw down the tailgate before hauling up the heavy iron door. The metal is quite cool. Inside, Jade and Dorothy lie next to each other. I climb in and feel a steady pulse from Jade's throat.

'She lives.' I'm relieved.

Next, I check the firebox and find the ash cooling. I prepare to start afresh, raking out the cinders and taking a shovel of embers from the edge of the house fire. I add some wood—also from the house—and then scatter on coal. We boil water in a pot on top of the firebox, make tea and then boil up a stew with a little of the smoked morh-beast flesh. While that cooks and the pressure in the steam valves builds, we dry ourselves in the heat of the house fire.

'We still have to get past the Darklings somehow,' I say, watching steam rise from my coat.

'I've been thinking about that,' says Roach. 'What we need is a distraction.'

*

Tonight we burn a gawper camp. It's the one near their roadblock by the woods. Parking at the far edge of the neighbouring woodlands, we take the canister of *Old Fisher's Wick Grease* and creep silently closer, hiding in the shadows. Unseen, we sneak to the fringe of the camp using the trees for cover, pour the whale oil around the outer edges of the gawpers' great, domed tents in the dark. When every canopy we can reasonably reach has been fuelled, we light torches and scurry from tent to tent, setting the oil ablaze. Roach makes a sign in the air with a stroke of his hand and we hurry back to the truck. From there, we watch as chaos awakens across the camp, hear the rasping shrieks of the startled gawpers and see the gawper guards at the roadblock run to help their fellows.

Ain't no better feeling than the one rising in my chest, right now. A feeling that we're gonna win. Like they can't stop us. And they don't. In the cabin of the Clansly, the steam valves are fit to burst, the turbines and jibes juddering like they're gonna blow any second. I release the brake and the truck chugs forwards. Moments later the wind is tearing at us in our seats as the truck speeds ahead. We hurtle towards the unattended blockade and rattle through, smashing vehicles aside as we go. And howling in victory, we leave the Darklings behind.

15. THE CLIMB

Sometimes you got to take precautions. I mark out a route on the map, avoiding the few scattered towns before us. It means weaving back and forth along smaller roads, which also means using more fuel, but the risk of being surrounded by other Darklings in a town feels too great. Better to stay clear and take the country roads. The course takes us into foothills again and there, as we follow a deep valley, our eyes are drawn by a fire in the sky. Roach is the first to spot it.

'What's that?' he asks, drawing the truck to a stop in the middle of the road.

We watch as the fire descends slowly over a hill. Finding my telescope, I extend the rings to focus on the drifting flames and see the twin gas skins of an invader's airship.

'It's a kattalang,' I tell Roach. 'One of the smaller ones. It's caught fire.'

The kattalang drops steadily. Roach releases the brake and cranks a gear.

'They may need help.'

The Clansly chugs on. Following the road, we climb the hill, all the while keeping the crippled airship in sight.

'But what if they're Urthians?' I ask. 'They invaded our country. Don't you want to let them burn?'

'No. People are people,' he says. 'What if it was you or me up there?'

The ship seems to plummet faster the closer we get. Roach halts the truck by a dry stone wall bordering a field. Beyond, the kattalang hits the ground with a great burst of flames. Smoke and cinders swirl as the last vestiges of the air skins take fire. I hear Roach's door open and shut before realising he's running for the wreckage.

'Wait!' I leave the truck to hurry after him.

He stops in the field around twenty feet from the fire and collapses to his knees. This is as close as we can get. I join him in the intense heat, watching the flames consume everything. No way anyone's surviving that.

*

For seven long days we drive. Highlands and more highlands. Ain't nothing else in sight. It seems that's all Scolanda's made of from here on. The land is desolate, cast in shades of grey and white. The higher we climb, the colder we grow and I soon find myself wishing the glass in the cabin of our battered old truck had not been lost to the Darklings' fire. The Clansly's like an old friend to me now, which makes it all the harder to part with her when a turbine blows on a particularly steep stretch of track up a long mountainous ridge. The old girl's done well, but that's it. She's gone. Ain't nothing can be done for her now. No parts, no tools and anyway, there's only half a tug of coal left and we'll have to head off-road soon if we're to climb any higher.

I leave the cabin for the last time to survey the snow before us.

Wrapped against the cold in his ragged layers of clothes, Roach leads Dorothy down the truck's ramp and we hitch up tethers around her shoulders with which to drag the bier. Jade lies still, cocooned in her coats and all the blankets we have, only her face exposed. I lean down to place my hand upon her brow, feel her skin clammy and cold to the touch. I worry she's passed the point of return, that she'll never be roused by Roach's ma-jick or anything else. I fear that inside she's already gone.

We bind her to the bier with rope to hold her in place and I choose the best of the spears to take with me. We load up with our bags, a few coils of rope from the truck and what little supplies we have left, and wading the deepening snow, trek ever higher into the mountains.

A feeling grows stronger in my mind as we climb—has grown stronger ever since the roadblock—a sense that Skalla-grim is near, as though he knows we approach. That his eyes are upon us. It troubles me as tangibly as the ice that chills my feet and creeps so thoroughly into the marrow of my bones that I feel I may never be warm again. This is no place for the living. I watch a lone crow cross the barren sky and wonder what it might possibly find to eat up here. Us, per-haps, in a day or two?

Dorothy slows, looking weary, ice clinging to the feather-ing of her bony legs. We're asking too much of her but nei-ther of us say so and I wonder, is it out of love for her master that she plods on?

The afternoon light seems to fade before its time. As night sweeps over the surrounding peaks, we search for a sheltered place, find a sheer rockface where the snow can-not cling. At its foot, we dig a hole in the snow large enough for us to all lie in, out of the rising wind. The temperature plummets with dusk's last light. And then begins a tortuous night with us curled up in the snow pit, huddling together for warmth.

Terrified that we might freeze and never wake, I sleep little but enter a hideous state of stupor, conscious yet with-out control over the horrors plaguing my mind. Bodily I'm trapped, unable to move a single finger or toe. This drags on for hours while an ominous shadow slithers nearer before rising to tower over me. I sense a dread so vast, that I fear succumbing and falling into its depths. A pair of burning ruby eyes watches me and I know Skallagrim has come for my soul. Doom stretches before me, like an endless chasm.

At dawn, sunlight pierces the heavy grey clouds, a welcome, golden ray. I feel its warmth on my face and stir, glad to be free of the night terrors. I glance around. Jade looks dead. So does Roach, his head resting on the neck of the mule. Stink's nowhere to be seen. Off hunting, no doubt. He seems to like the snow. Crazy animal.

I shake Roach to be sure he's alive, relieved when he stirs. He reaches up to ruffle the mule's mane, but Dorothy is unmoving. The old girl is lifeless, stiffening with the cold. Roach runs a hand lovingly down her neck, his eyes laden with sorrow.

'I'm sorry,' I say. 'She was a good mule.'

While he grieves and makes his farewells, I study the map and with a nub of charcoal, mark a course of vales through the tall ridges leading to the mountaintop marked as Grim Gore.

Roach removes his boots and massages his feet through his stockings.

'What are you doing?' I ask.

'Are your feet cold?'

'Like ice.'

'Rub them. Unless you want frostbite.'

I do as he says and soon feel my toes warming. We do the same for Jade before cocooning her once more in her blankets.

We sip water from our canteens and stuff them with snow before tucking them into our clothes to thaw. Roach packs a few of his more treasured possessions into a single manageable bag. The rest he leaves with the mule. We chew on tough strips of morh-beast flesh and when we're ready, load up with our bags. Stink joins us, looking hungry. He bolts down a share of the meat and pads the snow restlessly. Then taking a front corner of the bier each, we set off, hauling Jade behind us.

Roach is quiet for most of the day. I'm unsure what he feels about the loss of Dorothy. It's hard to tell. He seems to withdraw like a hermit crab into its shell.

In silence we climb.

*

Another day passes. And another. Our meat rations are running low and sleep is hard to come by up here in the heights. I'm either too cold or hungry or damp with sweat from the effort of climbing. I quickly learn to hate the nights.

*

I begin to lose track of the days when the slopes broaden before us to reveal the tallest mountain for miles around. Grim Gore's jagged arêtes run steep and sharp, pitted and gnarled. Perilous and foreboding, they jigger-jag upward to a crooked white peak, veiled by a haze of low cloud.

We scrutinise the possible routes up while Stink snuffles about in the powdery snow nearby.

'The western edge would be faster,' I say, pointing out the way.

Roach squints in the glare from the snowy slopes. 'Yet we may never make it hauling the bier. The central path is more viable.'

We both consider a route up the steeper eastern side and soon decide it's impassable.

I concede. 'Alright, we take the central path.'

A storm is building from the east—cold winds, swiftly joined by large flakes of snow that sting my face and blur the landscape to a haze of grey.

The central path runs along a line of channels gouged into the mountainside by some ancient force of weather. That's the easy bit; our climb simply becomes steeper than before as we inch closer to the summit. But soon enough we reach the end of the last vale and the way ahead is blocked. We're forced to clamber out onto a knife edge, flanked by drop-offs that would mean certain death in a fall. Still, we manage to traverse a path, rounding jagged outcrops and skirting gullies until the rock beneath our feet becomes treacherously fractured, as though in a bid to outdo us. The weather, too, seems to be angered by our presence as the skies darken with storm clouds. In the distance, thunder cackles and booms.

We drag the bier along a narrow ledge, clinging to the mountainside and fearing a hundred-foot fall while the rising wind threatens to cast us into oblivion. Stink takes the path swiftly, his paws skipping nimbly over the ice, rock and snow. And rounding the mountain, I see it: a triangle of sky framed by two huge rocks that lean in against each other, a slab of the mountain forming its base. The kissing stones.

I stop.

'That's the place I saw,' I tell Roach as the wind whips up powder from the crags about us. 'That's Skallagrim's lair.'

I feel the hairs on the back of my neck prickle. There is fear in me—I sense it—but it's far beneath the surface of a pool that boils with hatred, like blood screaming for vengeance. It's a compulsion I've carried all this way and now that my goal's in sight, it churns all the harder.

But where's Skallagrim? Ain't no sign of him on the mountain.

Dragging Jade behind us, we climb and let down the bier in the mouth of a cave that worms deep into the rock. Between us and the leaning stones, a cleft in the mountain drops away, a sheer fall for a thousand feet or more. Setting down our baggage, we collapse, exhausted from the effort and the thinness of the air. The snowstorm lashes down upon us. I feel small and insignificant, spent on the climb.

Stink trots straight into the cave, sniffing a line of scent.

Roach drags himself to his feet to peer inside after the dog. A planum horis has been daubed on the cave wall in blood that has dripped and is now blackening. I glimpse piles of human skulls in the shadows: trophies of the king's conquests.

Roach's voice startles me.

'Skallagrim!' The name echoes back to us from the far recesses of the cavern. 'He's been here.' The old man enters and stoops to feel the ashes of a fireplace. 'Cold. Perhaps he's moved on.'

'The book?' I push myself up from the ground, forcing my aching legs to move. 'Is it here?'

Roach doesn't seem to hear. I lay a hand on Jade's cheek and kneel to listen for her breathing, but I can hear nothing over the driving wind. 'She's like ice. We're too late.'

If I could only get her warm, perhaps there might be a chance...

'We must search.' Roach ventures deeper into the cave.

I drag the bier in, out of the wind, and look around. Beyond the skulls lies a woodpile. I gather kindling and arrange it over the ashes before taking tinder and my flint and steel from my pack, my fingers so numb I can barely feel what I'm doing. I split sticks into matchwood with my knife and set sparks to the tinder cloth until it glows. Blowing gently, I coax the tiny ember to grow and flame. I light the kindling and watch the fire come slowly to life.

The sounds of Roach's search reverberate to me from the inner darkness and soon he returns to the stormy light of the entrance, his face drawn.

'The Codex is not here but there are others—tomes that I doubt Skallagrim would leave behind. There are other possessions, too, though he would have greeted us by now if he were here—and when I say greeted, I mean–' Roach falls silent as a new sound steals our attention. A rhythmic gusting of air. The beating of gigantic wings.

I peer out into the sky and grab my spear. 'He coming!'

We rush from the cave. Beyond the precipice, a monstrous war bird alights on the rock platform between the leaning stones just twenty feet from where we stand. Mounted upon its back is a red eyed gawper, the tallest I've ever seen. Stink's hackles rise. He fixes upon the gawper, his growls rumbling low. Skallagrim dismounts as the bird folds its ragged wings. The bird is a battle-torn wreck, patched with missing feathers, the stippled skin beneath showing red and raw. An iron shackle about its naked neck has bruised it purple. Its buzzard-like face and beak are battered and scarred, its head almost bald. Skallagrim throws the chain through an iron hoop that's been anchored into the bedrock and taking a stone, hammers an iron pin through two of the links to secure the creature. He straightens to pierce me with his gaze.

One Eye...

The voice in my head is the sound of granite slabs grinding.

Taking a book from his robes, he speaks. 'One Eye desires what Skallagrim possesses.'

Roach steps between us. 'Leave the boy alone, Skallagrim. You can deal with me.'

Stink comes to my side, hunkering at the spectacle. The book hangs in the claws of Skallagrim's hand. He laughs, a disquieting noise like boulders shifting and sliding. His next words sound only in our minds.

What will you do, old man, weak as you are?

I hear Roach's reply like a thought in my head.

I am not weak. I am broken. There is a difference.

Eyeing the book, I lean down to hiss into Stink's ear. 'Take!'

Your death approaches, old man. It is whispered on the planes.

177

Before Skallagrim's words die, Stink launches into a run. He reaches the edge and leaps the precipice, his teeth tearing the book from Skallagrim's grasp as he lands. Skallagrim rounds on the dog, but too late. Stink slides into a turn and pitching up snow, scrambles back towards the gap. The Gawper King's claws close on thin air.

Stink leaps again—a distance no gawper or human could ever clear—and lands, running to my side.

'Drop.'

He deposits the book at my feet. I snatch at the tri-lobed bone around my neck and tear it free, let it drop to the ground. I ready my spear as Skallagrim watches in fury. His gaze passes from the war bird to the book and back again. Although a stretch of rock sweeps around to join the mountain peak, I can see that way would take a little time. The bird is his only fast transport from his side to ours without ... conjuring.

In a breath he's there before me, eyes like hot coals, boring into my mind, delving through my soul. Staggering, I drop to my knees. My spear clatters to the icy ground, forgotten, as the voice in my head envelopes me.

Now this one... WILL DIE!

I feel my back arch as my mind reels and those eyes consume my vision. A searing pain swells in my head as I lose all sense of my surroundings. Stink and Roach are lost to me. I am alone in a world of torture, aware of nothing but one simple fact.

I. Am. Dying.

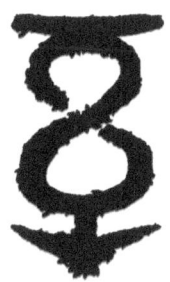

16. DEATH ON THE MOUNTAIN

Red is everywhere. It spills from those eyes into me, a liquid fire, seeping into the distant reaches of my being, flooding my every thought. It dims then, darkening to black like the dried blood on the wall of the cave. On it comes until the darkness overflows, a nocturnal velvet absorbing my consciousness.

Skallagrim's words find me in that terrible place, his speech slow and crawling.

The old man's ma-jick is weak. He will not redeem the girl. The rite will claim him and the girl will die. So will fall the last of the ma-jickers.

I am drifting and tumbling, down and on. A spiral with no end.

All perception of time has left me. Has it been a moment or a thousand years? I cannot say. It is strange and cruel and limitless.

I get a sense of Skallagrim's mind, then. Feel what he feels. He is done with humankind, the originator of war, the cause of the poisoned lands, the murderers and thieves, the ruin of the good green Earth. No more will he seek out the worst, weed out the killers. For all are guilty, all are tainted. And to prevent the return of such ruin, all must perish.

On and on it goes, the nothing unravelling before me as I tumble and turn.

Until...

Distant sounds disrupt the emptiness about me. They call to me, tug at my ebbing mind like memories. Sounds familiar to my ears.

The voice of an old man, and the growl of a Draker's dog.

Let it go, Ebadiah. Let go your hate.

I hear my own distant murmur. 'No. I can't. I won't.'

You must, Ebadiah. Let go your hate.

I see the truth of Roach's words, then, although I'm torn. How can I relinquish something that has become a part of my life—part of me? Like a disease on my soul, it has birthed and grown. Yet I glimpse it now for what it truly is, perhaps for the first time. It is a deformity as real as my blind eye or twisted foot. And Skallagrim knows it rules over me. I feel a tip in the balance of my mind, then. See that I can end it. That it is within my power to release it. I give it up—relinquish the anger, let go of everything. Push it away with all I have. And with it, the darkness recedes. The echoing sounds slowly thicken from dream-state to reality. I open my eyes to the howling storm, the biting wind, gasp for breath and feel my heart thumping in my chest. I am alive.

Across the chasm, Stink has Skallagrim by the arm and is hanging there, mauling at the gawper's upper body. The apparition before me contorts, twists and fades, swallowed by the maelstrom light as the conjuring fails.

Skallagrim swipes at the hound with a clawed hand. Stink squeals at the lacerating blow but holds fast, his teeth locked. Staggering, the Gawper King raises his free hand. Across the platform, a boulder shudders, breaks free of the mountain to rise into the air. He draws back the claw and with a flick of his wrist, sends the missile arcing.

'No!' I scream.

The rock strikes Stink's side, the impact knocking them both to the ground. Yelping, Stink rolls away while Skallagrim rights himself and prepares to bear down upon the stricken dog.

A whisper comes to me, a sound like the murmur of the gentlest breeze. Like the trickle of a highland stream. For a moment, I pause in the eye of the storm and all is strangely still—all is quiet.

Take up your spear, Ebadiah. Aim fast. Aim true!

The words shake me from my stupor.

I turn, seeking the speaker, but Roach is kneeling over Jade's bier back in the mouth of the cave, conducting the rite. On Jade's chest, the ancient book lies open. The trilobe rests on her brow.

Reaching down, I grasp my fallen spear and raise it, draw it back to throw with all the strength left in me. It flies fast and true, the tip thumping into Skallagrim's shoulder, piercing his robes of weed and lodging deep in his flesh. His howl grinds in my ears. With one arm limp, he clambers to his war bird, chained between the stones. The creature squawks raucously and jitters its bill. Skallagrim grips the chain and frees the iron pin to mount up.

Stink staggers to his feet.

I fear the king will use his powers to lift Stink from the ground and cast him into the chasm, but Skallagrim's wounded shoulder seems to have disabled him. Mounting the great bird, he clings to the chain with his one good arm as the bird unfurls its tattered wings. They beat at the air to lift the creature slowly from the mountain.

But Stink ain't through. He runs, launches himself after the bird, snapping at its tail feathers. For a heartbeat that seems to slow time, all three are airborne. And then Stink has the bird's tail in his teeth. With a squawk, the bird lurches sideways, dropping back to the mountain top, clawing at the edge yet slipping. And together the three of them fall, tumbling past the leaning stones and out over the edge beyond.

'Nooooo!' I scramble to the side of the precipice, unable to cross the gap as the bird reappears, recovering its flight. Unladen, it gains air with mighty sweeps of its wings, lifting up into the sky. Skallagrim and Stink are lost somewhere below. I watch the war bird until it's no more than a speck and before long, it's gone.

Stink is well and truly unreachable, surely lying dead at the foot of the drop on the far side of the platform.

The rope!

I turn back towards the cave, only to find Roach collapsed face down in the snow beside Jade's unmoving form. They both look dead. I run to them and roll Roach's body face up. As I turn him, the tri-lobed bone tumbles from his lifeless hand. His eyes are fixed and glassy.

It's then I recall his words.

The rite may only be performed once. If it doesn't work, there's no second try.

And now I know the truth of it. The rite has taken his life as he knew it would—as Skallagrim said it would—yet still it has failed! Jade's face is stricken and pale. It is the face of a corpse.

All hope drains from me. It slips away like blood on a battlefield, leaving me abandoned and surrounded by death on the mountain.

Stink!

I will myself to rise and find the ropes we've carried with us. Tying the ends together to form a single, long length, I coil it and loop it over my shoulder, set off in search of the path that must join his cave to the platform. Backtracking past the entrance to find the way, I haul myself up a rockface that leads around and up to the very summit. It soon levels out to circle the peak and there before me is a narrow causeway that leads to the platform and the kissing stones.

I run to the edge where I last saw Stink and, leaning out, search for him in the chasm. At first, I can see no sign of the dog or Skallagrim—and figure they must have fallen far below to be dashed upon the rocks—but then I see their distant bodies: dark specks in an icy gulf.

'Stink!'

There's no response. My words are swallowed by the wind. He ain't moving and it's too far for a climb, even with the ropes. If I'm to recover his body it must be by descending the mountain the way I came.

I turn at an unexpected voice.

'Hey.'

Jade stands there, looking ashen and sickly.

'You're... You're...' I blink to be sure she's real and not some trick of my tortured mind.

'I'm starving hungry—that's what I am—though I found some dried meat in the bags and there was a canteen of water. Sorry. All gone. Ain't never had a thirst like it. I've a headache like no other.'

'It's alright,' I say between breaths. 'There's plenty of snow to melt for water. I thought you were dead.'

She falls into my arms and I hold her, set her upright.

'Where's Stink?'

'Gone.' I peer back over the edge at the bodies below. 'He took Skallagrim with him.'

Jade walks to the edge to look down.

'Poor boy,' she eventually says. She looks me in the eye, her face sombre and tear streaked. 'Roach is gone, too. He's back there.'

'He died saving you,' I say. 'He knew it would happen. Did it willingly.'

'Everything he did, he did for us.' More tears well to dampen her cheeks. She sniffs and wipes them away with a sleeve. For a moment there's only the sound of the dying storm.

'When I first met him, I thought he needed me—thought he'd be a nuisance,' I say. 'But now, after everything... I'm not sure what I'll do without him.'

Jade nods and mops at her face again with her sleeve. 'I know.' She squints around at the mountains and hills that surround us. 'How did I get here?'

'That night I went out searching and left you and Roach in the house—you must have found the gawper skull in my bag and tried to use it, or you used it by accident. Either way, Skallagrim found you through it. Without knowing, you mind-walked and he did something to you, something that Roach died fixing.' I move a strand of her hair to see her eyes. 'How do you feel?'

'Tired and hungry. Like I've gone a month without a bite.'

'You've been asleep all this time. Well, not asleep... We carried you all the way from Threadmoor to Grim Gore.'

'Is that where we are?'

'Aye. On the tallest mountain.'

'So, what now? I suppose you'll go after Skallagrim's followers.'

'I thought I'd want to—need to, even—but I don't.'

'Good,' says Jade. 'You'd probably get yourself killed anyway.' She cradles the side of my face in her hand, the hint of a sad smile lingering in her eyes. 'I don't want that to happen.'

I slide an arm around her waist to draw her close. 'It doesn't matter now. I think I've found something more important. And I'd rather just hang on to what I got left.'

*

A cold north wind blows drifts of powdery snow across the mountain. We shelter in Skallagrim's cave and light a fire. Warm ourselves. Brew heather tea. And in each other's arms, find warmth.

BEN MEARS

When I next wake, its morning and Jade is curled in
against me. The memory of Stink's and Roach's deaths hit
me afresh to twist my gut. The snow has stopped falling and
the air beyond the cavern is clear, the sky a vivid sapphire.
Roach's body has frozen where he fell, his leather bag at his
side. I take the bag and stow it with mine. The tri-lobe bone I
pocket and the sacred book I wrap in the oil skin that used to
cover the gawper skull. I place it safely into my pack.

We can't bury his body up here—there's only rock
beneath the ice. Neither can we carry it all the way down
from the mountain. We're drained and we need to descend
quickly or risk freezing to death along the way. We decide
the best thing to do is carry his body up to the summit and,
there, pile stones over him to cover his remains and mark
the place. It's a grave of sorts, and an act of respect.

Looking mournfully at the finished mound, I try to think
what he would have had me say but feel lost—have felt
lost since the moment he died. Instead, we simply stand in
silence and look upon the cairn. I think about Roach and the
sacrifice he made.

We stay at the cave for a further day, while Jade recovers
a little of her former strength and on the second morning
set out at first light. Our descent is faster than the climb. The
weather is kinder and by noon of the first day, we're stripping
off our outer layers of clothing, warmed by the sun and the
effort of hiking. But the first night is the coldest yet. We dig a
snow hole and crawl inside to shelter, shivering, once more
clinging to each other for warmth. For another two days we
trudge down the mountain, all the while searching for Stinks
body, but the site eludes us. We're disoriented and don't find
the place. At least, if we do, we don't know it 'cause the bodies
must now be covered by snow.

On the third evening as the sun sets, I realise we must
have already passed his resting place when the wrecked
steam truck comes into view beyond a sparkling lower peak.
We stand in silence for a long time looking back up the

mountain before descending further, and reach the Clansly as the night closes in around us. It affords us a little shelter from the cold and huddled in the back beneath layers of empty coal sacks, we fall asleep.

*

The mountains don't seem so harsh now. They're beautiful in a majestic kind of way. Moving slowly, we walk south, glad to reach the first highland stream we've seen for more than a week. We fill our canteens with crystal waters and bathe, wash our clothes and set camp in the shadow of a hill.

Over the following four months we maintain our bearing, crossing the estuary east of Firth Glaggan by night in a stolen boat and leaving Scolanda behind. We stay a few days in Threadmoor to rest, trade rope for supplies and forage seaweed and shellfish. A few miles north of Fenlock on the western coast, we stumble upon a place that seems abandoned and full of potential.

*

Summer 1803, north of Fenlock, Londaland

The woods are green and bustling with life at this time of year. Birdsong trills the air. The sunlight plays in warm dapples across the forest track as branches sway in a cooling breeze. Blackberries grow here, and mushrooms, hazelnuts and sweet chestnuts too. Rabbits burrow at the lower edge of the woods where the grass runs down towards the sea, and there you can net fish and shrimp, gather mussels and clams from the rocks below the shoreline.

Up from the woods roll hills where hares hide in the wild grasses of the old fields. Wheat still sprouts there, though, so there'll be something to harvest come Honourmoon, and it won't take much more work before we have our first field yielding a good crop. There's a great deal of weeding to do—backbreaking work.

Stink would have loved it here. He'd have chased the squirrels and snuffled in the fallen leaves, barked birds to flight and leapt the fallen boughs. Ain't no morgue rats in these woods. No dragons either.

I push a sprig of spiniker aside as I leave the forest. Stepping into the sunlight, I feel its warmth on my face and peer up at the land before me that opens onto meadow and then on into a garden. Beyond that sits a timber cottage. It's only small, but is warm and dry, and inside, Jade is waiting.

17. UTOPIA

For a long time, Roach's bag sits on a shelf in the cottage. I feel strange about it, intrigued though reluctant to open it. It catches my eye when I'm shovelling out the ash from the fireplace and each time I bring in the logs. In the evenings I often gaze at it for hours on end, recalling the old man and the things he did and said. I have so many questions.

Jade's colour returns after a week or two. We walk the woods and she slowly regains her former strength. We heal, and rest when we can, still deeply weary from the mountain trek. Jade works on my twisted foot—after a whole heap of nagging.

'Ain't no point trying but carry on if you must,' I tell her.

That earns me a scowl. 'Ebadiah Joseph, you are a stubborn blinder.'

The thing is, after a time, I feel the tightness in my ankle lessen and my limp ease. That means I'm also faster and more agile. So I should be grateful.

One night, I'm watching her stitch the tear in my spare shirt by the light of the fire when I realise my feelings for her have only deepened. She's somehow taken root in me, and it's a good thing, a feeling I like. As my attempts to resist it fail, I'm overwhelmed with admiration for her. I allow myself to dream that we might survive here for good and be content. Happy even. Is that too much to ask?

Several more months of this routine go by, until I feel ready to loosen the straps and take out the sacred book that I returned to Roach's bag up on the mountain. I take the Codex and set it aside to look through the rest of Roach's things as the waning sun casts long shadows in through the cottage's crooked windows. There's his metal cup and bowl, his little three-legged cooking stand, his pipes... I pick them up and blow across the ends of the wooden tubes like he used to do. Notes that remind me of the wind on the moors, rise and fall. There's a ball of string and some leather twine, a tinder box, a tin still half-full of ground black beans—that makes me smile—and a small bottle of ink, a quill and a few dog-eared pieces of parchment. Tucked in among these are two envelopes, one bearing my name and the other Jade's.

'What's that?' Jade carries in a basket of foraged greens and berries.

'A letter from Roach.' I pass her the envelope. 'There's one each. Found them in his bag.'

For a moment she's still. 'You finally opened it, then...'

There's a hesitant quiver in her eyes before she sets down the basket to take the letter outside. I sit by the fire and stare at my name, unsure I've the strength to do more. But curiosity wins out. Opening the envelope, I read.

Dearest Ebadiah ~ Wolf Brother, Scourge of Skallagrim, Spear Thrower, Defender, Protector, Student, Companion and more importantly, Friend,
By now you must surely understand the nature of the mission bestowed upon me from the Great Elder Light, whom I serve. As with all things, I do not know the precise details of my passing, yet having glimpsed it in part, perceive that I may not be offered

189

*a chance to say goodbye. In that eventuality, this letter must
serve as my farewell.*

*My humble possessions I hereby leave to you. I'm sorry I do not
have something more, yet I hope these few things will be of use.
They may perhaps prove to be of some consequence. Learn to
play the pipes. They were passed to me by a great man who was
my mentor. Music can be a connection to your soul and so, to the
Light also.*

*Protect Jade. She is special, as you are special. And be in no
doubt that the fate of humankind lies in your hands. Do not let
your broken eye and twisted foot limit your actions - nor so the
deeper scars you carry, those of loss and rejection. They may
always be a part of you, though they do not define you.*

*The sacred book is neither mine to give, nor yours to own - yet
it is enough that you be its keeper for now. If it is in your possession, as I suspect it is, guard it well and know this. The codex is
as evil as it is good.*

*Farewell my friend, and Godspeed. You are more marvellous
than you will ever know.*

I take Wolf Brother as a reference to Stink. The words hit
deep and take me back to a time when I asked him about
his ma-jick.

*'It's not ma-jick,' he had said. 'Not in the sense you are meaning.
I'm not a wizard or sorcerer, Ebadiah. I'm a follower.'*

'Who do you follow,' I'd asked.

'The Light, of course. I follow the Light.'

There's no signature on the letter, which seems typical
of Roach, but it leaves me wondering if he was finished. Was
there something else he wanted to say? Suppose I'll never
know.

Setting the letter aside, I look at the book he called the
Tanak Codex. The cover's leatherbound, fragile and worn,
the corners and edges tattered. It looks a thousand years old
and I wonder when it was made and by who. I run my fingers
over the two lines of embossed symbols on the front. The

characters remind me of the writing on the walls of gawper caves, and of the planum horis. There's nothing on the back—or at least—if there was, it wore away long ago. Was it written by an ancient race of gawpers, or by people? I can't know for sure. Opening it, I find the pages look just as old as the cover. The ink is pale brown, faded, the parchment yellowed with age. The language is a mystery to me. I search the bag for anything else that might help—another book or perhaps some notes left by Roach—but there's nothing. There seems only one way I might truly make sense of the writing.

I've retied the trilobe on a twine around my neck and have worn it there since finding the cottage. Lifting it over my head, I weigh the risks of trying to reach Magwitch or Deadlock. Is that what Roach had in mind? Skallagrim knew about the trilobe though he's dead. But are others waiting for me to use it? Others just as dangerous? For now, I close the Codex and slip it back into the bag.

In the back yard, I find Jade sitting on the oak stump I use for chopping logs, her letter in her hands, tears streaking her face.

*

We make it to a second summer and I play the pipes often, soothed by melodies mostly stolen from Roach. The cottage feels like home now, but I miss Stink. Without him, the place feels incomplete. We've worked hard to fix it up. The crops in the nearby fields are doing well and we even have a little grain left from the harvest we gleaned last year. Ain't no sitting around here. Our time's spent on daily tasks: weeding the fields, hunting, fishing, foraging, scavenging, gathering firewood, chopping logs with the old axe we found out back, cooking and cleaning. A portion of each day we set aside for training, too. I surprise Jade by showing her a new assault course through the woods, but she just stares at it as though I've lost my mind.

'How do you know this is how the troopers trained?' she asks, when I've explained what I've done.

'Back when I wanted to join the army, I used to go down to the encampment west of Camdon City to watch the infantry. They spent a lot of time shooting guns. We can't do that, but we can do the other stuff.'

There are ditches to crawl through, fallen trees to duck beneath and others to scramble over. I've used a little of our remaining rope to make a climbing net and a tightrope to traverse, which stretches below. There's a stream to cross, a rope swing and a log wall to clamber over.

We practice with our spears and knives, sparring, and I hunt with my slingshot for rabbit and hare, even deer and boar, and with a four-pronged spear I fish for rays and eels in the shallows of the sea. That keeps my aim sharp.

I think again about using the trilobe. I need to do it, I decide, even if only for a second. I must contact my gawper friends once more and ask for help with the book. So, one night while Jade is asleep, I try.

Hands trembling, I take the bone and place it against my brow.

Magwitch, are you there? Deadlock?

There's a moment of noise as their images flash through my mind. I hear fragments of their voices amid the clamour, glimpse shadows of their faces before a silhouette that can only be Skallagrim floods my vision. And then it's gone. I lower the bone, unsure if the Lotharians heard my call or not. It will have to do for now. But does what I saw mean that Skallagrim is somehow still alive? How could that be? I cannot say, but the thought leaves me disturbed.

*

The following day a cold dawn breaks, clear and still. Good fishing weather. I'm up early to gather my gear and, heading out of the cottage, ease the door closed behind me while Jade remains asleep in bed. The sky promises plenty of sun. Warmth. Ain't nothing better than feeling the sun on your back. My memory plays tricks and I see Stink padding at my side, glimpse his shadow, hear him pant. But he ain't really there. It's just a ghost that won't leave my head. I see him often these days.

The cottage feels safe now. I've patched the roof and shored up the back wall with timbers from the forest. I've put Skallagrim out of my mind and there ain't no worries in my head as I stroll the little winding path down to the sea.

But the fish don't bite today. It's like an omen, though Roach would chide me for saying so. Still, it's there in my head. I got the whole ocean full of fish before me with not a single one on my line or in the gill net left clamped between rocks beneath the cliff where the water's deep. By ten in the morning, I'm heading home with the ghost of a dog, and we're both disappointed. The net I can check again later. Perhaps the tide's wrong. Perhaps my luck's just not in. It don't matter. We have bread, a little rabbit stew left from yesterday, apples. We'll not starve.

I'm on the path again when I hear it: a scream that chills my core. It's coming from the cottage.

'Jade!'

My fishing gear hits the ground. I run. Trees block my view while sounds reach me: wood splintering, a grating, creaking noise and a creature's piercing shriek. I clear the trees as my path bends closer, racing to the cottage. There before me is a beast the size of a coach 'n' four. It's heavy set with a battering ram of a head, which sweeps back to a splay of curved horns over its neck. From each of its heavy fore-limbs extends a long scimitar claw.

Another scream comes from the cottage as the creature charges at the wall with its armoured head. The building

193

shudders and groans, listing dangerously. The timbers rattle. The monster lets fly another shriek.

'Jade!' Through a window I see her inside, backing away, a spear clasped in her hands.

The shrieker's mottled green-grey skin ripples with muscle as it slams into the wall again and again. The boards split and rend. Jade bolts from the back door while I stand, helpless: *What can I do against such a beast?*

Use the axe, Ebadiah!

I skirt the cottage, sprinting to the woodpile as Jade joins me. I yank the axe from the oak stump and turn as, with an almighty groan, the building collapses sideways. Dust billows up into the air. Beyond the flattened cottage, the shrieker stands glaring with both sets of eyes through the haze. It's a curious animal, with one pair of eyes sitting beneath its horns and the second closer together and over its formidable mouth. It snorts and shrieks, stamping the ground.

As the dust settles, the planum horis painted in blood upon its brow becomes clear.

'He's controlling them. Setting them onto us like he did with the Morhs.'

'Who is?' Jade frowns, brandishing her spear at the beast.

'Skallagrim.'

'I thought he was dead!'

'So did I. Whoever's doing this is using the fourth plane and growing stronger. Maybe it's Tacitus, his captain.'

This creature ain't going nowhere. It just stares at us as, catching its breath. Then it charges. We run as it thunders between us. When it passes, Jade brings her spear down. I swing the axe at its flank, hacking deep into the flesh between ribs. The beast roars and groans, turns to charge again, only now its fixed upon me alone. I'm sure this is the end. Ain't no escaping this monster. In a moment I'll be ground into the dirt, trampled, flattened. Gore drips from the axe blade. I stand and prepare for one final swing. It will be the last thing I ever do.

194

Only the shrieker slows and stops. I hear Jade grunt with effort and glimpse her running in to strike again with the spear, following through with her full weight. Her spear lodges deep in the beast's rear haunch.

It's my turn to charge. With a two-handed swing, I launch myself, plough the axe into the centre of its skull, splitting the planum horis in two. Stunned, the beast releases a mournful groan. Its legs fold beneath it as it crashes to the ground. I move in again to plant another blow into the middle of its head. In a red mist I keep swinging over and over, until I feel Jade pulling me away.

'It's dead! It's dead! You can stop now.'

I step back and drop the axe, shaking, exhausted. Amazed to still be alive.

'What is that thing?' she asks.

'A shrieker,' I say, breathlessly. 'Come up from Mors Zonam. Michael told me about them.'

A distant rumble reaches us then, a thunder that builds.

'Quickly! Get your things!' I hear trees crashing to the ground.

We rush to salvage what we can from the wrecked cottage. On my belly, I crawl into narrow gaps between collapsed timbers, spy Roach's bag and snatch it. My coat and weapons are the only other things I bother with. When we meet up again, Jade has a bag slung over her shoulder, her coats and our small sack of wheat swinging from one hand.

The crashing grows louder as the approaching shriekers trample the forest across the meadow, and we see them spill out onto the tall grass, galloping towards us.

'Run!' I shout. And we do. I'd have liked to have returned to the sea path for my fishing gear, but that would slow us down and put us in danger. Instead, we make for the trees on the rise behind our flattened home, a place we'd named the far forest. For the first hundred yards we're exposed, but we drop into a ditch that edges the track as it winds up the hill, to hide ourselves. Reaching the slope, we watch as the lumbering pack of shriekers slows.

'They're still coming,' says Jade, breathless, peering down the hill from our grassy ditch.

'I doubt they'll keep their speed up for long. Too big. Too heavy. We just need to keep moving.'

We press on, climbing to the forest, glad when the land flattens out and there we leave the ditch to be swallowed by the trees. The shriekers' thunder becomes distant and small.

I sink against a large tree trunk. 'I gotta rest.'

Jade joins me, gesturing back the way we've come. 'If the gawpers have *them* in their power, what else are they controlling?'

'Who knows?' The shock of the attack ebbs away, only to be replaced by anger. My throat closes and I can say no more. We were doing alright. We had a home, were making a life. But now it's all gone, the cottage obliterated. Beneath my rage, I hate that it's my fault. Shouldn't have used the trilobe.

'Where we gonna sleep tonight?' asks Jade.

All I can do is shake my head—can't face telling her that I don't know.

'Suppose we'll find somewhere,' she says in the absence of an answer. Jade tries to cheer me. 'Hey, come on. We survived before, didn't we? We can survive again.'

Reluctantly I nod. 'I guess.' Rested, I drag myself up from the ground. 'We'd better get going, put some miles between us and those things.'

*

By the time night falls, we're approaching a salt-blown hamlet that's strung out above a rocky cove. Below us, waves smash against dark and jagged rocks. The sea is to our right, which confirms to me that we've been travelling southward for most of the day. We've never seen this settlement—haven't found it on any of our excursions hunting for food or game—so it's unknown to us.

'It could be dangerous,' I say.

'You think?' says Jade.

'Watch for the planum horis. Tell me if you see it anywhere.'

'You're gonna kill him, aren't you... Skallagrim?'

'What do you mean? Skallagrim's dead,' I say, but there's doubt in my voice. I scold myself for letting his name slip earlier.

'Is he?'

But I have a feeling Jade's sensing the same thing. That he's still out there somewhere. That perhaps he didn't die on the mountain.

The truth is I just don't know anymore.

18. THE PURSUIT

Steeped in drifting sea fret, the hamlet is ghostly quiet. I take a pebble from my coat pocket, slip it into the leather pouch of my slingshot and launch it down the main street. Ducking low, we watch the missile skitter from cobbles and walls before clanging the rusting shell of a clockwork car. When nothing stirs, we rise and walk in, seeking a good shelter and hoping the whole place is abandoned. It soon becomes clear that a battle has raged here. As with so many of the other places we've been, the dead lie scattered, skeletonised, their clothes rags. They remind me of flotsam and jetsam washed up along a beach. The salty air is thick with their stench. The houses are pockmarked with war wounds, many of the windows smashed or blown out. Part of me wishes someone *was* here. A few survivors... Something that could be called hope.

'Hello?' I call, feeling desolate. Is this the fate of the whole world? Or does a place still exist where peaceful people make their way, getting by, living? Somewhere where kindness has not died.

Jade picks a house. 'Let's try this one.'

We climb the steps and I test the door. It's unlocked so we enter.

'Hello?' My call raises no response. 'Reckon we're alone.'

In the front room, several windowpanes are missing and a sea breeze blows in.

'At least we have a place for the night,' says Jade.

The stairs creak as we climb to find the first-floor rooms empty. Out back there's nothing but a weed-strangled vegetable patch. We begin to believe we are indeed alone. Gathering furniture from around the house, I start a fire in the front room's grate using tinder from Roach's kit. While I break up chairs and a table to burn, Jade finds an old pan from the kitchen and grinds some of our wheat to make flour.

We warm ourselves around the fire and bake four small loaves of bread over the flames. The bread's dense and hard, like biscuit—we've no yeast—but it's still good. The endless rhythm of the surf soothes us from the dark expanse of water beyond the glassless windows, and I imagine Stink curled up before the fire.

I miss that thieving hound.

Using our coats and some mouldering cushions from the house, we make up a bed on the floor and fall asleep to the sounds of the sea.

*

For two weeks we travel south, knowing only that the shrieker pack is somewhere in our wake. Are they still in pursuit? There ain't reason to think otherwise.

We walk hard, pushing ourselves, resting little until one morning we come to a forest's edge that overlooks a patchwork of rolling fields. The grass is long, green and luscious. In several fields, old crops are losing their fight against the weeds. I think about harvesting what's left of the wheat for our supplies. The humped shapes of farm buildings clutter the land: barns, silos and a stable, and at the centre of the cluster sits a tall farmhouse built of grey stone. A sudden movement in a nearby field causes us to withdraw into the woodland shadows.

Two great cart horses amble into view on the rise ahead. The larger is a roan, the smaller a golden tan colour.

'Horses!' I hiss, excited by the prospect of taking them.

'But the farmer…' says Jade.

'Let's find out.' I can't help myself. Those horses could make a big difference to us. Better than a steam truck!

I lead the way out of the forest, not caring if we're seen. At the end of the field we watch them and catch a foul scent on the wind. Ain't no mistaking the stink of death. Further down, a third horse—this one black—rots in the sunlight, a chasm in its side buzzing with flies. Stink would've barked his face off.

'They're not for eating, boy. Come on,' I murmur as though he's still here, though I know he ain't. I head through a field of straggling plants, making for the house. The fields are running wild. One horse is dead, its carcass left to rot. 'I guess the farmers have died or moved on.'

'Be careful,' warns Jade.

We cross a meadow, passing a line of graves—shallow humps of soil marked with crossed sticks. In the yard by the house we ditch our bags and coats, keeping our weapons to hand. I'm so sure the place is empty that I knock brazenly on the door and when no answer comes, try the handle. It's locked so I hammer loudly and shout.

'Hello? Anyone home?'

A feeble voice comes from within. 'Hello? Who's there?'

Jade and I exchange a glance.

'We're travellers, passing through. Can we come in?' I shout.

'You may.' The voice is distant yet clear.

We wait but no one comes to the door so I begin to doubt what I heard.

'Did you hear that?' I ask. 'The voice?'

'Aye,' says Jade. 'They said, *you may*.'

'How do we get in?' I call back. 'Can you open the door?'

The thin voice reaches us again. 'There's a window at the rear.'

We skirt the house and find a window smashed out. I peer into a rundown hallway where mould and moss grow between the floor tiles and plaster flakes from the walls. I see no one.

'Hello?' I call again. 'Are you there?'

'I'm here. Come in. Come in.'

'Is it a trap?' asks Jade.

'For sure,' I whisper. 'Be ready to fight.'

I clamber through the open window and stand guard with my spear as Jade climbs in. In the passageway I approach a closed door, pausing at the sound of the voice.

'In here. I'm in here.'

'Ready?' I hiss to Jade, before shouting. 'We're armed! You don't want to fight us!'

She nods. I throw open the door and thrust the tip of my spear through the gap.

The voice responds. 'I surely don't.'

Through the opening I see an old woman, stricken and lying in a bed. The room smells little better than the dead horse.

'I'm dying,' says the woman. 'My family are all gone.'

'Dead?' I ask.

She nods. Her eyes are rheumy and clouded, her skin waxy and thin.

'No farmer?' I ask, still expecting some trick.

'My husband was killed by the painted men, like the others. I buried them in the meadow before I grew too weak to dig the ground.'

'Yet you survived,' says Jade.

'How?' I ask.

'I hid in the cellar. They never found me there. These foreigners don't know what a cellar is.' The old woman coughed into a filthy rag. 'Water...'

'Are you armed?' I glance at the bedclothes, wondering if they're concealing a gun.

'No.'

'I'll go.' Jade steps towards the door.

'Be quick,' I say.

'I've nothing left to live for, so you've nothing to fear from me. Some water is all I need.'

'You'll have it soon enough.' I cross to a grimy window, rub a patch clean and peer out to check for others, but the yard outside remains eerily quiet. Footsteps sound in the hallway beyond the door. I meet Jade with the tip of my spear before lowering it to let her in. She takes a canteen to the woman, who drinks, nodding gratefully.

'You have horses,' I say.

'Three.' She wipes her mouth on the rag. 'Three beauties.'

'Two,' I tell her. 'One's dead.' She looks sad so I add, 'I'm sorry.'

'It's not your fault,' she says, resting her head back against her pillow. 'Which is dead?'

'The black,' I say.

She nods. 'My husband named the roan Gun. You'll have to watch her. She's headstrong. The other's Brimstone. You should take them. I can't look after them now.'

'Thank you,' says Jade.

'Is it just the two of you?'

'Aye.'

'One each, then. Perhaps you could leave me a supply of water to keep me a while.'

'We will.' Jade places the canteen within reach of the bed. 'Can you walk?'

'I can't even get out of bed, but I'm ready for what comes next.'

'Oh.'

'It's alright. There comes a point when you welcome it. Take whatever you want. You seem like nice folk.'

Jade turns to me, lowering her voice. 'Leave us a while. I'll wash her, make her more comfortable.'

'Do you have food?' I ask the woman.

'A little. In the kitchen.'

'I'll make us something to eat.'

With a final glance from the window, I go to explore the rest of the house. In the kitchen I find oats and the dregs of some honey set solid at the bottom of a jar. There are a few other bits and pieces: some apples going soft, the stump end of a salted ham hanging in a cold store and a pot of dried peas. It's enough for a decent stew. I set the peas to soak, rummage through the rest of the house and take a good pair of crossed daggers from the wall. They'll make fine spear tips for Jade and me. From an upstairs window I can see the horses feeding in the field. Now they're mine, I get a crazy fear of losing them, so I go outside, walk back to the field and bring them into the stable. In the yard is a large brass bell hanging from an iron bracket on the wall. I lift it down and take it over to the stable. There are a few lengths of rope inside. I use one to rig an alarm, looping the length through the hooped handles of the double doors and throwing the end up and over a roof beam. I tie on the bell so that it hangs in the air. If someone opens the doors it will ring. I check there's hay and water for the horses before climbing out over the gap at the top of the doors.

Before returning to the house, I visit a pine copse that's nestled beyond the barns. There I hack down two straight branches, each one twice the length of our old spears, and carry them into the house.

Outside the old woman's bedroom, I stand and knock.

'Come in,' says Jade.

Leaving the spears, I enter to see the woman sitting upright in bed, looking a little brighter and happier for the company.

203

'Jade tells me you'll stay the night.'

'If you don't mind,' I say.

Jade smiles. 'This is Eleanor.'

'I'm making a stew for later. The horses are stabled, watered and fed.' I show them the daggers. 'I found these. Do you have any other weapons hidden away?'

Eleanor shakes her head. 'The men took them.'

I nod. 'Pity.'

*

The stew's the best thing I've eaten in a long time and there's enough for all three of us. Stink would've loved it. In the evening I set a fire in the old woman's bedroom grate and another in the farmhouse living room, where Jade and I settle.

'We could stay here,' says Jade. 'For good, I mean.'

'Skallagrim's beasts will soon find us. It's best we move on.'

'You think they're still following.'

'I reckon so. We shouldn't wait too long.'

I can tell she's hiding her disappointment as she stares into the flames. But she knows I'm right.

'At least we have horses now. And look.' I show her the long pine branches. 'These will make fine lances.'

She glances at them before curling up in a big old chair, blanketed beneath her coats. Shutting me out, she rests her head to sleep.

I console myself by working on the new spears, stripping the bark, honing the shafts and carving sockets for the dagger tangs in the thicker ends. When they're all cut and ready, I heat pine resin in a pan over the fire and cover both joins with the glue before wedging in the daggers and binding up the ends with twine. I daub more resin over the bindings to make it good and strong, then sit back, pleased with the new weapons.

BEN MEARS

'What d'ya think, boy?' I ask the dog who ain't there.

*

For a further day we rest at the farm, look after the old woman and prepare to leave. We forage greens and rescue a little grain from the fields, gather all the food we can find and place most of it by Eleanor's bed, along with an old milk churn full to the brim with fresh water from the farm well. She insists we take a little of the food for ourselves. As evening sets in, we pack our gear ready to ride out in the morning at first light. We're bedding down for a second night in the house when the bell sounds from out in the stable.

Jade scrambles to her feet. 'The horses!'

We throw on our coats and boots. She grabs a long spear for herself and tosses the other to me as we rush out into the shadowed yard, though the place looks deserted. Running to the stable, I find Gun's broken loose from her stall and is rearing, pounding her hooves against the doors.

'Listen!' says Jade.

As Gun quietens, a deep thunder rolls in from the distance. For a moment I think the mare has been spooked by an approaching storm, but it ain't a tempest on the wind—it's the rumble of the pack.

'Shriekers!' I throw open the stable doors. 'Fetch our stuff!'

Jade runs back into the house while I saddle the horses. By the time she's back, laden with our bags, I'm leading the mares out into the yard and the first few shriekers are breaching the ridge at one edge of the farm. We hurry to load our bags onto the horses, strapping them in place behind each saddle. I help Jade mount Brimstone and pass up a lance.

'I ain't never ridden before!' she says, looking scared.

'Ain't nothin' to it,' I tell her. 'Just hold on!'

'What about Eleanor?' Concern lines her face.

'We'll draw them away. It's the best we can do for her now.'
Jade peers back towards Eleanor's window.

'She'll be alright,' I say, hauling myself up into Gun's
saddle. 'Someone else will come by to help her.' I don't fully
believe that, though, and I doubt Jade does either. Eleanor
has food and water enough for a week, two if she ekes it out.
Jade's quiet as we coax the horses into a trot. I think deep
down she understands we can't bring the old girl with us and
we can't stay, either, though she ain't happy about it. She
clings to the reigns as we speed into a gallop.

Glancing behind, I see one of the shriekers slowing. It
seems exhausted as it lumbers to a halt. For a moment it
wavers on its legs before finally buckling and crashing to the
ground.

'They're being driven mercilessly,' I call to Jade. 'We can't
stop.'

Armed with the horse spears, we ride out across the dark
fields to follow a track into the woods. Our mounts speed
us through the trees and out into an open nightscape of low
hills and shallow vales, and once more we leave the shriekers
behind.

*

Dawn light shimmers through an early mist. I bring Gun
to rest before a magnificent oak, a single tree at the centre of a broad, open meadow. A planum horis is carved deep
into its bark like a hateful wound—the third symbol we've
found this morning.

'Gawper territory... What now?' I ask Jade, fearing we
might be wandering closer to them without even knowing.

'We keep going,' she says. 'Ain't much of a choice, is there?
Not with those things at our backs.'

'Suppose.'

I think about teaching Jade how to ride, how to grip the saddle with her thighs and how to steer Brimstone with her heels and reins, but we've been riding all night. There ain't much I can show her now that she hasn't already worked out for herself. So, on we go at a walk, our horses weary, our spirits low. The symbol's everywhere after that: on a gatepost, a house, a watch-lamp, chiselled into a boulder by a stream that leads down to the sea, daubed on a milestone further south. Seems like we ain't never gonna be free of it. In a copse beneath a knoll, we stop to eat a few morsels from our meagre supply, only to set off again a few minutes later. Jade stares into the trees lining the road.

'Something's out there,' she says. We listen, wait, watch. 'We're being hunted.'

'By something else?' I ask.

'I don't know. It's just a feeling.'

That unnerves me 'cause I got the same bad notion churning my gut. I hear the Voice then, thin, like a distant whisper. The same small voice I heard on the mountain top.

Find another path, Ebadiah.

A shiver of energy drifts through me like a wraith. Up ahead our route will take us down between cliffs and the coast to the west. We'd be trapped down there if anything was to block our way. I point to a small valley leading inland, which from here looks more open.

'Let's try that way.'

We turn the horses for the vale but that feeling comes with us, like the stink on a dog. Ain't no shaking it. And a mile or two further on, a noise in the hedgerow at the side of the road makes me tug on the reins.

'Something's there, hiding.'

I glimpse a flash of grey fur in the foliage. Brimstone stamps to a halt, baulking, and then both horses turn about, whinny and rear. Behind us the familiar shapes of the shrieker pack break the skyline. A sudden snarl from our other side startles the mares further.

207

'Wolves!' cries Jade.

'Yah!' We dig heels in and take flight, our horses speeding as, one after another, wolves thread their way out onto the road at our backs. They give chase, snapping at our mounts' heels as we ride, a dozen or so, snarling, bounding, lunging. Jade lurches in her saddle, yet to match Brimstone's rhythm, but the mares are faster than the wolves. For now...

Around us, the valley steepens and snakes into a turn as we race. For a time we hold the lead, stretching out ahead of the pack.

Leaning into the bend, we see the craggy slopes at our sides climb higher to form a gorge where the road dips. Left with but one path open, I feel more trapped than ever, and glimpse dragons scurrying down the mountainous sides up ahead. As the chasm walls close around us, we are sur-rounded.

19. THE BOOK

Hooves pound dirt. There's movement around twenty yards away. Low down in the mouth of a cave at the foot of a rising cliff, two more creatures appear from the shadows. They're big cats, the like of which I ain't seen before. One's black, the other the colour of sand. Tall as a man, they pad into the half-light, each on six legs, their forelimbs doubled at the shoulder. And something else lurks there, obscured by darkness: *Skallagrim,* I think, *alive and hunting us with all his monsters.*

Near exhaustion, our horses slow. I feel Gun's heart pounding through the saddle.

'Ain't no good.' Jade sounds desperate as we watch our foes in turn. 'We gotta stand and fight!'

She's right.

We turn our horses to face the wolves as they close in.

It's over. We know it. The wolves know it. The odds against us are just too great.

'It's been nice knowing you, Jade Garaday,' I say, allowing myself one final look at her while readying my lance. My heart wells with a sadness I can't explain. I want to make a charge at the pack—go down fighting—but that ain't happening. Gun's spooked and finished. In no mind to run at the wolves. She skitters sideways, jostling into Brimstone. But then my name echoes out from the cave entrance.

'Ebadiah!'

Recognising the rasping voice, I turn to squint at the cave. The big cats have moved out to stand in half-light, their riders revealed.

'Magwitch!?' I gape in wonder, scarcely believing what I see. 'It's Magwitch and Deadlock!'

Deadlock calls across the gorge, gesturing to us, his voice commanding. 'If this one would live, he should hurry!'

Their cats carry baggage strapped across their backs behind the mounted gawpers.

I tell Jade, 'Trust me! They're friends,' and we ride for the cave along a rough expanse of gravel and stone, mere moments ahead of the wolfpack. The dragons close in, too. The nearest makes a grab for Gun's side. I aim my lance and thrust it into the creature, which twists in agony and draws away. I glance up at the overhanging cliff before following the gawpers and their strange cats into the cavern. The overhanging rockface there looks cracked and dangerously loose.

Pausing inside, Deadlock makes a fist in the air. As he brings it down, there comes a rumble and a scatter of gravel falls from the cliff outside. It is as though he is pulling at the very ground above us with an invisible force. Larger rocks follow his draw and a moment later, a huge mass of stone and earth cascades into the entrance behind us. Blocking the way, it fills the air with dust and dark as we hurry deeper in. Beneath the din of the rockfall, wolves bay and yelp, and before long all becomes quiet and still.

'What now?' I ask.

In the soft glow of the gawpers' eyes, we wait. Listen. And then the howling begins again—a mournful, haunting, hunting sound—the wolf survivors banding together in fury.

Stink growls but I know it's only a memory.

A sudden blue-green light shimmers from a glass orb that Deadlock reveals from his black-weed robes. It casts the cavern in otherworldly hues as he holds it aloft.

'This way,' he says.

We follow as the howling softens into the distance.

'You... You heard my call,' I stammer, still amazed to see the gawpers here before me in the flesh. 'You're here? Are you *really* here?' I fear they are conjuring us into their presence and may at any time vanish, leaving us trapped in the pitch black of an unknown cave. And who can say what lurks in its depths?

Magwitch nods. 'We are here and we are real. Magwitch heard your call. Though in such days as these it is unsafe to mind-walk. This one took great risk to reach Magwitch.'

'We've been hunted ever since,' I say. 'I wasn't sure you heard me.'

'*You* did this?' Jade narrows her eyes at me in the iridescent light. 'We're being hunted because *you* mind-walked?'

'I'm sorry. I had to.'

'*Why?*' She glares.

'I need to know about the book.'

'Of what book does this one speak?' asks Magwitch as the giant cat beneath him pads the cave floor. Its shoulders roll in the gloaming light.

I tell the gawpers all about the mountaintop fight, my recent doubts about Skallagrim's death and about the book Stink stole from him.

'Roach called it the Tanak Codex,' I say. The gawpers look at me as though they already know of the book and that they know more than they are saying.

'Who is this Roach?' Deadlock quickly asks.

'He was a friend.'

'And this one has read the book?'

'I can't read it. That's the problem. But Skallagrim didn't like losing it, so I figured it's important.'

The light of Deadlock's eyes seems to grow cold. 'This one carries the Tanak Codex? This one is certain?'

'Aye.'

We follow a winding passage through the cave system as somewhere water drips and echoes. The dank air is cold against my skin. I think about what we've left behind.

'Will the wolves find another way in?' I ask.

Magwitch explains. 'They will try, though they must travel many miles around the higher ground.'

'Where are we going?' asks Jade.

'Skallagrim's hoards gather on a hill some miles from here. Others join them as we speak. Magwitch will take you to the Lotharians. It is the only safe place for you now. We must journey in stealth.'

'Then it's true. Skallagrim lives.'

'It is so,' says Magwitch.

Disappointment and fear cloud my mind.

'What are you riding?' I ask, in awe of the six-legged beasts.

'They are sand cats, from Mors Zonam—loyal to us only because we have connected with them on the fourth plane. This is Doom. Deadlock rides Grimclaw. Keep your distance. At heart they are wild creatures. If the connection fails, they will kill any who venture near.'

Jade and I steer our horses further from the huge cats. I watch the beasts pace, the massive paws of their doubled forelegs almost touching the ground in unison. From time to time they twitch their long, tapered ears.

Magwitch continues. 'Skallagrim is using creatures, too.'

'I do wish you'd tell me what you're planning,' hisses Jade at my side.

'*Planning*? What makes you think I'm planning anything?' I ask.

'Don't you have a plan?'

I glimpse the fire in Magwitch's eyes sparkle and his cheeks rise. It's the closest thing to a smirk that I've ever seen on a gawper's darkly inscrutable face.

'The book this one carries is important indeed,' says Deadlock, seeming unaware of my plight. 'The Tanak Codex is infamous among our kind. It is an ancient book containing all that is known about both nackh and bah-nackh.'

'What's nackh and bah-nackh?' I ask, struggling to sound the words, which Deadlock pronounces with clicks.

'The terms mean good and bad ma-jick,' explains Magwitch.

Deadlock continues. 'The book has been the cause of much conflict throughout our history. Skallagrim has good reason to mourn its loss. Though he has likely committed much of it to memory.'

'Could he not just find a copy?' I ask.

'It is forbidden to copy the Tanak Codex. This was made law among our kind. A curse was sealed over the book to restrict its use by any but the royal line, and so it was passed down to Skallagrim. There is no copy in all the world, not in this kingdom or the next. It is a royal heirloom like no other, and he will stop at nothing to reclaim it.'

'I'm a dead man.' I contemplate my impending doom.

'This one lives yet,' says Magwitch, his eyes brightening.

I wonder how Skallagrim managed to survive the fall. Did he summon some other creature to carry him away when his war bird deserted him, or did he use another kind of ma-jick? How long did he lie at the bottom of the mountain cliffs? Another thought occurs to me. Is it possible he was never truly there at all?

'Can Dagomites conjure more than one place into their midst at once?' I ask.

Magwitch looks at me for a moment and again I glimpse that suggestion of a smile. 'This one should read the Codex. Perhaps it holds the answers.'

'Believe me, I would if I could.'

Riding on in silence, I'm left to dwell on my approaching fate. I start thinking about how things might have turned out differently. If Roach had not died during the rite, perhaps he would have found a way to finish Skallagrim. If I'd only been more resistant to the gawper's power... If I'd thrown my spear a few inches to the left, it would have pierced his heart. If only Stink had not fallen. If, if, if...

But there ain't no point thinking like that. I force myself to focus on what I might do. I have the book and Jade and, for now, the protection of the Lotharians. That's something, I guess. But can I trust them? The Codex is important, priceless, even. I fear the gawpers may try to take it from me. I ask myself, just how far can Magwitch and Deadlock be trusted? They could be leading me into a trap where I will be powerless to stop them. Now I'm not even sure we should be going with them at all.

We follow the beasts and their riders through miles of cavernous tunnels, and I wonder how long these passages are and what dangers might be waiting for us at the end.

'How far is your camp?' I ask.

'It is seven day's ride from here,' says Magwitch, 'beyond the caves. Though it will take longer to reach, for we must travel only at night and may be delayed. Magwitch and Deadlock will risk mind-walking to see the way ahead. We may need to take a longer road to remain hidden. We shall rest soon and await nightfall before continuing.'

'Is it safe in here?' Jade asks.

'It is safer than outside,' says Magwitch.

Before long the tunnel broadens out and the stone roof flutes upwards into a tall crevasse over our heads, like a vast chimney where the rippled walls glisten. Daylight filters down to us dimly. Magwitch and Deadlock dismount and lead the sand cats across a shallow rivulet that divides the chamber. They seem to have control over the beasts, who obediently lie down away from us on the stone floor. I feel a cold draft and wonder if we can light a fire to cook and to warm ourselves, but a moment later Magwitch arranges tinder and kindling on a flat area beneath the natural chimney. There, he sparks a small fire into life with flint and steel. I wonder what he will use as fuel, until he fetches some wood from a small supply they have brought in the baggage carried by the cats.

Heating rocks, they bake a kind of hard bread using dried and crushed gawper weed that they mix with some ground seeds, which I cannot name. This they moisten with a little water from their canteens. When it's baked, they share the bread with us and we share what we have with them. Feeling better for the food in my stomach, I ask them more about the Codex as we sit around the little fire.

'Do you mean to take the book from me? Will the other Lotharians take it from me?'

'The Lotharians will not take it from you,' Magwitch says. 'Only we two know what you carry.'

'Will you teach me to read it?'

'Bring out the book,' says Magwitch. 'Let us see what may be done.'

Tentatively, I slide the Codex from Roach's bag, unfold the oil cloth and pass the book to Magwitch. He opens it to study it briefly, turning the pages with a clawed finger.

'A little of this writing, Magwitch can read.'

Sitting cross-legged next to him, my first lesson begins as he points out individual characters and symbols, explaining their meaning.

'Nackh.' He points to a twisted symbol before moving on to another, which looks the same only reversed. 'Bah-nackh.'

'Good ma-jick. Bad ma-jick,' I say.

He nods. 'It is important to know the difference. A mistake could mean death.'

'Blinders.'

Little by little, I learn that the language is a kind of merging of sounds and pictures. Some of the symbols are stylised pictographs, which mean precisely what they look like. Water

is a rippling line and when spoken sounds like *sanfar*. Air
is a simple circle and sounds like *oft*. Other forms are perhaps older and have lost some of their origin over the years,
now only known by their associated sounds. The words feel
ancient on my tongue and I imagine a scene where altered
beings—somewhere between gawpers and men—huddle
around a similar fire in the caverns of Mors Zonam, thousands of years before, muttering among themselves, drawing
images in the sand or on cave walls, baking their black weed
bread, surviving, changing.

By the end of my first lesson I'm fighting to stay awake.
Magwitch seems to notice and tells me to rest, so lying down
near the fire, I lean my head on Roach's old bag as Jade settles down close by and, missing the warmth of Stink's body, I
fall asleep.

*

I dream of Stink: of hunting with him, roving woodlands,
sleeping at his side. His growl wakes me in the near darkness but when I open my eyes, he's not there. Yet the growl
from my dream is quickly followed by a skittering sound that
is there. It's the pattering of many legs over the hard ground.
I glimpse a movement across the cave but whatever it is vanishes before I can get a good look. A splashing noise comes
from my other side, over at the rivulet, and I turn in time to
see a low, segmented body slither into the water.

I scrutinise the obscured reaches of the cavern.

'Wake up.' I shake Jade by the shoulder. 'We ain't alone.'
She stirs, looks around. 'I don't see nowt.'

'They're here, Toxic slinks. Wake the gawpers.' I take my
lance. Set my back to the fire.

The skittering continues as my eye strains to make
out flickers of movement in the shadows. A moment of
near silence is broken by a sand cat's roar, followed by the

unmistakable hollow rattle of a slink's tail. My blood chills. It's the sound of death.

The black sand cat erupts with movement, swiping at a slink. The other rouses, leaping up and spinning to confront another of the giant insects. Behind me I sense movement. The gawpers scramble to their feet, their staffs at the ready. Deadlock snatches a brand from the fire to probe the near dark as the insects scurry closer.

The killing begins.

They scuttle out of the water, from the hollows and down from the void above, while we form a ring around the fire. Magwitch lifts an orb of flame, one hand outstretched. He sends it shooting, to explode over a large slink that crackles and hisses as it burns, writhing on the cavern floor. Close by, another scurries away from the burst of heat. The air fills with fumes and the ominous rattle of the slinks.

'They're afraid of fire.' I stoop to claim a burning stick to ward off a rearing slink that hesitates and twists away. I chase it down and skewer it to the ground with my lance.

'Fetch the horses. Gather your belongings!' cries Deadlock, plunging his brand into the fanged face of another squealing insect. It's feelers sizzle as it reels and screams. 'We leave! Make a line of fire!'

I pin the corpse with a boot and tug my spear free, then race to collect my gear, all the while fending off the slinks. We take fire sticks and hurry after Deadlock, leading the horses further into the cave system. The sand cats seem to know exactly what to do, pacing ahead of us into the continuing tunnel where they wait. The gawpers toss burning wood behind us to form a line across the cave and, as we add our brands, they use their powers to cast more fuel from the campfire and drop it along the line.

Dead slinks lie scattered, broken or burning in their shells, and with the tunnel roof sloping lower over our heads, we move on.

THE JICKER MAN

*

Twilight glows faintly in the cave ahead. We see it long before the mouth comes into view: a point of light that grows as we near. Beyond, the land drops away into a steep-sided, forested valley. Fresh air hits my face. I smell an earthy taint. The trees hang damp with dew. I'm relieved to be out of the claustrophobic cavern and yet a new fear grips me—every manner of beast is out to get us, and out here we're vulnerable. I see wisdom in the gawpers decision to travel at night, and will the darkness to quickly cloak us as we mount up to ride.

It feels safer travelling with the gawpers and their mighty cats. We settle into a simple routine, riding by night and sleeping by day. Each time we stop to make camp we seek out a new hiding place—somewhere a soaring war bird cannot spy—and hope to remain hidden from the creatures that hunt us. We shelter beneath dense woodlands with thick canopies of green, in caves and crags, ruins and abandoned buildings.

On the third night, a group of tall figures approach our camp from a fringe of trees, their outlines bulked by furs. I snatch up my lance but Magwitch stays me with a clawed hand as the newcomers call out.

'Lo, lo! Lo, lo!'

The words mean nothing to me, though they seem to put the Lotharians at ease.

'Friends from the North,' mutters Deadlock. 'Come to join our cause.'

More Lotharians join us each time we move. They drift from the shadows and gather through the woods, each time calling the greeting to make safe their approach. And little by little, our number grows.

During the nights as we ride, Magwitch teaches me more of the gawper language as best he can, but it's when we're

camped and working by firelight that I make the most progress. I find myself eager to learn and soon feel the book is
no longer such a mystery to me, but that I'm getting to know
it. I can easily find a chapter I seek and, when I do, I can
read some portions of it well enough to gain their meaning,
though as much is still unreadable.

I read a line aloud. 'Erd-bah-dannackh fah nachantai
dauh.'

'Erd-backh-dannah,' says Magwitch, correcting me and
laughing. 'Dagomites do not eat stones.'

On I work, learning, reading, absorbing all that my
strange teacher conveys. I realise the ma-jick in the Codex,
whether nackh or bah-nackh—I've yet to find a way to tell
them apart—is routed in a source beyond the realm we
are in. There is something other, something more, that is
beyond the known even to the author of these texts. The
book calls it the *nackh-moor*, a shorthand term meaning the
source beyond ma-jick, although I struggle to understand
how the good and the bad can come from the same place.
When I ask Magwitch about it, he shakes his head slowly.

'The nackh-moor is beyond our understanding,' he tells
me. 'There are some questions to which we have no answers.'

It's then I realise I will probably never fully understand it.

Nights roll by and the Lotharians gather around us, riding
in from creeks and crags, trickling like streams to join a river.
They slip into our line as we move, find us each time we stop,
until we are fifty strong.

I learn that many chapters of the Codex are made up of
distinct sections of ma-jick script all scribed in the ancient
gawper tongue, and each created for a unique purpose.
These, Magwitch tells me, are called *nackh-sahar*. And each
nackh-sahar has six parts. The first is called the skitzerhelm,
and is a statement, a little like a complicated name for the
nackh-sahar. The second part, named the fruhazen, sets
out the situation and intent of the nackh-sahar. The third
is the brahadran, which denotes the nature of the wielding,

for which there are various methods. The draconbrah gives direction. The omnadran describes the action. And the closing command is known as the camplanodrix.

My lessons continue and my progress is quick, partly because Magwitch is an excellent teacher and in part because I do little else. Even during the days, I work on, unable to sleep for hours on end. I can't get used to sleeping without Stink around. He was my protector, my alarm, my peace of mind. And now he has gone. I have only a shadow to haunt me. We're in a burned-out barn one day when Jade stirs. Noticing me studying the book, she comes over to my spot by the fire.

'Can't sleep?' she asks.

'Nah. Ain't the same without that dog. It's like part of me's missing or something.'

'You were bonded to him as he was to you. You miss him. It's to be expected.'

'I guess.'

Gently, she takes the book from my hands and closes it. Placing it down on my bag, she lies down, curling in beside my like Stink used to do. She pulls my arm across her so that I'm holding her, and there we fall asleep.

*

The next night we thread a path through dense woodland until the trees give way to a clearing and a sprawling camp of green, conical tents. I marvel at the number—perhaps five hundred or more. The scent of smoke is in the air. Here and there, campfires gleam beneath canopies while gawpers huddle miserably around them.

Magwitch glances about at his fellows. 'They chew the corners of their cloaks.' When I look at him questioningly, he adds, 'We are starving. The battle *must* come soon or we shall be too weak to fight. Yet we are not ready.'

I reason the encampment must already be known to Skallagrim. It's too large to have remained hidden. Checking around for Stink, I catch myself. He ain't coming.

As we ride in, a pair of glowing white eyes peers out at us from beneath the door skin of a nearby tent. The eyes quickly disappear as gawper murmurs carry on the wind. The sounds spread like a catching fire until more eyes appear from other tents and out come the tall, dark shapes of the Lotharians. Curious, they gather around us in the night. Among them are youngsters, males and females, which makes me think this is an entire community, whole families on the road. They fall silent, watching us plod in, and the newcomers with us disperse into the camp.

Magwitch tells us to dismount. Other gawpers step forward to take the horses from us. Gripping her spear, Jade glances nervously around.

'Do not fear,' says Magwitch. 'They will be well cared for and returned to you when you need them. We must gather in the moot tent.'

A female gawper glides gracefully up to us. 'Magwitch has returned.' As she embraces Magwitch, the fires of her eyes burn delicately small.

'Dagmar,' says Magwitch with a softness to his voice I've not heard before. I presume Dagmar is his wife. Do gawpers have husbands and wives? I do not ask, for there is a sense of urgency in the air now that we've arrived. In the shadows gawpers are moving. Several enter the large tent before us at the centre of the camp.

Our hosts dip their heads to the watchers as they pass, also heading for the tent. The other gawpers give the sand cats a wide berth. Leaving the beasts to settle either side of the entrance like a pair of magnificent guards, Magwitch and Deadlock stoop to enter.

Exchanging nervous glances, Jade and I follow.

20. ALARIC

A central fireplace casts the gathering in flickering, golden hues. I ain't never seen a crowd of gawpers before. Not like this. They're a dark mass, like a forest of pines in the night, most of them armed with tall staffs or spears. Our arrival does nothing to lift the sombre air. I feel many eyes upon me. Young gawpers bring us cups of a dark liquid.

'Drink,' says Magwitch before downing half of his.

'What is it?' asks Jade as I give the liquid a dubious sniff.

'It is beer made from the black weed.' Magwitch directs us to the middle of the tent, where we sit. Across the fire, a dozen murmuring gawpers encircle a figure on a bier.

I sip the strange brew and find that it has a rich, earthy flavour, bitter-sweet, with a herbal edge.

'What are they doing?' I ask Magwitch. Deadlock joins them, reaching out a hand towards the gawper at the centre of the huddle.

'This Dagomite has been scraithed. Those gathered are giving of their energy, in the hope of healing.'

'Scraithed?'

'There is no one word for this in your tongue. It means drained, robbed and crushed, all at once.'

'How?' asks Jade.

'Skallagrim, or one of his followers, has done this. Their bah-nackh uses a power, which has to come from somewhere. It is drawn from those closest to the spellcaster and is often fatal. Others lie stricken within our encampment. Many are the buried.'

Wondering how it works, I ask, 'Does it only affect Skallagrim's enemies?'

Four gawpers carry in another of their wounded and others gather around.

'The spellcaster can direct the scraithing,' says Magwitch. 'It can be aimed as a weapon. It is a deed of great evil.'

'Is it in the book?' I whisper. 'My book?'

Magwitch lowers his voice. 'It is surely written in the codex you carry—but listen now and watch.'

I hope for the world that the scraithed gawpers get healed and rise from their biers, but instead, the healing ceremony comes to an abrupt end as other gawpers carry them out, and all eyes turn upon Jade and me.

Matching Deadlock's great height, a commanding gawper with a long face turns from the healing group to stand before us. 'Who is this Magwitch brings into our presence, risking our safety?'

I feel a cold terror descend my gut. I'm about to answer when Magwitch speaks.

'This one is Ebadiah, of whom Magwitch has spoken. Friend of Lotharians, scourge of Skallagrim. The woman, Jade, is a trusted ally.'

'Then, welcome, Ebadiah,' says the commanding gawper. 'Welcome Jade.'

'This one is Robespierre,' says Magwitch. 'Leader of Lotharians.'

I bow my head before asking, 'Is it true that Skallagrim lives? How can you be sure?' I watch the lines of

Robespierre's leathery, black-skinned features but if his expression changes, it's too subtle to read.

He nods solemnly. 'This is truth. We sense him on the fourth plane. Skallagrim yet lives.'

'Are you to fight him?' I ask. 'All of you?'

'Our conflicts have been many, though a deciding battle is inevitable,' he says, leaning upon his staff, which is knotted and carved with gawper runes. 'Our fate will be decided by this.'

'When?' I ask.

'Soon,' says Robespierre. 'Our enemy draws near, though we grow weak from hunger. Will Ebadiah stand with us? Will Jade?'

'We will,' we say together. I'm tempted to tell Robespierre all about the book, there and then, but think better of it when I remember what Magwitch told me. I get a feeling that I can't explain—like a cool wind blowing through a distant, unreachable thought—but it tells me I must not give up the Codex to the Lotharians, however tempting the idea seems.

As Deadlock comes back to us, I think about the barrels of salted fish lying hidden and wasted in the sand, and realise I've been travelling for so long without checking the map that I've lost track of where we are. Taking out my tattered map, I unfold it to show Magwitch. 'Where are we?' I ask.

Magwitch studies it briefly before pointing to a spot with an outstretched claw.

'Here.'

I stare at the location in disbelief.

'Would eleven barrels of salted herring help?'

Robespierre stares at me for a long moment. 'What is this herring?'

'Fish,' I say. 'It would feed many.'

'Do you have it?' he asks.

'It's here.' I point to the location on the map. 'Buried safe in the sand.'

'A day's ride. Perhaps more,' says Magwitch, judging the distance. 'It would be dangerous. Enemy spies are everywhere. They seek to infiltrate our camp.'

'We'd need a cart,' I say.

'A waggon can be found,' says Robespierre. 'Who will go?'

Magwitch's silence leaves me thinking he'd rather not, having only now returned to his family.

'Deadlock will go,' says Deadlock. 'If Robespierre will send him.'

'Take a guard of six, a waggon and horses. Travel by night. Find food. Return.' His command delivered, Robespierre turns to leave.

'So, we're going for the fish?' I ask.

'Ebadiah is to show us where they are hidden,' says Deadlock.

'But you're staying here,' I say to Magwitch.

'Deadlock will keep you safe,' says Magwitch.

Deadlock swallows the dregs from his cup.

'Prepare yourself. We leave within the hour.'

*

Deadlock dumps a folded tent into the back of the waggon with the other baggage before closing the tailgate. Mounting up onto Grimclaw's sleek back, he views our small gathering dourly. Five of his chosen guards—Cerimon, Vipsanius, Pingala, Marcos and the largest, Gadshill—wait on horseback, armed with spears. The sixth is Rhesus, a stooping gawper with mean-looking eyes, who drives the waggon.

'Move out.'

Now the moment has come, I'm nervous. At the edge of the camp, I look back before climbing up onto the bench alongside Rhesus, and Jade.

'You sure about this?' I ask her.

'If you're going, I'm going,' she says.

'You don't need to. You could stay here and rest. Mag-witch would look after you.'

'I don't want to rest.' There's determination in her voice.

Rhesus flicks the reins and the horses plod forward. Our little company moves out through the encompassing trees: a waggon surrounded by six mounted Dagomite spearmen. Harried by a fear of what awaits beyond the relative safety of the camp, I glance behind for a second time, but the forest has already swallowed the view and soon, even the scent of woodsmoke is lost. Here, the trees hamper the moon-light, though the sky is cloudless. It's not until an hour of travelling has passed that the way opens to scrubland, and we pass down a rutted track to a village that slumbers in shadow. We're quiet but not silent. I'd be more comforta-ble if we were. I feel the gentle tramp of the horses and the soft rattle of the waggon would be enough to summon the ghosts of a thousand years. In the surrounding stillness, the sounds seem deafening, yet nothing stirs as we thread our way through, not even the phantoms. Perhaps Deadlock knows the settlement is deserted. I don't know, and I don't ask. I just kind of trust they know what they're doing, and watching every window and door for signs of life, I grip my lance tightly. Jade leans in at my side, resting her head on my shoulder as the trundle of the waggon lulls her to sleep. I'm not sure at what point I fall asleep myself, but I must have eventually relaxed enough to lean my head against hers, too, 'cause the next thing I know, voices startle me awake. They're stern and dangerously loud. When I open my eyes, we've stopped and the gawpers are gathered around.

Deadlock sounds furious. 'The child has endangered us all!'

'What should we do with him?' asks Gadshill from horse-back.

'Turn back,' suggests Marcos.

'Perhaps we should,' says Deadlock, peering intently down at the side of the waggon. I try to see what he's looking at beyond my view. Up ahead on the track, Grimclaw rests, scanning the night like a sentry. 'Come out here. Now, Alaric ag Magwitch!'

I climb down from the driver's bench as a small figure, about half my height and wearing gawper robes, crawls timidly out from beneath the load bed.

'Magwitch?' I ask no one in particular.

'Alaric is the son of Magwitch,' explains Rhesus. 'This child should not be here.'

I guess Alaric has somehow stowed away on the waggon, perhaps hiding with the baggage.

The gawper child hangs his head.

'What do you have to say for yourself?' asks Deadlock.

'Alaric helps get the food. Alaric is fast and strong. Alaric is a warrior.'

Deadlock gestures to Rhesus. 'Turn the waggon.'

'No!' says Alaric, his voice a lighter version of his fathers. 'Don't take me back. Alaric goes with you!'

'Why?' Deadlock towers over the child, who is visibly shaking.

'Alaric wants to help,' says Alaric.

'And what help would this one be?' Deadlock glares.

Vipsanius, the shortest of the gawper guards, says, 'Captain, if we turn back, precious time will be lost. Our enemy is poised to fall upon us in a matter of days.'

'Yet our warriors need food!' says Gadshill.

'Silence!' Deadlock looks around at the nightscape. We're on a muddy track too narrow to call a road, halfway across a field overgrown with tall grasses. A hundred yards to one side, a patch of woodland conceals who knows what. To the other, lies a hedgerow and beyond, a burnt field and a single bombed-out farmhouse. As though to compound the situation, it starts to rain—great, heavy droplets that quickly grow in number so that even before he's finished speaking, we're soaked through. 'This place is too exposed. Take shelter. We shall talk more in a safer place.'

A distant, ominous thunder booms. Unnerved, the horses stamp and neigh. I think about the troopers setting sail from Camdon City's docklands to fight in the war, me left behind with my damaged foot and eye.

'He can ride with us,' I say, feeling bad for the boy.

Slowly, Deadlock's narrowed gaze turns upon me and for a moment he stares. 'Very well.' To the company he says, 'Onward!'

Alaric scrambles up onto the bench beside Jade. I follow and notice he's shivering.

'Are you alright?' I whisper.

He nods. 'Just cold.'

Jade and I close the gaps between us to warm him.

In a moment, Rhesus has turned the waggon towards the ruined house and our company moves on. As we approach, it becomes clear that around three quarters of the building has been smashed. Ain't no one gonna sleep in those bedrooms. The entire roof's gone, the upper floor exposed. I'm guessing there's two—three at most—leaky rooms left downstairs. Looks like we're in for a *fun* night.

We're chilled and wet by the time we get inside with our baggage. The place is empty. Not even a broken chair left for firewood. But it don't matter. Deadlock wouldn't let us light a fire anyway. Out here, the smoke might give us away, even at night. Instead, we huddle on the bare floorboards, trying to keep warm as the first light of dawn rises through the shattered windows. It's easier to sleep once we've dried out a bit. Cerimon takes first watch.

I wake after an hour or so. Across the room, Alaric sleeps curled up. Light falling from an empty window catches on a dagger that pokes out from his cloak. The haft bears a row of symbols I recognise as gawper text. A while later, when he wakes, I quietly ask him about the weapon.

'Father gave it to me,' he tells me. 'This is an heirloom as old as my ancestors. Alaric is honoured to carry it.' Slipping the blade from its sheath, he passes it.

While I'm admiring the dagger, he slips away to the nearby corner where my lance leans against the wall.

'This is razor sharp. A fine blade,' I say.

'Dagomite smiths are highly skilled.'

I turn to find him wielding my lance, thrusting and sparring in play. 'Yah! Yah!'

'Hey! Careful with that!' I hiss. 'And be quiet before—'

We turn at the sound of a deep voice, see Deadlock filling the doorway.

'Put the spear down, child!'

Alaric replaces the lance and sinks against the wall to hug his knees. Deadlock leaves the doorway and a few moments later we hear the gawpers' hushed voices as they consult in another room.

I sit next to Alaric. 'I guess you want to be like your father,' I say to him.

He nods. 'Father has respect among the tribes.'

'You'll have respect, too, one day. It takes time to get that, and you're only young.'

'I'm a Dagomite warrior,' he says defiantly.

'I don't doubt it. Here.' I hand the dagger back to him. 'Look after that. It's a beauty.'

'I want Father to be proud of me.'

'Of course, though I bet he already is. What does it say, the words on the haft?'

'It says Truth. It is the name of the blade.'

When the second night comes around, I'm glad to be leaving the damp, wind-blown house. Deadlock must have decided to take Alaric with us, because no more is said on the matter. We bump along in the waggon for several hours before fording a stream, and I wonder if it's the same one Della and I found. It could be, but I don't see the beach. The waggon's wheels splash through and on we go, into soft-floored woodlands that roll through the landscape. Deadlock directs us off the track to skirt a town. It's slow going, the ground either too boggy or stony and cluttered with trees, but we make it through and back onto a path that plunges into dense forest again, where our tall riders are plagued by low branches.

Every so often, Deadlock pauses, taking a parchment map from his cloak to study. He glances up at the position of the moon and stars when they appear between the trees, before directing the driver, though as the night progresses, clouds scud in to blot the sky and our murky world is further dimmed. I give a cry when the trees before us part to reveal a small settlement that I recognise even in the gloom. At a junction of roads stands a familiar signpost.

'I know this place,' I say.

Raising a claw, Deadlock brings the company to a halt at the treeline.

'The beach is that way,' I add, pointing. 'Fordby Sea Town. That's where I buried the fish. These houses were abandoned when I was last here.'

'There may be enemies lying in wait.' The captain eyes the scattered dwellings with a cold fire in his eyes.

'Wait.' I dig out the slingshot from my coat pocket and load up with a pebble. 'Be ready.' Drawing back the rubber, I let fly at a window across the junction. Glass smashes loudly and tinkles from the frame. Still nothing stirs.

'See?' I say, peering from house to house. 'Noth– '

A deep rumble issues from further in. It's a sound I know well.

'Shriekers!' As the word leaves my mouth, a huge shape lumbers from the shadows between two houses, a second following close behind. From the other side of the hamlet more of the monsters thunder into view, Skallagrim's mark pale on their foreheads. In the darkness beyond rise a collection of glowering, glowing eyes.

'And Darklings!' says one of the six.

Deadlock waves us back into the cover of the trees. 'Retreat.'

'What are they doing here?' I ask, aggrieved.

230

Deadlock rides alongside the waggon. 'Skallagrim has learned there is something we seek.'

'How?' I ask.

'He spies on the fourth plane. His war bird riders watch from the skies. We can only hope he does not know what we have come for. That may yet help us.'

'So, we're not giving up?'

Deadlock's eyes burn fiercely. 'We are not.'

When he leads us back through the woods and off the track, I realise we must be heading for the coast on the northern side of the beach. Sure enough, not half an hour later we arrive at a craggy clifftop overlooking the sea. Deadlock beckons to me and I follow him closer to the edge. It's a vantage point from which we can see the lay of the land, both north and south. To the south, the fish beach stretches out, the dark hulks of its wrecks dotting the sand. We talk alone.

'I fear we have a spy in the company,' he tells me quietly, his eyes narrowing.

'Do you know who?' I ask.

'Deadlock is trying to discern. There is movement on the fourth plane. The spy creeps in shadow.'

From then on, I watch the others with suspicion.

I take the telescope from my bag, with which to scan the dunes below. They're unoccupied, but a little way further in I catch the glimmer of Darklings' eyes and their outlines moving between the domed shapes of a dozen or so tents.

'It's like they're protecting the whole beach,' I tell Deadlock as he extends a scope to view the scene. I search around for shriekers. 'Where are their monsters?'

I take his silence to mean he can't see them either.

He switches focus out onto the sea and something resembling a smile alters his face.

'The fools have left the storm brakers unmanned. We must find a boat.'

We ain't looking for long. Our view of the coast to the north shows us the cove of a fishing village and a little harbour built of concrete and stone. I peruse an array of boats through my telescope, some modest, others large, many wave-broken and half-submerged beneath the tide.

'Come,' says Deadlock.

*

Like most places, the village is empty, the signs of war everywhere. I'm relieved. I don't like stealing from the dead, but it's easier than stealing from the living, who tend to object. When it comes to the boats, no one tries to stop us and we have the pick of the crop. We choose a sturdy-looking fishing boat with a small cabin towards the stern. The deck is large enough for our entire company, so leaving the waggon with the horses tethered, we board and at Deadlock's command, salvage oars and load up around fifty good boards prised from the decks of the surrounding wrecks. With nine hands to the job, it doesn't take long. When I ask him what they're for, he tells me his plan as Alaric and Jade listen in.

'The Darklings have learned we come from the land to the north. They do not expect an approach from the sea. You say the barrels are buried beneath a dune...'

'At the foot of a big dune, on the landward side, aye.'

'Ebadiah will take us there. The company will dig through from the beach side while the Darklings sleep. The dunes will hide us.'

'The boards are for a tunnel?'

Deadlock nods and I glimpse that maybe-smile again.

The gawper boy steps closer. 'Alaric will help.'

'Indeed. You three will stand guard while we dig,' says Deadlock. 'You are small and nimble. This will be your task—three lookouts to warn us of danger.'

The three of us exchange glances and nod.

Grimclaw ain't keen on the boat. He paces and growls objections, so Deadlock leaves him behind to guard the horses. I've a feeling he'd eat them if it wasn't for the psychic connection with his master. Once the boat is fully loaded, the six loose the mooring ropes and push us away from the dockside before taking to the oars. They take us out and around the headland, keeping well clear of the rocks before the long beach comes into view. It's eerily quiet with nothing but the sound of the oars slipping through the water and the lapping of small waves hitting the bow.

'Eyes to the open sea,' says Deadlock. The gawpers hide the glowing of their eyes by turning their faces seaward. Stealthily, we cross the shallows between the storm brakers and the beach.

Alaric glances my way, fear welling in his shimmering eyes.

'Remember, you are a warrior,' I whisper to him. 'Do what Deadlock tells you and you'll be alright.'

The boy nods but seems no less afraid. Jade takes his hand, though fearing what lies ahead, he glances back towards the beach.

'Look away, child,' says Deadlock, and Alaric obeys.

Our voyage is short and the sea relatively calm. For a time, Jade and I are the eyes of the company, guiding our way. With the six rowing strongly, the boat slides quickly to shore and the slight surf pitches the vessel gently onto the soft sand. Our gawpers leap from the gunwale to drag the boat further in and without a word, begin hefting the boards up towards the dunes. Deadlock gestures for me to show them the place, but it's dark and I worry the dunes may have shifted since I was last here. For a moment I'm lost and think I may never find the barrels, but then my eye settles upon the halker that first held them. I hurry to look it over and satisfied that's it's the same ship, peer up the beach and point to the nearest large dune.

'There. The barrels are in the ground on the other side,' I whisper. 'Wait. I left a marker.' I hurry up the dune and lie flat to the sand near the crest to look down at the board still sticking up from the sand. Returning to Deadlock I confirm it's the right dune.

I've seen the caverns that gawpers have used, and been in tunnels and chambers they've excavated, but I've never actually seen gawpers dig. Not until now. There's a reason their leathery fingers end in substantial claws rather than fragile nails, like those of people. It was an adaptation necessary for surviving in the sands of Mors Zonam. Their large hands tear into the damp sand with great powerful swipes and in what seems like no time, create a hole. Their efforts are silent but for the faintest swish of sand in the air as it's flung aside. I have no idea why they're so confident their tunnel will hold, until one of the six takes something from beneath his cloak and lights it.

A firebomb!

The others leave the hole. The gawper ignites the bomb before hurling it in. The resulting blast turns the sand to glass.

Deadlock glances around at the dunes. 'Go now. Keep watch.' We set off but I feel his hand on my shoulder. 'Tread lightly upon the sand,' he says.

Jade, Alaric and I look at the expanse of sand with concern. Cautiously, we climb the dunes and, looking back, I glimpse a gawper carry in the first of the boards to shore-up the glass-walled tunnel entrance. Reaching the crest, we drop low in the lyme grass to peer over the Darkling camp. All is quiet. I find myself thinking, *This will be easy.*

Down behind us, the Lotharians dig on, blaze more sand to glass, shore-up with boards, and repeat.

The three of us sit exposed on the peak. Looking around, I reckon we'd be safer watching from a few lower positions that still offer good views of the Darkling camp—somewhere our bodies are not breaking the skyline. I gesture for Jade to move down to the right and for Alaric to go further to the left. Spotting a bushy strand of lyme grass a little closer to the camp, I slip down the far side of the dune to hide there with my lance. The other two take up their new positions and there we wait, watching.

For an hour we hold our positions and with that wait comes a new fear. We're running out of night. As the first hint of dawn dapples the horizon, a tension settles over me, a tightness that feels as though an invisible net is closing in. My feet are like ice when a pebble hits my back. Turning, I see Deadlock's silhouette peering cautiously over the mound of the dune, and scramble quickly back over to join him on the seaward side.

There's an urgency in his whisper. 'The barrels are found. The six are digging them out. We leave soon.'

Below us, one of the six leaves the tunnel, rolling a barrel to the boat. As he returns, another appears from the entrance. I watch as they load a second and a third barrel quickly aboard, before I head back to look for Jade and Alaric. I'm nearing the peak of the large dune when a tremor in the sand makes me turn. Down on the beach, one of the six stands frozen, stooping over a barrel. A look of concern flashes across Deadlock's face.

For a breath, no one moves.

But then the dune to my left erupts. My heart jolts. A shriek splits the night and, to my right, another dune bursts apart, sand flying.

'Alaric! Jade!' I run, my boots churning up the slow mountain of sand. All down the beach, the soft dunes appear to explode, as though from a barrage of bombs. From beneath, the splayed horns and green-grey skin of Skallagrim's squealing monsters arise.

'No!' The word escapes me.

'To the sea!' Deadlock runs for the boat as an orange glow lights the air over the Darkling camp. A moment later they send their firebombs arching over the dunes. Our gawpers scramble for the safety of the surf as orbs of flame rain down across the beach. Shriekers close in as fear streams into my blood. The first of the six immerse themselves in the waves before returning to continue loading the boat. I glimpse Deadlock, his arms outstretched, steering the falling bombs aside with the focus of his mind.

'Hurry!' he cries between bombardments. 'The last barrel...'

Rolling the eleventh barrel, a gawper hurries from the tunnel. He runs halfway across the beach before a plummeting sphere of flame engulfs him. The sounds of his screams twists my gut and I turn to search for Alaric and Jade. To my side, the hulking form of a shrieker breaks the dune ridge, its cry ringing in my ears. I feel its thunderous approach vibrating the sand. Another blaze of light comes, and another terrible scream, but I can't turn back. The others are out here somewhere, closer to the Darkling threat, and I must find them.

Jade appears ahead, her form a slight shadow darting down a dune as, beyond, Darklings advance on us from the camp. I see Alaric then, in the light of the firebombs as they flash overhead. He's sunk up to his shoulders in the loose sand of a shrieker's burrow.

Digging frantically, he calls out, 'Help me!'

Jade's nearly there but the Darklings are closer, the first of them almost upon him. I hoist my lance and launch it. *Thrump!* It strikes, lodging deep. The Darkling staggers back with the impact before falling to the sand.

Reaching Alaric, Jade grabs his outstretched claws and pulls, though he's stuck fast. A moment later I'm there, hauling Alaric's arms with Jade, and his body loosens and shifts in the sand. On the Darklings come, a tide of imminent death.

'Heave!'

We heave and, at last, Alaric slides free as the Darklings move in. I make a dash for my lance. Alaric uses his gawper powers to blow a storm cloud of sand at the Darklings' eyes.

They raise their arms to shelter their faces. Behind them, a second line of oncoming Darklings appear, these holding firebombs in their thrall. Darkness dispels as more and more of the incendiaries take flame. The three of us turn but stop before a shrieker that blocks our path. The creature roars and shrieks. Ducking away, we scurry along the sand-slippery hill to avoid the beast as fire streaks the dawn, and climbing with all our strength, make for the peak. The beast turns, lurches and screams, lunging as we pass, but we're quicker. Reaching the downward slope, we rush for the boat through the firestorm, while shriekers charge after us onto the flat expanse of sand.

'Move!' cries Deadlock.

With the barrels stowed, our remaining gawpers shove the boat into the shallows. The surf drags at our legs as we wade in to pull ourselves up and over the gunnels. Two of our gawper guards lift a burned fellow into the bow as Deadlock reaches the boat. Glancing behind, I see our fallen guard lying dead and burning.

Clambering aboard, we row for our lives.

21. LOTHARIANS

The waggon horses whinny at our arrival as the gawpers guide the fishing boat in and lash the mooring lines. Watched by the great sand cat, we hurry ashore and soon have the cargo transferred to the waggon, along with the wounded gawper. As they lift him in, I ask, 'Will he live?'

'Cerimon will survive.'

I think of the body burning on the beach and look around at the faces of the others. 'So Gadshill was the one we left behind?'

'This is truth,' he says with a sorrowful look. 'Gadshill was a great warrior.'

At Deadlock's word, Rhesus gives the reigns a skip and the horses pull away. The captain mounts Grimclaw as the waggon rolls out from the fishing village. Soon, we're bearing north to distance the company from the Darklings, who are presumably hunting for us in the growing daylight.

For a while I'm quiet. Ain't in the mood for talking.

'Drive the horses!' says Deadlock. Rhesus coaxes the horses to speed. Our waggon clatters down an old, cobbled street that becomes a country lane and then a forest track.

For two hours we travel without stopping, but eventually Deadlock gives the word and Rhesus slows the horses. The forest has grown thick around us, the dense canopy of evergreens concealing us and giving a little shelter from the wind and rain. Fifty feet in from the track, we hide for the rest of the day, our ears primed for the sounds of pursuers.

When we set off at nightfall, Deadlock drives us hard. It feels reckless, but he seems more determined than ever to deliver the barrels with all speed.

Our hasty night's travel brings us to the rebel camp as a red dawn breaks. Gawpers gather around the waggon, eager to see what we bring. They share out the fish and it feels good to watch them eat. After that, everywhere we go, gawpers greet us with cups raised and with words of cheer as we pass their campfires, though recalling the death of Gadshill, we struggle to share their celebration.

I accompany Deadlock to deliver Alaric to his parents. The boy stares at his feet as his father takes him by the shoulders.

'Foolish child! Go to your mother.'

Dagmar is kinder, embracing Alaric and leading him away while Magwitch thanks us for returning him.

Once rested, we're called again to meet in the moot tent and there gather around the fire. Magwitch draws Deadlock aside to talk in whispers. Trying to eavesdrop, I catch but a single word: *spy*.

The two rejoin the group. We're listening to discussions about the coming conflict when a stillness descends over the gathering, and Deadlock turns his head in one quick motion, searching the gawpers standing opposite.

'A spy is among us,' he says with quiet assurance. I can't tell how he knows, though the others seem to understand. Deadlock has noticed something, perhaps, on one of the *planes*. Closing his eyes, he appears to enter a state of meditation. His body becomes perfectly still. What comes next happens so fast I barely perceive it. His eyes blink open into sharp focus. The gawper on the receiving end of Deadlock's gaze gasps as his staff is ripped from his clawed hand by an unseen force. The staff lands across the tent as other gawpers leap aside. The spy squeals—a sound like steel on steel—and Deadlock launches himself across the fire to pin him to the ground.

'This one has betrayed us,' says Deadlock. 'This one must be taken.'

A nearby gawper steps away from the accused. 'Marcos, is this truth?'

'This one has deceived us all!' says another.

'Restrain this one!' cries yet another.

'Take him,' says Deadlock.

At his command, others move in to take hold of Marcos and drag him out of the moot tent.

'What did he do?' I ask.

'This one is reporting our preparations to Tacitus,' says Deadlock. 'He is the one who informed the enemy of our journey for the fish. Deadlock has seen it on the planes.'

'What will they do to him?' I ask Magwitch.

'He will be confined until the war is over.'

I think about what the gawper said on the road. *Our enemy is poised to fall upon us in a matter of days.* 'Will we win the battle?' I ask.

Magwitch is slow to answer. 'None can say. Skallagrim's followers are more numerous than the Lotharians. He holds sway over the beasts, though we shall not give up while yet we live.'

The room around us slowly empties as gawpers return to their tents. All of a sudden, I have a strong desire to see the enemy and know exactly what stands against us.

'Robespierre said the enemy is near,' I say. 'Are you watching them?'

'The spies who were last sent out did not return,' says Magwitch.

'Then we should go and see for ourselves, don't you think?' I turn to Jade. 'Don't you want to see what we're facing?'

'That would be dangerous,' says Magwitch, his eyes dimming to an intense smoulder. 'Remember the beasts that hunt you.'

'We're not afraid, are we?' I look to Jade.

She folds her arms and throws Magwitch a determined look.

'Show us.'

*

An hour past midnight, the three of us mount up and leave the rebel camp: Magwitch, Jade and me. Magwitch leads the way, riding Doom through the trees and over a high stony ridge. The land beyond softens, sinking down into a valley and onto a course of low, rolling hills. We keep to the lowland, following the great cat and its silent rider along a murky path. Magwitch seems pensive.

'Are we close yet?' I ask, breaking the quietness.

'A few miles more and we shall see the camp.' He's nothing but a black shape in the moonlight. 'Magwitch has not yet thanked Ebadiah and Jade for saving the life of his foolish son.'

'It was nothing. But I don't think him foolish. He's just too keen.' I don't know what else to say.

'It was a worthy deed. Dagmar and Magwitch are forever grateful. The child should never have gone with you. He must be punished.'

'I think being grilled by Deadlock was probably punishment enough,' says Jade.

'Aye.' I nod and grin.

'You would not punish him further for his disobedience?' asks Magwitch, seeming troubled.

'I don't know,' I admit. 'It must be hard, being a parent.'

Magwitch shrugs and we ride on for another hour or so. When we break the crest of a wooded hill, our guide dismounts from his sand cat to draw us off the path.

'Keep low,' he says, narrowing his eyes.

At his direction, we tether the horses to a nearby tree and crawl on our bellies out onto a ridge that overlooks another hill. This one is dotted with dark tents like those of the Lotharian camp. Points of firelight speckle the slopes and streak the star-peppered sky with smoke.

'Behold, Skallagrim's army,' he says, watching the enemy camp, his eyes glowering.

I shiver at the sight. The camp is huge and all around the lower slopes are what at first glance look like herds of sheep, cattle or pigs—animals all gathered to feed an army, perhaps. But studying the scene, I realise they're not livestock at all. They're rank after rank of Skallagrim's beasts: wolves, morhs, slinks, shriekers and other terrible creatures from Mors Zonam or from foreign lands. I take out my telescope to focus in on them, though it's too dark for much detail.

'Blinders.' My heart sinks. We're outnumbered by the gawpers alone, but with the monsters... 'What chance do we stand?'

'We must not concede,' says Magwitch. 'We Lotharians will fight to the death if need be.'

I nod. 'Is Skallagrim there?'

'My instincts tell me no, though he may arrive at any time to lead his legions.'

'He's using the war birds,' I say. 'He could fly in whenever he wants. I reckon there'll be others riding the birds.' Through the scope I see more of the creatures coming in from the surrounding woods and fields to swell the ranks.

'There must be a way to defeat them,' says Jade.

'The Lotharians must find a way.' Magwitch takes a telescope from beneath his robes and extends it to scan the camp. 'He is gathering his animal hoards. It is a bad sign. He will march soon.'

I think of the book and the looming battle. I could sure use more time to study the Codex.

'We must leave.' Magwitch retreats through the under-growth back into the cover of the trees, and we follow. 'Come. We will tell Robespierre what we have seen.'

*

G uards call Robespierre from his bed. He lurches dourly from his private quarters to lead us through the Lotharian camp and into the moot tent once more. The entrance is now guarded by two gawpers armed with spears.

'What is so important that you disturb my slumber?' he asks.

'Our time is shorter than we thought,' says Magwitch as we gather around the embers of a waning fire. 'Skallagrim musters his beasts.'

'More arrive each passing moment,' I say. 'A great number preparing to march.'

'How long do we have?' asks Robespierre.

'I would say a day at most,' says Magwitch. 'We should not delay. Skallagrim's hill overflows. The slopes below are full of his creatures.'

'Then the time has come,' says Robespierre, nodding with an air of regret. 'We may hide in the shadows no more. Rest a while. We march at dawn.' He turns away to speak briefly with the guards, who then hurry away.

'It seems we are going to war,' says Magwitch, turning to us. Dagmar and her two children enter the tent. Running to us, Alaric throws his arms around Jade and me. The younger one, a timid girl, is more cautious.

'This is Elke ag Magwitch,' says Dagmar as Elke clutches her mother's robes. The little one's large eyes remain fixed upon us. 'I hear you have already met Alaric the trouble-maker.' Dagmar bows low to the ground. 'Alaric tells me he owes his life to you both. You have my gratitude, always. We have prepared a tent for you.'

Alaric remains close and takes Jade's hand in his.

'Come,' says Dagmar, turning away.

They lead us through the camp to our tent. Inside, we drop our bags and make ready to sleep, but I'm restless and filled with a sense of urgency I can't explain. Dagmar sets Elke down and the girl eagerly takes Alaric's hand. When Dagmar calls for them at the entrance, they move deeper into the tent, watching for her reaction.

'They desire to remain with you for a time. Is this well?' asks Dagmar.

I tell her I don't mind.

'We'll watch them,' says Jade, seeming as intrigued by the gawper children as they are by us.

Before leaving, their mother tells them not to stay too long. Jade begins stitching a tear in her bag, working by the light of the fire.

I can't think of anything to say to the youngsters, or how we might satisfy their curiosity, but soon Alaric glides across to my bag and begins poking around inside. When I step close to take the Codex, he flinches and withdraws.

'It's alright. I don't mind.'

He's soon back, his long, clawed fingers probing the remaining contents. Sitting on the ground, he takes out the ink bottle and Roach's old fire-starting kit, examining each piece with great interest and sniffing at them before placing them down. Elke joins him on the floor by Jade, watching her work. The next item Alaric finds is the set of pipes.

'What is this?' He studies them closely, though when his breath plays an accidental note, he drops them and leaps away.

'They're pipes. You know, for making music.' I collect the pipes and gesture for him to come back. As he settles by his sister, I begin a playful tune and the white flames of their eyes brighten, warm and dance. I pipe another tune stolen from Roach, this one a gentle melody that always brought me peace.

The children lull where they sit, seeming entranced. I find myself sinking back into that peaceful retreat somewhere in a far corner of my mind, and it's as though the tune I'm hearing is being played not by myself but by Roach—like the memory of a bird that's been plucked from my head by another and released. And I hear a voice, though it ain't Roach's. It's a voice like a distant whisper.

Take up your pen, Ebadiah. Take up your pen and write.

And I begin to catch a glimpse of what I must do.

A few minutes later, I'm shaken from my trance when Dagmar returns to collect her children, though she's loaded with folds of the gawpers' black fabric. She kneels to present the bundle to us.

'Dagomite robes, altered for your stature. They will guard against fire.'

Approaching, I hesitate. 'But they're made from the black weed. Should they not be ground for bread to feed the army?'

A shadow falls across Dagmar's face.

'These robes belonged to the fallen. They may not be ground for bread.'

Thanking her, we take the hooded cloaks to try them on, and find they've been trimmed to the perfect length.

Dagmar gathers Elke into her arms as the child clings around her neck, but Alaric glides to me and anchors himself by taking my hand.

'Alaric stay, learn music.'

'Come now, Alaric,' says Dagmar, but the boy remains. 'We must leave our guests in peace.' When he refuses to go, she says, 'It seems he is fond of you.'

'They ain't no trouble,' I say.

'Alaric?' She gives the boy a long stare and her eyes seem to simmer. Relinquishing my hand, he goes to her.

'Rest well,' she says with what I take to be an apologetic look, and she leaves with Alaric in tow.

I return the book to Roach's old bag, though it's as though it's taunting me. I see a corner of it protruding from the fabric, and it seems to call my name as that song continues to ebb and flow in my mind. There's something I must do, something I must find or learn or read.

Take up your pen and write.

I must write! This I feel as much as hear, though why or how is beyond me. Yet there it is, nonetheless: an undeniable notion. But write what? And suddenly a fog lifts and all becomes clear—as clear as the fire that some kind gawper has set for us at the centre of our tent. I must write a piece of ma-jick, a nackh-sahar of my own making.

With a new sense of purpose, I take out the Codex and flip through its pages. Where to start? I don't know. I'll need a new page but turning to the back of the book, I see there are no blank pages. The writer, scribe or bookbinder has collated a work complete. To add a page with a new nackh-sahar— which is what I'm now convinced I must do—I'll have to find a sheet of parchment and somehow fix it in place. Why does it matter? I cannot say. I only know that it *does* matter. It matters a great deal.

A quick study of the Codex's spine tells me the pages are bound with stitches, so that is how the new page must be added. I delve into Roach's bag and find the few loose pieces of parchment that were with the letters he wrote. There's a small bottle of ink and a quill also—everything I need— except the words, of course. And they're the hard bit.

Across the tent, Jade lays out a bed of blankets and coats.

'What are you doing now?' she asks as I rummage purposefully through the bag.

'I ain't sure,' I say, selecting the best of the loose pages which is a good match in size to those of the Codex. I change my mind and take a dog-eared sheet instead: I'll need to draft out the text in rough before writing it up neatly on the good piece. 'Though I have an idea. I'm going to try some ma-jick of my own.'

'Do you think that's wise?'

'I don't know what I'm thinking. I'm just following a notion.'

'You'll probably get yourself killed.'

'Quite possibly.'

I don't know if my hastily learned knowledge of the ancient language is good enough, or if my attempt at a nackh-sahar will actually work. How does any of the ma-jick from the Codex work? I don't know, neither do I dwell on it. For days I've been wondering if the book can somehow help us in our fight against Skallagrim and his followers, and now I think this is it. In fact, I'm certain. Just don't ask me how. Driven by some force beyond my ken, I begin work as Jade settles down to sleep.

Of course, it helps to have the examples of nackh-sahar already in the book. I refer to them constantly while trying my hand, stealing parts from various forms and mixing them with others. There come moments when I feel entirely lost with little understanding to the symbols I write—for Magwitch could only explain them in part—and at other times I have an irrational confidence, and sense I'm being led by a greater power. In those moments the words flow from the quill as though someone else is guiding my hand. I can only hope that is it the Great Elder Light that Roach spoke about. I know with certainty that it is not Skallagrim, for there ain't that sense of dread I felt in his presence. Only peace in my mind.

When the entire nackh-sahar is written, I return to the beginning and make corrections and amendments. I change the skitzerhelm and rewrite the entire fruhazen. The bra-hadran seems good as it is. Don't ask me how I know... I just do. And I sense the omnadran needs shortening. I finish and stare at the page with an unaccountable feeling that it is complete, and somehow—inexplicably—perfect.

When I've copied it all out neatly on the good page in a style to match the other writing in the book, I wake Jade, who blinks at me in the firelight. She looks beautiful and I wish we were not about to go to war against an entire gawper army and a hoard of monsters. I wish we could just stay here and that the night would not end.

'Is it time?'

'Not yet,' I say. 'But I have a job for you.' I show her the finished page and explain that I need it stitched into the book.

'Why can't you do it?' she asks, rubbing her eyes irritably. 'This is the third time I've mended this.' She shows me the repaired tear in her bag. 'I must be doing something wrong.'

'Well, you stitch better than me,' I say. 'I can barely thread a needle. Only one eye, remember?'

She takes the page from me. 'It's hard to forget.'

*

Dawn breaks over the horizon, setting the distant clouds ablaze with a fiery light. I think of the coming battle. There'll be fire enough. Across the dew dampened camp, word has spread that the Lotharian army will now move out and gawpers everywhere ready themselves.

A sudden horn blast jolts me—the call to march.

'Already?' The night has slipped away like sand between my fingers.

The vanguard begins to file out of the camp in a line four gawpers deep, an imposing sight. While the first of them move along a path and disappear into the trees, I help Jade up onto Brimstone before mounting Gun. We leave most of our things in the tent and carry our lances. The mares are skittish around so many moving gawpers. I rein Gun in, whisper softly in her ear and stroke her neck.

'It's alright.'

The Tanak Codex sits in Roach's bag slung around my shoulder, with its new page stitched carefully in place. How it might help us against the guile of Skallagrim and his multitude, I can only wonder.

'Jade and Ebadiah will ride with us,' says Deadlock as Magwitch and Dagmar embrace.

We join the line with our gawper friends and ride, unspeaking, yet of one mind, and up ahead the formation pauses as a horse-drawn waggon trundles from the woods to join the line. Another and another follow quickly behind before Robespierre appears, imposing on a great grey horse and calling orders to his men. Behind him stream rows of other horse-mounted gawpers—too many to count—each one armed with a long spear and carrying a circular shield of polished black wood. A dozen more waggons follow before the sand cat riders emerge from the trees to join the line. My spirits rise as my jaw drops.

'How many?' I ask, watching them pad out, four abreast like the foot soldiers.

'Our cat riders number but forty,' says Magwitch. 'The cats are hard to find in the wilds of Mors Zonam, and harder to master.'

It doesn't matter. The sight leaves me in a state of awe. 'Does Skallagrim have sand cats?'

Magwitch glances at me knowingly and, I think, with a hint of pride. 'He does not. Neither Skallagrim nor his followers have the required skill.'

'Could the Lotharians not use more beasts, like Skallagrim?' I ask then.

'We Lotharians will not do this.'

'But the sand cats...'

'Our riders commune with their cats on the fourth plane,' he explains. 'This cannot be achieved with just any creature. Skallagrim forces control of his beasts through bah-nackh. It is a cruelty that sets us apart.'

'We ride,' says Deadlock.

Following his lead, we spur our mounts on to join the cat riders at the end of their line. More carts and waggons file in behind us, their contents hidden beneath covers.

'What's in them?' I ask.

'They carry tents, supplies and weapons,' says Magwitch.

Glancing back at the emptying camp, I see those left behind: gawper women and children, sombre and silent amid the drifting smoke of the campfires.

We ride in silence for a time, our forced pace slow to match that of the foot soldiers up ahead. Gun settles into an easy rhythm that allows me to take out the Codex and in my saddle with my lance propped over my shoulder, I read through the new page. I start to memorise the nackh-sahar line by line, while keeping the book low and as hidden from other gawpers as a can. But riding at my side, Magwitch sees me studying it and I glimpse what I take to be a wry smile.

'Will he be there in person?' I ask.

'Skallagrim will be there. He is powerful yet must remain close to control such a vast army of Dagomites and beasts. Skallagrim *must* be there.'

'Good,' I say with a nod. 'Can you get me close to him?'

'This one has a plan.'

'I have something to try, though I don't know if it'll work.'

'Ebadiah should not gamble his life.'

'It ain't a gamble,' I say, thinking back to the way I felt the quill being guided in my hand. 'More like a hope.'

'Is hope enough?' asks Magwitch.

His question goes unanswered as we ride in line. We track what must be a similar path to the journey we took the night before, only now it looks very different in the daylight. We pass ruined villages—the small streets strewn with the dead—and traverse a landscape of once-green hills, now blackened and burned, pitted with the craters of Urthian bombs. The corpses of dragons and war birds rot in the sun alongside the broken remains of the invaders' airships.

Closing my eyes, I glimpse it in my mind's eye at a happier time, when the streets ran with life: children play games, dance and sing. Men and women stroll arm in arm, and ponies pull carts piled high with harvested crops. I sense a presence nearby, a black dog with pointed ears, a wolfish face that sometimes looks like a bear's. I glimpse the shadows of his running paws and turn to look, but when I open my eyes, he's gone, the ruins have returned, and I see again the work of Skallagrim all around. My heart feels like lead, its weight bent on crushing me.

'Skallagrim must die,' I mutter, wiping moisture from my eyes.

Magwitch nods. 'It is the only way.'

'Promise me this,' I say to him quietly. 'If I should get close to him but fail, destroy the book. He mustn't be allowed to reclaim it.'

He nods. 'Magwitch will do as the brave one asks.'

22. THE HILL

The longer we ride the more I'm convinced I ain't no ma-jicker. I've too many questions and with Roach gone, no one to answer. Magwitch and Deadlock can teach me a little of the ancient language, but they don't know ma-jick. In truth, they understand the book no more than I.

When I use the nackh-sahar, must I say it aloud? Does the target of the ma-jick need to hear what's said? Are there other things I must do to make it work? I realise I need to trial it and practice, that I really know very little at all, and I'm surely doomed to fail. What was I thinking! And yet, the one thing I'm sure of is that this nackh-sahar is for Skalla-grim. The Great Elder Light has told me so.

Riding in my saddle, I can do little but learn the words and watch the landscape roll slowly by. We thread a low path through burned forest and on into a valley to edge a babbling brook. At the peak of the following hill, Robespierre calls the line to a halt as the enemy camp comes into view. There's no attempt at stealth with our approach. Ain't no point. Skalla-grim will have sensed our presence before we even reached the hill. He probably knew the moment we set out. I don't know everything about gawpers but of this I'm sure.

Robespierre gives a command.

'Make camp.'

The line breaks and gawpers all around get to work.

'Are we not going to attack?' I ask.

'We will prepare. Robespierre will call for his captains and send out his spies. He has brought us to this hill because it is directly to the east of the enemy camp. If it is possible, he will wait until morning, and strike when the low sun is in our enemies' eyes.'

'But if Robespierre knows this, won't Skallagrim know it, too?'

'He knows, though Skallagrim believes he cannot lose, and *that* is another disadvantage he carries.'

Jade and I help pitch a tent that's large enough for the two of us, Deadlock and Magwitch. An hour or so later, the captains are called to Robespierre's tent. We follow and are given the honour of joining the meeting. I can only imagine that Magwitch has spoken well of us and that Robespierre has become convinced of our loyalty. Eight captains gather in all. Robespierre listens to them talk.

'Skallagrim will not leave his advantage of high ground. We would be foolish to leave ours.'

'But if we do not move, we cannot engage.'

'And Skallagrim will take Lotharians one bite at a time. He will send covert forces in surprise attacks to weaken our number.'

'We must devise a strategy,' says Deadlock—a voice of reason that seems to go unheard.

'Our number is already weak.'

'Skallagrim must be made to pay for his insolence. We must attack now before he grows stronger still—or all hope of victory is lost!'

'Victory? What victory can possibly lay ahead? He will crush us. Have you not seen his swarms? His forces are already too great.'

Magwitch drums the ground with the butt of his staff. 'Enough! We cannot afford to lose hope now. It is the one thing that will surely be our doom.' He glares at his fellow captains.

In the brief silence, Robespierre looks around at his council and his gaze falls upon Jade and me. 'What say the humans?'

'Deadlock is right,' says Jade. 'Our only hope of victory is in a clever strategy. We're outnumbered.'

I try to think of what Michael would have said. 'Skallagrim is strong, but he knows it. We should use that against him.'

'Yet what strategy?' asks Robespierre.

Deadlock speaks. 'Attack him where he sits on his hill but feign a retreat. Draw his army down into the valley. Divide his ranks and fight them on level ground.'

'That would at least remove one advantage,' says Magwitch, nodding.

The discussion continues for the remains of the day and on into the night. Robespierre's spies return to report the finer details of Skallagrim's camp and the positions of his hoards. When there is finally a general agreement upon the plan and the captains disperse, Robespierre turns to us.

'With whom will you ride? Magwitch or Deadlock? You must make your choice.'

Jade and I confer briefly.

'Magwitch,' I say.

'Very well,' says Robespierre. 'I place you in his charge.'

'How may we best serve you in battle?' Jade asks Magwitch. 'We ain't got powers like you gawpers.'

'Though you are strong, small and quick,' says Magwitch. 'Perhaps these ones could help supply the front line. You will need your cloaks of the black weed.'

*

At first light our rebel army advances down from the camp on the hill, eight captains, eight divisions, and at their head, Robespierre astride his pale war horse, flanked by a cohort of spear guards. A hundred yards to our left, Deadlock leads his sand cat riders. Beside us, Magwitch rides Doom. War birds carry spies in the dawn-reddened sky. Across the valley on Skallagrim's hill a sudden commotion draws our attention. It's followed by a series of resonant horn blasts that send birds into the air from the nearby forest.

'They order ranks to engage,' says Magwitch.

Garbed in our gawper cloaks, Jade and I watch it happen as we ride closer, descending the slope of our hill and all too soon reaching the flood plain of the valley floor. If Skalla-grim's army falls for our ruse, this will be the killing ground.

From the hilltop ahead, more of the war birds take to the air, these bearing darkling warriors. We ride in a formation that encompasses a pair of waggons, our mounts picking their way across a small stream before crossing more of the valley floor to begin the climb on the far side. The wooden wheels clatter over wet stones. I shudder at the sight of shriekers, morh-beasts and wolves awaiting our arrival as fear pervades my mind. The air turns foul with the stink of beasts.

Magwitch withdraws his hood. His hair—thick, black and banded—falls beyond his shoulders. His skin is like black leather in the morning light.

'Our enemy is near. Do you fear death?'

His eyes narrow and gleam with an intense fire.

'I do.'

'It is what he wants. Cast it from your mind.'

I try, though it ain't so easy.

There must be other beasts among the enemy lines, hid-den somewhere in the grim mass that is the force gathered against us. Watching them muster, my hope falters at the sight. *What chance do we have?*

'Halt,' cries Magwitch, while we are still a good way from the enemy. 'Stay the waggons.' He dismounts.

The gawpers driving the waggon horses rein them to a halt. Other gawpers ram wooden chocks behind the wheels and throw back the hide covers. The load bed of the nearest waggon is filled with blackened ceramic pots.

'Sulfurium incendiaries,' says Magwitch. 'Firebombs.' Reaching the waggon, he takes a bomb and tosses it into my hands. I fumble the catch, for a moment fearing the thing might explode. It's heavy. The pot has been filled with some-thing, the opening sealed with hide, and the entire outside coated in pitch. A grainy substance adheres to the dried sur-face and I smell the pungent, metallic scent of gunpowder, realise that I've already seen the bombs used to devastating affect on the fish beach and up at Firth Glaggan. And that Roach and I had felt their impact on the steam truck as we'd fled the darklings.

Magwitch seems to sense my reticence.

'Be in no doubt, our enemies will use these against us. Such is Dagomite warfare.' He reaches out to the second cart and takes a waterskin as others gather to do the same. This skin he holds over my head, so I don't really see what he does next, though I'm quickly soaked beneath a sudden, cold torrent. In a moment, all around me there are gawpers doing the same to themselves—releasing water to drench their bodies, their heads, their cloaks and shields. I notice the gawper robes seem to remain damp, holding the water. Mag-witch saturates himself before taking another waterskin with which to drench Doom, who complains with an indignant roar and a body shake. Lastly, he soaks Jade with water and tells her, 'Stay with the waggons, be ready with the incendi-aries.'

Jade nods and a quietness descends over us. I look up to see an ill-looking grey fog creeping down the hill. It rolls and thickens to envelope the enemy before spooling on towards us.

'Ebadiah, with me until our first volleys fly,' says Magwitch in a soft voice. 'This is Skallagrim's conjuring.' To his warriors he announces, 'Do not fear. It is nothing but mist.'

Still, the effect is clear. Our gawpers hesitate and view the approaching fog with apprehension as they collect fire-bombs. Horses neigh and snort. Doom hisses a warning and claws at the ground. And then they come: fireballs, hurtling at us through the air from the higher ground. They burst on impact, though this first volley mostly falls short. Gawpers who scatter from the flames, return to dowse their less fortunate companions. Gun rears at a fire burst nearby. I cling to her mane and steady my lance.

'Forward!' commands Magwitch and his gawper division obeys. We advance blind into the thickening fog. My hands tremble as I ride and glance back at Jade by the waggons.

The sounds of the enemy reach us. The first part of our plan has worked: keen for blood, they've been drawn further down the hill, closer to the level ground. A shrill scream rises, quickly swallowed by the din of battle cries. It begins in the enemy ranks but is soon joined by the calls of our Lotharians. The noise is deafening.

It begins.

A gawper atop a huge morh-beast comes charging out of the fog, spear levelled. I thrust my lance up to meet them but Gun balks in terror as they loom up in the murk before us. It's all I can do to hang on. The gawper's spear flashes past, an inch from my head, withdraws. Sweeping the blow aside with my lance, I reverse the weapon to hammer the gawper square beneath the chin. Head flying back, he tumbles from his mount.

In the chaos I turn about. Horses plunge and rear. Beasts roar. The smell of blood and guts fills the air, and all around the battlelines clash in a thunderous blur.

Now the riderless morh leaps and I'm ready with my lance, skewering the beast's neck as its weight bears down. Clinging to the haft, I'm dragged with the beast as it falls. The impact with the ground jolts my entire body. Unhorsed, I force myself to rise, and yank the lance free with a gout of hot blood. The creature's eyes grow dim.

I reach for Gun, but the next enemy is already upon me: a wolf bent on killing, its eyes crazed. There's nothing inside, it's a shell driven by another's command—senseless and unthinking. It will be easily fooled—I see that and know what to do. Lowering my lance, I let the beast sense a chance to take me. As it launches, I spin on me heel, whip the lance around and thrust the tip between the wolf's open jaws. It lodges deep within. There's a sickening, sucking sound as I drag the blade free and make a grab for Gun's reins.

At my side, Magwitch and two of his gawpers surround a shrieker, stabbing with their spears while one flank of the monster burns from an exploded firebomb. The creature shrieks and squeals before a deadly thrust from Magwitch brings it to a lumbering stop. Magwitch heaves his spear free of the creature's ribs.

Something hits me from the left, throwing me to the ground. Dazed, I grope for purchase in the slick mud, slip, slide, try to breath but my lungs are stunned. I roll onto my back, gasping.

Breath! Breath!

War birds swoop from the skies, plucking warriors from the ground to rise and drop them to their deaths. Our enemy's veiled advance has us startled and this ain't our plan. I was supposed to be with Jade, running firebombs to the front. Forcing my arms and legs to move, I crawl onto my front and drag myself up.

The bombs!

I turn for the waggon and stumble, searching for Gun, for a moment adrift in the fog. Jade must be nearby, though I've lost her, too.

258

'Jade!'

Her reply pierces the battle noise as smoke billows from numerous fires.

'Here! Ebadiah! I'm here!'

I head for the sound as the hazy shape of the waggon appears before me and there, see Jade collecting firebombs, and Brimstone tethered loosely to the load bed.

'Hurry!' she shouts. 'They need more!'

I gather an armful of the bombs and follow her through the deepening smog to the line, where our gawpers struggle to hold back the oncoming terror. Caught up in their control, the pots rise from our arms and rush through the air. The receiving gawpers touch smouldering match chords to the bombs' gunpowder and pitch seals, igniting them one after another, and sending them flying at the enemy.

Unburdened, we run back for more, load up and deliver them, all the while weaving between explosions and the falling firebombs of the enemy. Behind the frontline, it's safer from the advancing monsters, but for how long? With this mist and confusion, it's hard to know how we fare.

A war bird screeches down through the mist to grasp a gawper nearby. As it lifts away, a spear hurtles from somewhere behind me to take the bird down. The gawper falls a few yards back to the ground, unharmed, while others hack the bird apart.

I'm collecting more ammunition when a movement in the load bed catches my eye. There, a young gawper face peers back at me.

'Alaric!'

He's mostly buried beneath the firebombs.

'Alaric, get out of here! Now!'

He emerges from the bombs. 'Alaric is warrior. Alaric must fight with Dagomite kin!'

'It's too dangerous!' I shout.

A call rises over the clamour.

'Retreat!' The command comes from a gawper captain—presumably passed down the line from Robespierre—who is beyond view, lost in the haze. Magwitch must recognise the voice because he takes up the cry.

'Retreat!'

'Quickly! Hide yourself!' I throw the tarp over Alaric.

Our line wavers. Gawpers step back. Some manage to disengage from their opponents. Others are pressed hard and forced to fight on or be hacked to the ground from behind. A few of our number turn and run, but it's bloody chaos. Ain't the clean and clear retreat we need. Instead of a single wave of fleeing warriors, the enemy must surely only see a messy, partial abandonment of our line. They remain on the slopes, holding fast to the higher ground, and I see our ruse has failed.

Disaster.

Magwitch reaches the waggon with Gun in tow and thrusts the reins into my hands.

'It's not working!' I cry, fearing we've already lost and that we'll soon be overrun and slaughtered. 'What can we do?'

'Watch!' he calls back to me. 'And listen for my command.'

He gives orders for the waggon drivers to turn back, but then stops to survey the battle stretched out across the hill in the now-thinning mist. Through the mayhem, I sense a quietness that must surely birth from some other place. The world around me slows and stills, and with it comes a small voice—nothing more than a whisper.

Mount up, Ebadiah. Mount up and ride!

'Who are you?' I cry and the Voice responds.

I am Nackh-moor, the source beyond ma-jick. I am the Great Elder Light.

Lance in hand, I mount up onto Gun. On the far side of the waggon, Jade loosens Brimstone's tether. 'Don't tell me to stay behind. I'm coming with you!'

'Could I stop you if I tried?' I dig heels, feel Gun set forth as she carries me.

'See Deadlock and his riders?' Astride Doom, Magwitch points with his spear. 'He knows the retreat has failed to draw the enemy. He is breaking through their line instead! Rally to him!'

I look and see that's it's true. Deadlock's cohort has become a wedge that's biting into the enemy line, gaining ground, the captain at its point. The sand cats are unstoppable.

Glancing behind, I see Jade climb up into Brimstone's saddle and ready her lance.

Magwitch spurs Doom up the slope, screaming, 'With me!'

Doom takes a spear to the shoulder. Magwitch pulls it free and with a resonant growl, the cat drives on. The spearthrower screams beneath a barrage of teeth and claws.

Gawpers take the last of the firebombs from the waggon while, higher up across the slope, the cat riders surge ahead, forging through the enemy lines. In their wake, creatures lie dead or dying.

Our ranks form up behind Magwitch as he rides and this second wedge quickly merges with Deadlock's cohort. As Jade and I keep pace with the waggons, the new line smashes into the enemy and caught up in the riders behind the cats, we cut a bloody path ever closer to the hilltop. I realise something then: we don't need to defeat the entire enemy force. Just Skallagrim. Without his control, it would all soon be over. If only we could penetrate deep enough to reach him...

Our depleted waggons drop back, unable to stay the pace. Soon they are abandoned and left far behind.

Skallagrim is here. I feel his presence. Like the thinning mist that we breathe, his ma-jick touches all. Either side of the spearhead formation, dragons and gawpers fall, yet a glance around tells me Deadlock's and Magwitch's divisions are ahead of the others. A fear of the sand cats contorts the faces of our enemies.

Lotharian warriors hack through a thicket of enemy gawpers. It's brutal, hand to hand fighting. Ahead, a gulf opens up as their warriors withdraw. Briefly, I think Skallagrim has ordered a retreat but then through the haze, figures grow clear. A wall of creatures emerges and beyond, Skallagrim sits upon a raised throne where a tall guard of spear warriors gaze back at us. It's an odd thing to see—a throne placed on the hilltop—a sign of his arrogance. Behind the throne, his war-battered bird waits. Before the spear warriors spans a line of seething dragons.

Magwitch turns to me. 'Your chance approaches. Ebadiah will have but a moment to act.'

I try to bring the words of the nackh-sahar to mind, but fail. Instead, an image of Skallagrim's burning red eyes floods my head, clouding my mind. I try to shake the invasion off. Pulling the Codex from my bag, I hurry to find the page and begin reading in a loud voice. At once I sense Skallagrim stir. It feels as though he's aware of my every breath. My gaze meets his as he rises to his full height from his throne.

'The hairless one by the throne is his captain, Tacitus,' says Magwitch. Tacitus is either naturally bald or has shaved his head for the occasion. His leathery lined face wears a permanent scowl.

Skallagrim's gaze intensifies and I know he has sensed the ma-jick. I wonder if he senses the book's presence, too. His mouth moves: a command beyond my hearing. In response, a wind rises across the hilltop, sudden and cold. It builds swiftly into a gale that rakes at our hair and clothes. The rank of creatures before him parts and there in the gap stands a lone, black dog.

A Draker's dog.

'Stink?'

Confused, I freeze. But *Stink died on the mountain. Didn't he? Another dog, then. Another that looks just the same...*

Yet it *is* Stink. I recognise him at once, though this dog don't act like the dog I knew. *This* dog is mean and snarling, maddened, and dead set upon killing all who stand in his way.

And *this* dog is coming for me.

23. THE DARKNESS WITHIN

The book forgotten, I slide from my saddle to shout. 'Stink! Stink!' But either the dog ain't listening or he don't hear over the roar of wind and war. He charges at me, snarling, eyes wild, foam flying from his jowls. I see that, if it truly is Stink, he's been changed—perhaps beyond redemption.

The gawpers surrounding me level their spears.

'No!' I scream the word while, beyond them, the battle rages on. I can't watch my dog be speared, even if he *is* in Skallagrim's thrall. But if he ain't stopped soon, he's gonna tear me to shreds. That's clear. Closer he bounds, speeding, sleek and agile, a dark fury bent on killing. I'm powerless, in torment, raising my lance one moment, lowering it the next.

Jade wheels Brimstone around. 'Magwitch! That's his dog! Do something!'

Pulling his spear from a dying opponent, Magwitch dismounts. Doom opens the throat of a morh-beast that drives insanely into our line. Blood sprays. The cat drops the limp body to defend his master, who stands, head inclined, arms raised towards the oncoming hound. As Magwitch utters words unheard, I sense the energy he projects, and caught up in that power, Stink's bounding form lightens, his body rising until his paws leave the ground. Pounding at thin air, the dog continues to run, but he ain't going nowhere.

'Whatever it is you wish to try, do it now!' says Magwitch, exertion lining his face. 'Skallagrim's power over the hound is strong.'

I know Magwitch can't keep this up for long.

The dog's now close enough for me to see the darkness within his eyes. Stink ain't there—or if he is, he's smothered somewhere far away, deep down. I peer instead into the soul of the one controlling him.

A hideous voice booms in my head.

One Eye...

I shake myself. *The book!*

I scrabble on ground slick with the blood of gawpers and monsters. To my side a firebomb explodes, spraying liquid flames. Gawpers scream. Smoke billows thick in the air as my fingertips find the bag. My head feels about set to burst. Blood runs from my nose.

'Hurry, Ebadiah!' cries Magwitch, his face pained, the glow of his eyes dimming.

I snatch up the book, riffle desperately for the new page but it's gone. A thread hangs loose in the wind where it used to be. The torrent tears at the remaining pages, threatening to tear them away. I see something strange then: something that makes no sense to my battered mind. To be sure I look again, see a gawper child amid the battle, stooping to grab a page cast to the wind. Alaric...

'Alaric!' I scream. 'The page!'

Snatching the page in his claws, he runs to deliver it to me.

'Now go!' I shout, taking the parchment. 'Get far away!'

I wipe the parchment clean of mud and gore on my cloak as he flees and, glancing up, see Skallagrim, his arms outstretched, locked in a battle of wills with Magwitch as Stink is held captive in the air between them. Shoving the book into Roach's bag, I begin to read the page aloud.

'Tag-ma ken, furtmah-na-manti thru-ka-namabdah...'

Closer Skallagrim drifts, a tall, dark shape with eyes of ruby blood. The dragons and gawpers before him part as he comes. On I read.

'Nambir-hank dormitch da-nakim throminatriam furt-mah-na-manti.'

My words are interrupted by a hideous, piercing sound. Trying to refocus, I'm vaguely aware that the fighting around us has ceased and that we are surrounded by a clearing encircled by the enemy. Beyond this the distant battle continues.

The terrible cry comes from Magwitch.

'Magwitch!'

His body spasms. The flames of his eyes flicker and fade.

'No!' My words have no impact on the Gawper King. His laughter in my head thunders like the cold echoes of a cavern.

Crumpling to the ground, Magwitch lies lifeless.

I sense a force encroaching as my body tenses. The page is torn from my grasp as I'm lifted from the ground, my actions no longer my own. Skallagrim is all I see. He is all I think. The world folds in on me as my hearing fades. All is slow. All is pain.

Before me, Stink remains suspended in the air, a captive once more under Skallagrim's dominion. My eyes are closed by the overwhelming force. A fleeting image flickers through my mind: the Gawper King and Stink tumbling from the mountain top in a death fall, then slowing as Skallagrim uses his bah-nackh. High overhead a bedraggled war bird flees. The tumbling figures slow as they drop—slow and slower—until coming to a stop, they hang motionless in the air. They hover there for a moment before descending to settle gently upon the snow-covered rocks below, unharmed. There Skallagrim begins his bah-nackh on the dog.

My eyes flick open. Stink is before me almost within reach, though now he is himself once more. No longer the ferocious puppet, he paws the air, trying to reach me while Skallagrim holds him still.

'Stink! You're still there!'

I see a yearning in his eyes, quickly overwhelmed by fear as a figure slides into view at my side: Jade floating in the air, captured in Skallagrim's control, her lance drawing back to strike the dog.

Involuntarily, my arm flies out to my side. The cold wood of my lance hits my palm and my fingers close around it. Like a child's toy, I am a doll obeying Skallagrim's every whim. Fighting each movement, I watch my hands bring the lance up and know my enemy's mind. He would have us slay the dog. The dog we know. The dog we love. It will be both a demonstration of his control and a punishment for the upstart humans who dared defy him. It is a death sentence for the dog and a final agony we must endure before we, too, are slaughtered.

I feel my hands drawing back the lance to stab and to my horror, thrust the tip at Stink's chest. It's an inch from impact when Jade parries the blow with her lance. She sweeps my lance up and away. I feel it break free of my puppeteered grip.

'You hold no sway over me, Skallagrim.' She rounds on the Gawper King. Raising her lance she launches it at his heart. For a moment I think it will strike—that he will die— but he extends a palm towards the flying lance and holds it mid-flight, captured and halted in the air. With the flick of his claw, he lets the weapon fall harmlessly to the ground. So too, Jade drops, free of his levitation as she fights for control.

'You will submit to your master,' roars the Gawper King, gesturing for his spear guards to rush in. They seize Jade roughly by the arms and drag her before him.

'Kneel before your King!' They shove her down, her face in the blood and mud of the hilltop.

'He's no king of mine.' Struggling against their hold, she spits at his feet.

Skallagrim glares at her, his eyes narrowing.

I'm carried closer and set down as other guards hold me at spear point.

'The book,' says Skallagrim to his guards. 'Find the Codex.'

'No!' I gasp.

A gawper grabs my bag—Roach's old bag—from the ground and delivers it to the throne. It feels like a sacrilege for them to even touch it. Skallagrim takes out the book and flicks slowly through the pages. His voice is like grinding rocks, an ill-sounding scraping noise, drowning even the pounding gale.

'One Eye has caused much trouble. Much trouble, indeed. One Eye must pay...' He pauses, staring at the open book in his hands. 'What is this?' He studies the dangling thread and a pain explodes in my head as I sense him probe my mind.

'A page is missing!' He turns to his closest guards. 'Find the page. Bring it to me!'

His guards search the clearing and soon return to the throne to present the recovered page. Skallagrim examines the parchment, and a chugging noise begins in his throat. It builds into a slow and humourless laugh that hurts my ears.

'Skallagrim sees One Eye. This one has learned much since our meeting on the mountain. Yet this one has failed.' He bows mockingly. 'Skallagrim is grateful. One Eye has delivered the words that will end the war. One Eye shall witness the ruin of all he holds dear before his end.' To his guards he commands, 'Bring a prisoner.'

They bring forward a bound Lotharian. The captive looks around, but there's no escape. Fear contorts his features.

Held in Skallagrim's invisible grip, I can barely move, though I manage to form one word.

'Stink...'

Skallagrim spell-casts the nackh-sahar. 'Tag-ma ken, furt-mah-na-manti thru-ka-namabdah. Nambir-hank dormitch

268

da-nakim throm-inatri-ahm furtmah-na-manti.' The sky overhead begins to darken and swell with cloud. The captive's eyes widen as his head tips back. His body stiffens. He shakes.

Skallagrim reads on and I sense him add to the ma-jick of the words as the movements of his arms and the claws of his hands correspond. In what other way he weaves the spell, I cannot tell. Still, I know there is something more, a skill beyond my understanding—a hidden language of signs, of thoughts or communication.

The bound Lotharian screams. His body trembles. His eyes burn bright. Around us the squall builds with Skallagrim's ascending voice as he proclaims the final words of the camplanodrix. The clouds churn and thunder rolls from the heavens, giving pause to every creature on the hill. And then in a trice the wind drops. The prisoner tenses as blood gushes from his eyes, his nose, his mouth. Abruptly, his scream ends. His body falls lifeless to the ground. I sense a shift in power as a charge flickers in the air. There comes a moment of unfathomable silence.

Chaos follows.

Released from the king's control, the dragons scatter, some turning upon their masters. Skallagrim stumbles, as though drained by his efforts, his face contorts. He, too, is bleeding.

Seeing this, Tacitus bolts away into the masses.

Somewhere behind me, Deadlock shouts a command. 'Kill the bird!'

His cat riders rally, converge around Skallagrim's tethered war bird and attack. In a moment the creature succumbs beneath tooth and claw.

Skallagrim peers at the darkened sky before glaring around at the rampaging threshers and his other beasts running wild. Blood runs from his eyes while across the hilltop, a different sort of battle begins, one in which the fear-startled creatures attack friend and foe alike in their hurry to escape.

Those that don't fight, flee, between gawpers and the dominating sand cats. Like a wave, the change ripples over the hill.

Skallagrim staggers to his throne, crumples into the seat. Quite what he expected to happen, I cannot say. I never truly understood the nature of the nackh-sahar I constructed. Though it's clear to me now in this one lucid moment. The words were indeed meant for the Gawper King. And they were his undoing.

Jade slips keenly between warriors and dragons to reclaim her lance.

His hold leaves me. 'Skallagrim is broken!' I yell.

Dazed, though free from his grip, I look around at the battle and see the curse has truly lifted. His control is gone. Like the dragons, the enemy gawpers and beasts run or fight, but no longer for Skallagrim. Each is once more its own master. Across the slopes, pockets of the killing ground grow still as the fighting abates. In the valley below, creatures stream away, back into the wilderness. Dotted among them are the dark forms of gawpers fleeing.

Astride Grimclaw, Deadlock appears through the pressing madness of the hilltop, his spear held high. Around him, his cat riders cut a swathe through the remains of the darkling army. Grimclaw pads to the throne where Skallagrim slumps in the shadow of the great sand cat. For a moment, the two gawpers lock eyes. Deadlock raises his spear and thrusts. The shaft passes though Skallagrim to thump deep into the wooden seat. But the laugh returns—the mocking, grinding laugh—and Skallagrim rises to his feet while the spear remains lodged in the throne.

I shake myself as though from a trance.

'He's not here! He's conjuring!' In a flicker of light, Skallagrim's phantom vanishes. 'He was never really here!'

'He must be close by to have wielded such power,' says Deadlock, turning his cat about to scan the hill. He dismounts to lever his spear free. Kicks over the throne in frustration.

I see Jade then. She's leaving the clearing, pressing through the ebbing battle in pursuit of a tall gawper who is fleeing.

'There!'

Jade slips between two darklings who seem frozen to the spot while all around, their battle is lost.

Nearby, another tall figure rises, and then another.

But which is the real Skallagrim?

They are all a match for his immense height, each one a copy of the Gawper King.

The battle ebbs, the hillsides patched with the last of the warriors. Few of Skallagrim's creatures remain. Darklings run, some fight among themselves while others escape on stolen horses.

I delve into a pocket, take out my slingshot to load a pebble into the leather cradle. I draw, aim and fire at the tall figure beyond Deadlock. The stone bullet zips right through: a conjuration, then. Deadlock sees it and fixes upon the remaining two, one of which must surely be the real Skallagrim. Jade closes on her mark as I load a second missile, take aim and let it fly. The stone hurtles through thin air—a phantom, like the others.

Jade!

Deadlock and I sprint, watch as the world seems to slow. The remaining figure turns, a dagger flashing from beneath his robes as Jade brings her lance up to thrust its tip at his head. Jade stiffens. Skallagrim stills. For a moment, nothing moves. The lance falls to the ground. Jade follows. I glimpse a hateful smirk beneath the king's hood as he turns away. Hear his laughter rattle in my head.

A blur of darkness from my side.

An animal rush.

A black hound tears after the fleeing figure. Like a phantom, Stink leaps.

He is speed.

He is rage.

THE JICKER MAN

He is vengeance.

His attack is a frenzied rending of flesh, gripping and shaking. The Gawper King topples, his screams cut short as his throat is torn apart. Blood spurts. Teeth grind. The dog releases, steps back. The Gawper King lies quivering on the ground, soon to move no more and, quieting, Stink stands over his kill, looking at what he's done.

I fall to my knees beside Jade and take her in my arms, see the king's dagger protruding from her side. Her face is a deathly shade of white. 'Two Coats!'

'Is he dead?' she asks. Fleetingly, her eyes blink open, though they're unfocused. 'Is Skallagrim dead?'

'He is. He is truly dead.' I glance at the fallen, unmoving body, wanting proof, needing to see that he has not somehow deceived us again. But there he lies, solid, as dead as anything can be, the lifeblood flowing from his veins into the churned mud.

Jade closes her eyes and rests her head against me.

'We go home now, right?' she asks. 'We can forget about the darklings...'

Home... I think back to the cold space under Rook's Bridge where I sheltered as a street urchin, of the house on Bunson Street—now rubble, to our cottage flattened by a shrieker, and of the many ruins we've sheltered in along the way.

'Where is home?' I ask.

Deadlock is suddenly there, stooping over us to examine Jade's wound.

'Leave the blade in place. Our healers will remove it with care.'

I feel a cold, wet touch on my cheek, hear a soft whine, and turn as Stink prods me with his nose. Lotharians glide in around us, called by Deadlock—I reason—now that it is safer to mind-walk again.

'Ebadiah must let Jade go.'

At Deadlock's words I allow them to take her from me.

'Jade is in good hands.'

'We'll stay with you,' I tell her as they carry her away. Stink presses in close against my face and neck. I hold him as he stills and for a long moment, we remain locked together. My hands feel blood that's matted into his hair from battle wounds, but he is alive.

'Bear Dog...'

I see it then—the Tanak Codex lying in the mud to one side of Skallagrim's body.

*

'What of Tacitus?' I ask.

'Four of our captains are running him to ground,' says Deadlock. 'Do not fear. He will be found and brought to justice.'

Robespierre drinks black weed beer from a cup. 'Our enemy is defeated. The war is over.'

'Magwitch...' I begin but can say no more.

'Magwitch will be honoured forever in the libraries of our forefathers,' says Deadlock. 'His name shall pass through the ages, never to be forgotten.'

I visit Dagmar and the children, Alaric and Elke, tell them how Magwitch saved us and of the part he played in Skallagrim's downfall. Pride and sorrow flow in their tears.

'He would be glad to know his life was given in the great cause,' Dagmar says as Elke clings to her robes. 'He would have considered it the greatest honour.'

I hear her thoughts then, as she sends them to me.

We thank you, Ebadiah, for your part in our victory. What we share in victory, we share in loss.

'I owe him my life,' I tell her. 'We all do. The world will never be the same again because of what Magwitch has done.'

Sensing her resolve begin to crumble, I leave them to grieve.

24. DECISIONS

Before nightfall, we return to our camp on the neighbouring hill, eat a little and drink black weed beer. Gawpers collect our dead from the battle hill and carry our wounded in the waggons to tents, where healers tend to them. As work begins on the funeral pyres, our fallen enemies are left for the ravens. The grim birds flock in vast numbers to feast.

The gawpers take Jade away, but their healers are highly skilled and it's not long before she's returned to us as we gather around the hearth of the moot tent, her wound stitched and dressed.

'How are you?' I ask, glad to see her walking, albeit stiffly. She leans heavily upon Dagmar, who helps her to a place by the fire. The children follow closely behind.

'They say I'll live,' says Jade. 'So don't even think about running off.'

I grin. 'Blinders—you're back to your old self, already.'
She smiles.

In Roach's old bag slung across my shoulder sits the book, safely hidden, though I feel its weight and am compelled to keep a hand over it for surety. Jade notices and nods towards it.

'You still have it, then...'

'Aye,' I whisper, wary of every gawper in earshot. I haven't mentioned the book to anyone since quietly reclaiming it on the battlefield. I lean close to warn her.

'Not a word! They believe it lost in the mud.'

'What'll you do?'

'Don't know.'

Whatever I decide to do with the book, one thing's for sure: I ain't letting it fall into the hands of another. Ain't letting this happen again—and that realisation tells me what I must do. And that it must be done in secret.

*

Two days later, we are packed and ready to leave. Deadlock has given us a small gawper tent to help us on our way. I load up the folded tent and our baggage behind the saddles of our horses and we say our goodbyes to the gawpers we have come to know so well in such a short time. They have become like family. Alaric and Elke hug us tightly and for a long while refuse to let go. Only when Dagmar steps in to draw them away do they concede, and we are able to mount up and ride out of the camp. Looking back, we wave to the children, although the gesture seems lost on them. Dagmar whispers to them and they wave back as we enter the woods with Stink at our side, and soon we see them no more.

Jade and I talk about where we might go, where would be good, agree that the hills are probably safer, but I'm drawn back to my old home of Camdon, and so our path turns south. It's good to ride in the daylight once more, and camp at night. We can see where we're going, feel the sun on our backs and forage along the way. The first night we camp in some woods, pitch the tent on the soft ground and set a fire within a circle of stones. The trees about us are densely grown. I spent the day making sure we were not followed by anyone from the gawper camp, and I'm sure we're alone when we settle before the campfire.

Taking out the book, I look long at its cover, read again the loose page retrieved from the carnage of the hill and slipped back into place. And closing the codex for the final time, I lower it into the flames.

Jade watches the book burn. 'It's done, then. It's over.'

'It's for the best,' I say. 'Isn't it?'

She nods and takes my hand. 'I guess so.'

'Back there with Skallagrim—he couldn't control you. He had Stink, had Magwitch, had me... You were the only one.'

'Because of what Roach did,' she says. 'It was because of Roach.'

BEN MEARS

EPILOGUE

Jade works her healing on Stink. When his cuts have closed over, I watch her massage the muscles around his wounds, loosening them up each night before we sleep. After months of patient work, she's rewarded with an improvement in the dog's gait. He's quicker, too. Not quite as fast as he used to be, but close.

He's in his element here in the fields, just south of Camdon City.

But it's the woods he loves the most. He chases squirrels and snuffles in the fallen leaves, startles birds into the sky and leaps fallen boughs. Ain't no morgue rats in these woods, no Morhs—no dragons either.

He ain't the same since the battle. It's left him with a permanent limp, like mine, but he gets around alright and is fast when he wants to be. Smiling, I sit atop a fallen tree and watch him run.

I think often about Roach—wonder how much he really knew. Was he aware that Jade and I would make a life together when he said she'd be good for me? That when we climbed the mountain, he was heading for his death? The more I revisit past events, the further I'm convinced he knew more than he ever shared. One thing's for sure: I'm grateful and always will be. I carry the old man in my head and in my heart—and every day, listen for the whisper.

Stink finds me on the tree, throws me a look with a tilt of his head: *Why ain't* you *chasing squirrels?*

I hear Jade calling me home, then.

'Come on,' I tell him. 'Time to go.'

We find her in the kitchen tending a pot of stew on the old stove we salvaged from a wrecked house down the road.

'Boots off. I just cleaned the hall.' She greets me with a kiss as Stink circles us. 'You and that hound... He's like your shadow. Don't you ever go anywhere without him?'

''Course not,' I tell her. 'He's my dog.'

I think about Michael and Josiah, too, recall them leaving the house to ride for the docks. What became of them after boarding the gunship bound for Morracib. Are they surviving in that faraway land or injured and stuck in some bombed out shelter? Or do their bones lie mouldering at the bottom of the Eastern Sea? I visit the city once in a while—searching for perks—and decide to return one afternoon. It's a long walk to Dockside, but the weather's mild and Stink pads along next to me, so I don't mind.

Dust blows across the ruined city and I wonder if it will ever be rebuilt. I try to picture the scene: workers erecting scaffolding, ladders leaning, carpenters sawing timber and masons hammering out the imperfections of golden stone as the cityscape rises once more. But it's a fleeting fantasy and passing through Crowlands, I don't linger around Bunson Street. The place feels haunted to me.

Rook's Bridge is still standing. I cross it and follow the river Tynne out to the coast, where gulls cry and soar high above the sparkling sea. Mudflats spread far across the estuary and from here I can see for miles over a great expanse of water, out to the Eyes of Myrh and beyond, to the horizon. Following the shore, I walk down to a little beach and sit for a while, pondering. It's peaceful here, and war seems far away. Stink sniffs at seaweed and chews on a stick that's washed in on the tide. But my eye is drawn once more to the horizon. There the silhouette of a distant ship breaches the sky.

I blink in the sunlight, but the ship remains.

Getting to my feet, I view the spectacle through my telescope. It's a big old warship, a galleon, Londaland colours flying from one of three masts. I lower the scope as a closer ship breaks the line of the islands, sailing in towards the cove. Several others follow behind, each of them with the same flag, just across the bay. It's a sight to behold. A sight that makes my heart jolt. I make the sacred sign.

Running to the water's edge, I can barely contain my excitement.

Ships returning from war? Can it be?

But then I glance up the beach towards the harbour and see the tall masts and rigging of a ship already at dock. In a trice, I'm moving. Stink senses something's going on. He barks alongside me as I sprint up the beach. I run for the docks, my gaze returning to those tall ships drifting in, to the one already moored. Spraying sand, I dash to the path and there, pound my way up to the harbour wall. Beyond that, the ship is revealed in all its glory, berthed and sitting high in the water. Figures busy themselves with the sails and rigging, carry cargo down from the deck onto dry land. Stopping to catch my breath, I watch one fellow lead a horse down the gangplank, see other horses and gunners moving about the docks. Troopers in red coats carry stretchers bearing wounded men ashore.

I push myself too hard and come limping to lean on the wall of a dockside tavern, The Ship Keepers. I know it from before the war. From better times. It used to be the first stop a sailor would make once he'd disembarked from a voyage, there to be interrogated by the locals. I stop and stare at a line of horses tethered outside, searching for a pair I know—one a sleek, black gelding, the other a dappled grey mare—but they ain't there. Hobbling to the tavern door, I throw it open and with a deep breath, step inside.

The tavern is busy with troopers, though there's little drinking or eating being done. Their uniforms are worn, the colours stained and faded. They carry an air of fatigue as they arrange crates and barrels of provisions. One half of the room seems to have become a makeshift hospital.

I drag my aching ankle to the bar where a lieutenant with blood spattered epaulets is writing an inventory of supplies.

'You're back, then.' It's all I can think to say. 'Is it over?'

He gives me a cursory nod and a wry smile before turning back to the page he's working on. 'The war with the Urthians? Aye, for what it's worth. By all accounts the world's a ruin.'

'I'm looking for a silker, two of them really. They left on a gunship in His Majesty's Fifteenth Regiment, before the bombs came. They were bound for Morracib to strengthen the front.'

For a moment I think he'll ignore me but then his haggard face turns back.

'The Fifteenth, you say? Which battalion?'

'Don't know.'

'The Fifteenth... Well, their number was quartered in the first assault on Brinnah Pharos.' My heart sinks but then he asks, 'Names?'

'Michael Banyard and Josiah Mingle,' I tell him.

He frowns and I glimpse a distant recognition in his eyes. 'Banyard, Banyard...' He turns to a sergeant who's assisting him. 'Wasn't there a Banyard in the officers' mess back in Draymara?'

'I believe there was, sir,' says the sergeant. 'A Major, if I'm not mistaken.'

'When was this?' I quickly ask.

'Oh, six months back,' says the sergeant.

'So, he could be alive...'

'Could be,' says the lieutenant. 'If that's him.' He returns to his task.

It's funny, that small feeling growing inside. I think it's called hope. So small and yet...

I head out, back to the dockside to wait and watch the ships come in.

ABOUT THE AUTHOR

Ben first began writing high fantasy as a hobbyist, later working on a series of early-medieval whodunits before self-publishing the YA Tyler May Series.

In addition to his role as an author, Ben is a published songwriter, a published illustrator and an award-winning graphic designer. He is married and has three inspiring daughters. As a visiting author, he runs creative writing workshops in secondary schools and academies in the South West of England.

The Banyard and Mingle Mysteries were his first novels to be traditionally published.

Self-Published Titles

The Haunting of Tyler May (2012)
The Thieves of Antiquity (2013)
The Brimstone Chasm (2013)
Gallows Iron (2014)
Ghosts of Redemption (2015)
Dawn of the Sister (2016)

Published by Instant Apostle

A Sock Full of Bones (2020)
The Green Ink Ghost (2020)
The Shadow of Grayrton Mire (2021)
Seraph of the Sallow Grove (2022)

For more information, please see the following websites.

https://banyardandmingle.com/
https://www.bjmears.com/

BEN MEARS

https://instantapostle.com/author/mears-ben/
https://www.tylermay.co.uk/
https://www.facebook.com/authorbjmears

www.ingramcontent.com/pod-product-compliance
Lightning Source LLC
Chambersburg PA
CBHW031347070726
47496CB00017B/1817